THE MEDAL
Book 3

ONLY THE GALLANT

Kerry Newcomb

BANTAM BOOKS
NEW YORK • TORONTO • LONDON • SYDNEY • AUCKLAND

ONLY THE GALLANT
A Bantam Domain Book / October 1991

ISBN 0-553-29250-1

Published simultaneously in the United States and Canada

PRINTED   IN   THE   UNITED   STATES   OF   AMERICA

RAD   0 9 8 7 6 5 4 3 2 1

THE MEDAL: BOOK THREE
Only the Gallant

Jesse McQueen — A dashing, black-haired man of twenty-two, Jesse has learned the ways of justice from his father, Ben. As a spy for the Union Army, he must learn to keep his personal grudges—and infatuations—out of his perilous work....

Caitlin Brennan — A fiery-spirited lady; while serving as a Union spy she saved Jesse's neck from a vigilante mob in New Orleans. Now, the tables are turned and Jesse is faced with a cruel dilemma: Dare he jeopardize the success of his mission to repay a debt of honor no McQueen can ignore?

The Stark Brothers — Their blood feud with the McQueens had been running longer than the war. They'd tried to kill Jesse once but hadn't succeeded; this time they will be sure to finish what they've started—whether they wear the same color uniform as McQueen or not.

Ophelia Tyrone — A dazzling auburn-haired teenage Rebel lass of Memphis whom Jesse saves—and woos. Little does she suspect his real work—nor does he know of her dangerous family connections....

For Ann and Paul Newcomb with love

At the risk of sounding repetitious, I would like to thank my terrific editor, Greg Tobin, whose kindred soul and talents have made the journey from my typewriter to the published work a pleasure. My thanks to Linda Grey for her trust and support of this storyteller's visions and dreams. And my gratitude to Aaron Priest, my agent and friend, after all these years, nobody does it better.

ONLY
THE
GALLANT

Chapter One

Jesse Redbow McQueen bit the hand that tried to hang him. The man with the lynch rope, a Creole by the name of Maurice Charbonneau, was a stocky, thick-necked ruffian with a belly full of whiskey's false courage. No, he wasn't afraid of any man whose wrists were securely bound behind his back. Then McQueen clamped down, showing his fangs, and Charbonneau howled in pain, wrenched free, and stumbled back to safety. Jesse McQueen had bought himself a little time, but if he wanted to live through the hour, he'd have to come up with a better plan. He couldn't believe his luck. One moment he had been hurrying through the storm back to his warm dry room at the Orleans House on Toulouse Street. Suddenly he'd found himself cornered by a gathering of the crescent city's angry citizenry.

It was the twenty-fourth of April in the year 1862 and New Orleans was aflame despite a drenching downpour that obscured whole blocks from view. The nation was at war, split north and south by men with too many ideals and not enough patience. Cemeteries already teemed with the unfortunate blue-and-gray-clad victims of this tragic conflict. New Orleans had considered itself impregnable behind two mighty bastions, Fort St. Phillip and Fort Jackson. But Commodore Faragut had proved how wrong that theory was. After days of bombardment, the Union fleet had swept past the forts and up the mighty Mississippi and brought their guns to bear upon the city itself. At that point the city fathers surrendered. Word had spread like wildfire and ignited in the populace a sense of betrayal and outrage. As a result of this hysteria, strangers immediately became suspect, labeled as spies to be summarily shot, or in this case hanged. And Jesse Redbow McQueen was just such a stranger, touting a pack of law books and professing a desire to practice in New Orleans.

Jesse focused his dark brown eyes on the two men apprehended with him. One already dangled like a puppet on a string from the hotel's wrought-iron railing, a poor broken toy discarded by a violent child. The man was E. M. Todd, a fellow boarder at the Orleans House. Jesse knew him as a seller of wine and imported spirits, an Englishman and hardly a spy. The second of the mob's intended victims was a portly, middle-aged man whose shrill appeals for mercy went unheeded by the blood-thirsty crowd. Rumor had it that Union spies had caused the city's downfall, and there must be a reckoning. No matter if a dozen innocent folks were slain in the process, the guilty must not escape retribution.

"I'm from Atlanta and loyal to the cause!" the

portly man exclaimed. "My name is Robert Wilmont, portrait artist, nothing more!"

"And perhaps I am General Robert E. Lee," laughed a silver-haired Creole gentleman in the gray-and-red-trimmed uniform of New Orleans's home guard. He was a dapper, small-boned man with narrow features and blazing eyes. He sat ramrod straight in the saddle, oblivious of the downpour. His hair curled over his hard leather collar. Silvery white side whiskers all but hid his ears. "But you see, in truth, I am Colonel Henri Baptiste, defender of this fair city, and you, sir, are a spy."

"But I'm not!" the frightened artist cried, and lifted his quivering features to the rain. Rivulets streaked his face like tears.

"Oh, hell! I'm the spy, hang me and let him go," Jesse spoke up. His horse shifted and he had to grip tight with his knees to keep himself upright. Rain pummeled his head and shoulders and matted his shirt to his wiry frame.

"In good time," Baptiste remarked, glancing up at McQueen. It was obvious the colonel neither knew nor cared which if either of the men was a spy. They were strangers to him and that was guilt aplenty. "Private Charbonneau, put the noose on that man," the colonel called out, noticing Jesse's bare neck. Jesse was clad in nankeen breeches and a loose cotton shirt. The mob had stolen his hat and coat. His unruly black hair was plastered to his neck, and a black beard concealed the strong, clean cut of his jaw.

Charbonneau reluctantly walked his horse forward. Jesse took satisfaction in the crimson-stained bandage that the Creole had hastily applied to his mangled left thumb.

"Hang 'em both!" shouted a voice from the

crowd. And the throng, about fifteen men, most of them dockworkers and riverboatmen with a few merchants, heartily concurred. Time was wasting. There were other rainwashed streets to check and other traitors to apprehend.

"C'mon, Charbonneau," snarled Jesse, his dark stare full of malice. "Put your hand out and I'll bite it off at the wrist."

The Creole private hesitated. Then another Creole, a tight-lipped imperious-looking young man whose boyish expression could not conceal the blood lust in his eyes, brushed Charbonneau aside and grabbed the lynch rope from the cowed private. Someone in the crowd shouted, "There's a lad, Gerard. Show the scoundrel."

Gerard, handsome and much sought after by the young ladies of the city, blushed and acknowledged his accolades with false modesty. He walked his animal close to McQueen. Up ahead, Henri Baptiste had already thrown the length of rope up to another of the home guard who waited on the balcony. The militiaman quickly tied off the end, stared down at the portrait artist who continued to protest his innocence.

Gerard held the noose up to Jesse while a couple of the men in the crowd steadied his horse and held him about the waist. With a quick flick of his wrist, the handsome young Creole flipped the noose over McQueen's head and the mob cheered his dexterity. But his face was close and he forgot the lesson Charbonneau had learned: that a bound and cornered panther is still dangerous, still a panther.

Jesse lowered his head and butted the Creole square in the middle of his face. Gerard groaned and clasped a hand to his broken nose. When he felt the blood flow and saw the droplets work their way through his clenched fingers to be spattered by the rain and splotch his greatcoat, he could stand no more. He grabbed the noose and wrenched it tight about McQueen's throat.

"Damn you!" Gerard cursed. He nearly dragged Jesse from the saddle, the rough hemp tearing the flesh on either side of his throat. Colonel Baptiste at last intervened and walked his mount between his captive and Gerard, forcing the young Creole with the broken nose to release his hold.

"Each man in his turn," Baptiste said. Rain poured from the brim of his gray hat whenever he tilted his head, splashing his horse's neck. "This must be a proper execution, with as much dignity as time permits." He stared at his two subordinates, one with a cloth-wrapped thumb, the other cupping a hand over his disfigured features. The colonel glared at Jesse. "You, sir, are most troublesome."

"I've never been lynched before," McQueen rasped. "I am ignorant of the proper behavior. Why not take my place and I'll study you?"

His reply elicited grudging laughter from the less rowdy of the mob, who were patiently enduring the downpour in order to see another enemy of the Confederacy receive his proper dispatch.

"Study me?" Baptiste replied in a silken tone. "Study him!" He slapped the end of the hangman's rope down across the rump of the mare directly ahead of Jesse. The animal bolted forward, and the mob cheered as Robert Wilmont, lately of Atlanta, danced death's jig.

Jesse closed his eyes, his heart full of pity for the poor little man. The stench of smoke and death clung to the rain-drenched air. Throughout the city, warehouses of dry goods and cotton had been torched to keep these supplies out of Union hands. The city had turned on itself like a mad animal, destroying itself and its own people. Jesse looked into the faces of the men surrounding him. There was no reason here. Hatred and fear had reaped a bitter harvest among men of conscience. One death begot another, there was no stopping them. Two men twisted in the rain. It was time for a third.

Jesse Redbow McQueen struggled to free his wrists. The rope that bound him was soaked, and in another few minutes he'd be free. But Colonel Henri Baptiste wasn't going to allow him a few minutes. The mob was eager for blood and so was the Creole colonel. Jesse would have to stall them somehow. He closed his eyes and focused his thoughts. In his mind's eye, he drifted out over the bedlam of the city and soared above the burning warehouses and the smoldering bales of cotton to the branches of a magnolia in a garden apart from the destruction. And there among the ancient limbs, he imagined that a raven waited, fluttering its wings and preening its feathers. The bird's bold, keen stare revealed an uncanny intelligence. The trickster spirit of all ravens that had invaded his thought? "Raven, Grandmother Spirit, help me," he shouted in Chocktaw, the language of his grandmother's people.

Jesse glanced around him and saw that his strange outburst had momentarily held the belligerent crowd at bay. Even Colonel Baptiste seemed taken aback. He and the other two Creoles, Gerard and Charbonneau, blessed themselves as protection against whatever demons this stranger had attempted to summon.

But it was no demon or hell-spawned sprite that came to McQueen's rescue; it was instead a pair of frightened runaway mares hitched to a wagon whose load of hay was a pyre on wheels. Flames leaped from the bales of dry grass and singed the rumps of the frenzied horses, who raced down Toulouse at a reckless gait, desperate to escape the burning load to which they were hitched.

Jesse alone saw the wagon as it careened along the narrow street, trailing orange streamers of fire through the pouring rain. The attention of the mob was riveted to this next man to dance at the end of the colonel's rope. "I'll silence your hoodoo talk," Baptiste declared, and tossed the lynch rope up to the man on the balcony. The line slipped from the guardman's grasp and dropped to the street. A pair of rough-looking boatmen broke from the crowd. Each man fought to claim the rope as if it were some sort of prize.

"Tie off the end," came a shout.

"Raise him up with the others!"

Jesse ignored them. He tensed as the burning wagon bore down on the assemblage. It was close now, only a matter of seconds. At last the rattle of the traces, the pounding hooves, and the clattering wheels on the puddled surface of the street attracted the attention of the men on the fringe of the crowd. Their outcries alerted the rest. And the rabble that had called for another hanging suddenly lost its taste for death.

The runaway mares, mad with pain, plunged head-on into the mob, trampling one man and scattering the rest.

Jesse drove his heels into the flanks of the horse beneath him. The bay mare, already made skittish by the crowd, needed no prodding to escape the burning wagon and the terrified team. The bay plunged forward, away from the Orleans Hotel and out into Toulouse Street. Riding bareback, Jesse gripped the mare with his knees and bent forward,

lowering his head into the rain. Behind him the
team of mares swerved to avoid the hotel porch and
the bodies dangling from the balcony. The wagon
careened to one side as the mares lunged in the
opposite direction. The wagon toppled over, its axle
cracking under the strain. The singletree snapped as
the burning bales spilled onto the porch of the
hotel, crashing into chairs and setting the columns
ablaze.

"The rope!" shouted Baptiste, dodging a fiery
death and fighting to control his steed. Gerard leaped
from horseback as the frazzled end of the hangman's
rope slipped past. It flopped and bounded along the
street just out of reach. If the rope snagged even for
an instant, the man at the other end would have his
neck snapped. Jesse McQueen had escaped the frying
pan only to jump into the fire.

Back at the Orleans House, the Creole guardsmen
dismounted and led their horses away. The hotel's
residents had already begun to rush from the burning building. One woman saw the hanged man and
fainted. Baptiste and Charbonneau chanced a couple of shots. Jesse winced as hot lead whined past
his ear. Charbonneau was a good shot and Henri
Baptiste was fully his equal, but the downpour and
the decreased visibility ruined their aim. Both men
holstered their weapons as Gerard brought up their
horses and walked the high-strung animals away
from the spreading flames. The two mares dragging
the broken remains of the singletree fled down the
street after Jesse, further ruining the Creoles' aim.

"After him!" Baptiste roared. "He'll not escape
us, by heaven. I swear it!" Jesse had already
disappeared behind a wall of water, but the colonel
was determined to avenge the honor of the Baptistes
and that of the Creole guardsmen. He was confident

of recapturing McQueen. After all, just how far could a man get riding bareback through a downpour with his hands bound behind him and a hangman's rope trailing from his neck?

The frightened bay veered to the right and rounded the corner from Toulouse onto Bourbon Street. Somehow McQueen managed to stay astride the animal. Jesse McQueen had grown up riding bareback across the plains and foothills of the Indian Territory. He was a horseman first and foremost. But the downpour, while concealing him from his pursuers, also worked against him. It took all his skill to cling to the mare's rain-slick back. His legs were growing numb from the effort.

The mare splashed through a puddle and galloped past a half-dozen ragged looters who had broken into a bootmaker's shop and were helping themselves to his wares. The thieves were too absorbed in their ill-gotten gain to take notice of the mare and its hapless rider. As Jesse flashed by the shop the lynch rope worked its way to a corner step and a furrow in the splintery wood. Jesse felt the noose begin to tighten around his neck. For an instant he considered sliding from horseback and taking his chances, which were none too good without a pair of hands to break his fall upon the hard street. Then the last of the rope cleared the steps, sparing Jesse yet again. But he knew he was living on borrowed time. Sooner or later the rope would wrap around a hitching post or catch beneath a wagon wheel, and that would end it. Buildings skimmed past, blurred by the rain and the dense smoke that drifted up from the waterfront and hung like a pall over the city, choking entire blocks in its black embrace. The bay showed no signs of slowing. Smoke and flames, distant explosions, the bedlam of a rioting populace drove the animal onward in its headlong flight. Jesse McQueen needed a miracle if he was to see another sunrise.

He got one, a block from Canal Street. Fifty pounds of Mississippi blue-heeler darted from an alley alongside La Bonne Nuit Café. The short-haired hunting dog dashed out into the middle of Bourbon Street in front of the bay mare. Horse and hound caught each other off guard. The heeler's gray-speckled coat rendered him almost invisible in the rain until he bared his fangs, snarling and barking, hackles raised along powerful shoulders.

The bay mare skidded on the slick street, reared, and whickered in terror. Its hooves pawed the air. Jesse relaxed his hold, slipped from horseback, and landed on his back in a puddle. He sat up, sputtering, just in time to see the bay mare reverse its course. He rolled to his left and the mare missed trampling him by an arm's length. Jesse McQueen staggered to his feet and looked about at the empty rain-swept street. Well, almost empty. A silhouette of a narrow-shouldered man in a greatcoat and beaver hat materialized out of the shadows. Jesse retreated toward the nearest street lamp, which cast a dim circle of amber light that the storm threatened to obscure.

"Help me," Jesse rasped. "My hands are tied."

The man in the greatcoat reached up and shoved his wire-rim spectacles back up the bridge of his nose. He continued to stare at the torn, mud-spattered figure confronting him.

"Untie my hands," Jesse said. Still the man in the coat made no move. "At least take this noose off me. I'd do it myself, but you see I'm sort of at the end of my rope."

"Don't know you. Ain't none of my business,"

the stranger at last muttered. "But I could use your horse." And with that he brushed past McQueen and ran off after the bay.

"Son of a bitch," Jesse muttered. He was alone again, save for the blue-heeler, who continued to growl and bark. Every time the dog came within range to snap, the bound man aimed a kick at its head. At last the dog retreated, finding something new to inspect.

The blackened, shattered window of the café looked promising. Jesse staggered up onto the porch. The foyer of the café reeked of smoke. Its windows stared vacantly back as he peered inside. The place stood empty, its clientele frightened back to their homes and apartments once word had reached them of the impending arrival of the Union fleet. Jesse McQueen took a moment to catch his breath, grateful for the porch and the shelter it offered from the elements. He wrinkled his nose as the damp, charred smell of the fire-gutted café wafted out through the ruined windows. Jagged shards of glass still jutted from the whitewashed wooden frame like dragon's teeth. *Just the thing,* Jesse thought. He backed over to the remains of the window, chose the largest shard, and sawed at the ropes binding his wrists. Suddenly the lynch rope went taut and pulled him off balance even as it constricted his windpipe. The blue-heeler had found the hangman's rope to be of keen interest. Tail wagging, the dog clamped its powerful jaws around it and began to play tug-of-war.

"Not now," Jesse gasped. "Christ Almighty!"

The dog continued to pull and tighten the noose around McQueen's throat, enjoying this new game. Jesse held his ground, though barely able to draw breath. *Choked to death by a damn dog is a hell of an epitaph,* he thought. He continued to saw at his bound wrists. *Come on. Come on.* He was beginning to lose consciousness. The already murky street was beginning to darken even more at the edges, and slowly... ever so slowly... to tilt. Pain jolted him. He straightened and yelped as the glass shard sliced across his flesh. The bonds fell away and his arms swung free. He worked the slipknot loose, pulled the hemp necktie up past his ears, and tossed the lynch rope into the street. Then he sagged against the nearest post, where the café posted its menu for the day. Tonight's main course would have been smoked oysters, pork loins in a mushroom sauce, sliced wild onions and tomatoes with a vinaigrette dressing, and scalloped potatoes drizzled with butter. *And dog*, Jesse wished. He tossed a shard of glass at the animal, who retreated to the alley. Jesse's anger gradually subsided. He could not imagine anything sweeter than being able to breathe, even with the stench of burned cotton permeating the air. He was bruised and cut and his clothes were torn, but he was alive. He had made good his escape from Colonel Baptiste and his rabble.

Almost.

A bullet blew away a fist-sized chunk of the wooden menu board and thudded into the windowsill. Jesse dived for the street as a voice shouted, "Here! I've found him, Colonel. He's here!"

It was Charbonneau, and he was coming at a gallop, eager to atone for his past mistakes. He had a score to settle with Jesse McQueen.

Somewhere in the city there were streets that the looting and destruction hadn't yet reached. There were streets where families waited in the drawing room and parlor, discussing the tragic turn of events that had caused the city's surrender. Brave words were spoken about resistance to the bitter end, then the children were trundled off to bed, to sleep away the hours of invasion while their parents sipped sherry. And waited. Somewhere in the city men chose their favorite whores and tumbled into bed, all kisses and sweat and liquor and muffled cries of passion, and it made sense and sure as hell beat dying for a cause, any cause. These were the lucky ones. Had it not been for the driving downpour, the flames from the burning warehouses and stockpiles of cotton on the waterfront would have engulfed the crescent city and turned it into a wasteland of rubble. Still, where the fire could not spread, hatred found its way and violence followed close behind.

The Creole called Charbonneau was so intent on being the one to recapture and kill the fugitive that he never slowed his pace but rode headlong toward the dimly seen figure of the man he had tried to hang. He never noticed that Jesse no longer wore the hangman's rope. Nor did he heed how Jesse tossed the noose over the stone hitching post in front of La Bonne Nuit and then ran out across the street, playing out the lynch rope with every step. Charbonneau twisted in the saddle, preparing to ride past him and empty his pistol into the fleeing man.

The Creole had his shot but no chance to take it. Jesse hauled on the rope and it snapped from the rainwashed street, catching Charbonneau's stallion, leg high. The animal tucked its head under and neighed in terror as it fell forward, sending Charbonneau flying.

The Creole made a rough landing, rolled over a couple of times, and stopped spread-eagle, groaning and muttering faint curses facedown in the middle of Bourbon Street.

Approaching horses drummed an unmistakable

tattoo upon the stone-and-shell surface a few blocks away. Jesse heard the clatter of hooves and ran past the fallen Creole. A few yards farther along, at the corner of Bourbon and Canal, Charbonneau's horse struggled upright and stood trembling in the rain. Jesse caught the animal's reins, knelt, and checked its legs. Blood oozed from a number of superficial cuts. Other than that, the animal seemed sound. Jesse spoke soothingly to the frightened steed the way he used to calm horses as a youth in the Indian Territory. He had learned the ways of his grandmother's people in such matters, and their talents were his as well. The animal quieted.

Jesse walked the animal across the street and retrieved the gun that Charbonneau had dropped in the fall. It was a Walker Colt .44, a heavy, long-barreled cap-and-ball revolver with a kick like a Missouri mule.

Charbonneau groaned louder now and slowly drew his knees beneath him and pushed himself off the ground. He was in no shape to stop the man about to take his horse. McQueen swung up into the saddle as the surly guardsman lumbered toward him.

"Damn you!" Charbonneau growled. "I'll get you yet. If I have to follow you to the ends of the earth. There'll be a reckoning."

"Have it your way," Jesse replied as he thumbed the hammer on the Walker Colt and trained the heavy barrel right on Charbonneau's chest. The Creole paled and retreated a step. He held his hands out in a futile attempt to ward off the chunk of lead coming his way.

"On the other hand," Charbonneau added, tamed in the face of his own impending demise, "I ain't the sort to hold a grudge."

"Now there's a Christian attitude," Jesse remarked. He held his fire and the Creole spun around and limped off, losing himself in a rain-shrouded alley alongside a dress shop.

Things were finally looking up for Jesse. He was alive. He had a gun and a horse.

"Yankee renegade!" Colonel Baptiste shouted as he held his horse to a canter and rode with saber drawn, directly toward his elusive quarry.

Jesse swung the stallion about to face this new threat. So Henri Baptiste had found him. Well, no matter, this was one bastard he wanted to make pay for the innocent deaths he had caused. Jesse smiled.

"Come ahead, Colonel!" he roared, brandishing the Colt. His pleasure didn't last long. Gerard and a dozen or more of the Creole militia materialized out of the rain, guns blazing as they charged at a gallop and swept past the colonel as if he were standing still.

"Son of a bitch!" Jesse exclaimed, and drove his heels into the stallion. With a violent tug on the reins, he rounded the corner onto Canal, dodging a hail of lead as he headed toward the river. Behind him, the blue-heeler barked his defiance at the horsemen, then abandoned the field of battle, his defense of the city ended. Jesse chanced a couple of shots with the Walker Colt in hopes of slowing his pursuers, but the Creole guardsmen never lost a stride. They turned onto Canal and loosed another fusillade at the fleeing rider.

Jesse rode low on the stallion, leaning forward until the mane whipped his face. The gunfire behind him had cleared the street of rioters and merchants and the homeward bound citizenry of French, English, Indian, and African extraction. No one wanted to involve himself in this chase. Let the home guard and Colonel Baptiste handle their own affairs.

The closer Jesse McQueen came to the river, the worse the stench from the burning docks. Confederate blockade runners, two sleek-looking schooners, had been set afire to keep Commodore Faragut from hoisting the Union flag above the topsail. It was all a man could do to keep from weeping. Jesse would have pitied the populace if some of them hadn't been trying so hard to kill him.

Smoke stung his eyes and set them watering. Through blurred vision he recognized Camp Street just ahead. He chanced a glance over his shoulder and saw that Baptiste's men had lost a little ground. That suited him fine. He slowed the stallion enough to manage the corner on the slick road. A sharp tug on the reins and the stallion took the corner at a gallop. A puddle seemed to explode underfoot, and water slapped the stallion's belly and drenched McQueen.

Camp was a dark street, only a few blocks from the waterfront. Night and the smoke from the fires limited the visibility here. Jesse was counting on that as he swung out of the saddle and gave the animal a slap on the rump to keep it on its course. As the sound of Baptiste's riders filled the narrow thoroughfare, their quarry scrambled behind an abandoned, overturned wagon. The walkway was littered with fragments of shattered barrels. The ground underfoot was sticky with molasses.

"Oh, no," Jesse muttered, and then with a sigh, took cover as the guardsmen filled the mouth of the street and swept past at a reckless gallop. The noise of the horses was deafening in the confines of the street, with its Spanish, stucco apartments and walled courtyards rebounding the sound. Jesse McQueen, the length of his body pressed against the long-bed wagon, checked the loads in the cylinder of Charbonneau's dragoon Colt and found to his disgust that he'd fired the last shot back on Bourbon Street. He lowered his head and silently cursed the weapon and whatever gods were having such sport with him and waited out the din of the departing militia. Eventually the Creoles would discover they were chasing a riderless horse, but by then, Jesse intended to be safe inside a certain lady's warm, dry apartment.

His clothes stuck to the walkway as he stood and started down Canal. He grimaced and tried to pull the front of his shirt away from his body, then held his arms out to the rain in hopes of washing some of the molasses from his chin and chest and thighs. Not far away, he could see the wrought-iron gate in the courtyard of the Gascony, an apartment house that had once been home to men like Andrew Jackson and Jean Lafitte. Built around a square courtyard, the structure had once housed several generations of Spanish aristocrats. But the family's fortune had been lost in the changing times and the estate turned into a collection of handsome apartments run by the last surviving member of the family, Isabella Martinez. Right now those old, weathered walls and that rusty gate looked like the pearly portals of heaven itself. McQueen quickened his pace. The hairs rose on the back of his neck. He was too weary to pay heed to his own instincts. It was a mistake he wouldn't make again.

"Hold it!" A lone guardsman materialized out of the gloom, holding a revolver in his right hand. His left hand was thrust into the pocket of his greatcoat. The man's voice sounded curiously muffled, and when he had drawn closer, Jesse could see why. His nose was broken and blood was beginning to cake on his upper lip. It was Gerard, and his boyish good looks were definitely a thing of the past. "You're smarter than the colonel gave you credit for." Gerard drew closer but was careful to stay out of arm's reach. "I had a hunch you'd try something else. So I hung back and left my horse up the block. I reckoned as I'd have a better chance afoot. Makes less noise than a damn horse. Where the hell is Charbonneau? Well, no matter."

Jesse calculated his chances of charging the Creole and reaching him before the young man could fire his gun. Pitiful odds, he thought, but when that's all there is...

"I'm gonna shoot the legs out from under you so you can't run," Gerard continued. His round boyish features were bunched with pain. His thin blond hair was plastered to his head. He'd lost his sodden cap. "Then I'm gonna take this gun and bust your nose flat and let you see how it feels. After that, me and the others will finish what we set out to do and see you dance at the end of a rope." The Creole chuckled and puffed out his chest. "See. I'm smart, too."

"If you are, then you'll drop that gun and walk on up to Canal. And don't look back, or my friend in the gate back there will have to shoot you where you stand."

"I may have been born at night, mister. But it wasn't *last* night." Gerard raised his gun.

A shot rang out and a fleeting tongue of fire spat through the intricate whorls of the wrought-iron gate. Gerard staggered and fell to his knees and looked up at Jesse in astonishment. "No," Gerard gasped. "You weren't..." His eyes rolled up in his head and he fell forward.

Jesse staggered past the lifeless form lying in the middle of Camp Street and made his way to the wrought-iron gate that opened onto the courtyard of the Gascony, where a cloaked and hooded figure waited. Jesse had come so near to being lynched, his throat felt rope-burned. He'd been shot at and nearly ridden down. He was bleeding from a nasty assortment of cuts and scrapes. He was soaked and tattered and covered with molasses.

"Rough night?" Jesse's benefactor asked in a woman's voice. And she had the audacity to sound amused!

Chapter Two

Caitlin Brennan liked what she saw, but she wasn't about to tell that to Jesse McQueen. She had left the door to her bedroom ajar and couldn't resist an innocent look in his direction as he emerged from her copper tub and wrapped himself in a towel. Muscles rippled along his back. His hips and thighs were lean and powerful. He stood a couple of inches under six feet, and when he moved, it was with sleek, sure grace. His hair was smooth and glistened against his skull. His jaw was white where he had recently shaved off his beard. A ridge of scar tissue streaked his left shoulder blade, the legacy of an old knife wound.

He dried himself, oblivious of the woman in the front room of the apartment. Caitlin found him a pair of woolen trousers and a ruffled cotton shirt in a trunk by the Sheraton writing table next to a shuttered window. She carried the clothing in for him. Jesse turned and arched an eyebrow as she placed the garments on her bed.

"I was supposed to be waiting for my husband, remember. I thought it better to have some of his clothes in my trunk. What a coincidence—exactly your size." She sat on the bed, a tall winsome lady with an elegant neck and high cheekbones. Hair fine as corn silk and so light blond in color as to be almost white was coiled and curled in ringlets and gathered at the nape of her neck. She wore a blue flannel dressing gown and slippers to match. Her dress and the hooded cape she had worn in the courtyard had been draped across the footboard of her bed to dry. A four-barreled pepperbox, a gambler's gun made for purse or pocket, had been left on the bed table. Jesse started to drop the towel, then paused, for modesty's sake.

Caitlin winked, her green eyes twinkling, and returned to the drawing room, where she lowered the flame on the oil lamps and poured a brandy for herself and one for her guest. She opened the French doors leading out onto a balcony overlooking the courtyard. She could barely see the vine-covered walls in the feeble glare of distant lightning. The gate itself was a blur. The droning downpour hammering the tile-inlaid floor of the balcony filled the drawing room. She liked the sound, its melancholy beauty suiting her mood. She sat in a high-backed, velvet-covered chair and watched the rain as she waited for Jesse to join her by the balcony. She heard the door to the bedroom open and held out the extra glass of brandy.

Jesse sauntered across the room. The hot bath had eased the soreness from his limbs and cleansed his cuts and scrapes. He gratefully accepted the brandy and stood by the French doors, peering out at the night.

"A poor showing for a Union fish to be caught so easily in Confederate waters," Caitlin chided.

"Bah, Colonel Baptiste used a dragnet," Jesse replied. "I was one of many. That bastard didn't care who he lynched. Even when I told him the truth, I doubt he believed me. It didn't matter. And it didn't save the other poor innocent souls."

"Innocent?" Caitlin remarked. "They were Confederates."

"Merchants and artists?"

"It doesn't matter."

"It does to me."

"Then I pity you." Caitlin set her drink aside and rose from the chair. A night breeze felt cool and moist, but she found the smoky residue that permeated the air distasteful. She closed the doors, turned, and placed a hand on his forearm. "But let's not talk of war. Our task here is ended."

"We aren't safe yet. The Creoles are still after my head. More so when Baptiste finds the body of the man you killed."

"By then, Faragut will have landed troops in the city. New Orleans will be under federal control. And this Colonel Baptiste will have to flee or wait out the war in a prison ship." Caitlin parted the folds of his shirt. A shiny English coin hanging from a length of braided leather dangled against his chest. It was an old coin dating back to the days when thirteen American colonies rebelled against the might of the British empire and miraculously won their freedom. The letters "G.W." defaced the image of the English monarch stamped on the coin.

"Did George Washington really give this to your grandfather?" she asked.

"My great-grandfather." Jesse tilted her chin. He would have elaborated, but at the moment, the scent of her was so tempting. "You smell like lilacs."

Caitlin chuckled. "That's you, silly. Remember, I let you have my bath."

Jesse wrinkled his nose and sniffed his forearm. By heaven, she was right. He was about as perfumed as the belle of the ball. He grinned. She moved closer still, her breath fanning his lips and chin. They might have kissed but for the sudden rapping on the apartment door. Jesse tensed and his rope-burned neck began to ache anew. He took another whiff of the perfume and muttered, "Well, if it's Baptiste, he'll have to decide whether to hang me or just dance with me."

"Hide in the bedroom," Caitlin whispered.

"What about your reputation?" Jesse retorted, padding across the room.

"It will hang with me if you're discovered here," snapped the lovely Union agent. For a spy, the threat of execution was a constant danger. The hangman's noose made no distinction between sexes. Woman or man danced the same jig to the gallows' tune.

Jesse left the door to the bedroom slightly ajar. He wanted to hear trouble before it came. He noticed the pepperbox on the bed table and palmed the weapon. There were three shots left. Hefting the gun, he felt a certain sense of dismay. After the dragoon Colt, this popgun didn't feel like much of a weapon. But it had been plenty for Gerard. Jesse cursed himself for a fool. He had left Gerard's revolver in the street. Too late now. He cocked the gun, its four-chambered barrel offering meager comfort, and waited.

Caitlin gingerly approached the door to her apartment. Her mouth had turned dry, her flesh ice cold. She shivered. Someone dancing on her grave?

An old wives' tale? The story might come true. She leaned against the door. "Yes?"

"Señora...oh, Señora Brennan."

Caitlin sighed and sagged against the walnut panel. "Yes, Señora Martinez. I have just come from my bath and cannot open the door."

"No matter, Señora Brennan. I thought I heard gunfire. Outside in the street. I see two figures— men, I think—through the courtyard. Our courtyard. I dress and go outside, but there is no one. They have gone, I think. I pray. Still, I visit all my people here, to see if they are all well."

"I heard nothing," Caitlin replied. Lies came easily to her now, after two months of pretending to be a loyal Southern lady hoping to redezvous with an imaginary husband. "But I assure you, I am safe and sound."

"*Bueno*, señora. Such terrible trouble in the city, eh? Burning. Stealing. While the good stay home and wonder what will happen when the federals come. But I know what will change. Nothing. Babies will be born, the old will die, and life will go on. *Buenas noches*, Señora." The old woman's voice had already begun to grow faint as she continued down the hall.

Caitlin willed her hands to stop trembling, but the adrenaline pumping through her veins made it difficult. She took another deep breath, slowly exhaled, and chided herself. Here she was, twenty years old, two years younger than Jesse McQueen, and she was shaking like some old crone five times her senior. Caitlin took her own sweet time walking across the drawing room to the bedroom. Halfway across she noticed that Jesse was watching her. A blush spread to her cheeks.

"What? Spying on me?"

"Don't worry. Faragut needs no more of my

reports. New Orleans has surrendered, remember? Besides, why would the commodore be interested in knowing you are not the iron-willed, fearless lady you pretend to be." Jesse danced aside as she brushed through the doorway. In the few months they had been together he had never seen Caitlin so vulnerable. That facet of her character appealed to him as much as her stalwart, self-reliant side.

Caitlin gave him a shove that propelled him out into the drawing room and then, when he spun around, promptly shut the bedroom door in his face.

"Now what are you doing?" Jesse asked through the door.

"Waiting for Faragut to land his troops."

"That will take a while. Probably not until tomorrow," Jesse said. He glanced over at the couch, a short, hard-looking bench padded with cushions of russet-colored velvet. "Perhaps we could think of something to do to pass the time...."

The next couple of minutes took an eternity to unfold. Silence, save for the spring rain rattling the windowpanes and cascading from the eaves to splash and crash upon the stones in the courtyard below.

The bedroom door creaked open.

Caitlin Brennan waited within, her dressing gown fastened by a single bow, a tempting cream-colored thigh barely visible where the ribbons were untied. Her expression was haughty again, belonging to a woman in complete control of herself.

"Do you love me?" she asked.

"No," Jesse answered.

"Good," Caitlin replied, and pulled him into her arms.

The bedroom door creaked shut.

Chapter Three

Jesse waited on the hurricane deck of the *Cairo Belle* as Ethelred Jones, the riverboat's captain, a dour-looking officer whose right arm had been blown off by an exploding boiler, brought the side wheeler gently into port. As the sleek ship settled against the pier its crew escaped to the planking and tied off the ropes. Other men, clad in Union blue, hurrahed the ship and its crew and surged forward to greet their comrades at arms, whom they hadn't seen since the campaign against Fort Donelson upriver.

McQueen adjusted his hat to shade his eyes and studied the city spread out along the bluffs. It was the fourth of October, and the fall of New Orleans was just one of many memories tucked away to be relived in simpler times.

He'd spent part of May in Washington and had been planning a trip to the Indian Territory when orders came directing him to Cairo, Illinois, and two tedious months of inaction. A berth aboard the

Cairo Belle had been the answer to a prayer, as had the dispatch from Major Peter Abbot instructing Jesse to rendezvous in Memphis and there receive his orders.

The gangplank landed on the dock with a reassuring thump. Jesse bided his time as the crew and the dockworkers mingled and exchanged pleasantries and began to unload the riverboat. Captain Ethelred Jones had brought barrels of salt pork, crackers, and apples from the loyal people of Illinois.

"Well, what do you think of her?" Captain Jones remarked. He clamped a pipe between his strong teeth. The smoke curling from the bowl was as white as his hair and beard. "I'm always partial to a city when I don't have to run beneath its batteries just to reach harbor." The captain merrily puffed on his pipe, enjoying both the taste of the tobacco and the satisfaction of a job well done. Jesse studied the stone-and-wood buildings whose whitewashed outer walls all but gleamed beneath the sun's glare. He noticed the batteries overlooking the Mississippi and shared Captain Jones's relief that the nine-pounder rifled cannons were manned by federal artillery crews instead of Rebel marksmen.

Jesse spied a stern-featured young officer wearing a lieutenant's uniform similar to his own. The lieutenant appeared to be in charge of the supply detail, that ragged column of men eagerly ferrying foodstuffs from the riverboat to one of five canvas-covered military wagons.

"Say, Lieutenant," Jesse called down to the officer ashore. "Where might I find General Sherman?"

The officer wore a blue, short-brimmed cap, which he removed to further shade his eyes as he peered up at the hurricane deck. It took him a few moments before he realized where the voice came from. Then he waved to the man above, his smooth cheeks and freckled features lit by a grin.

"General Sherman is it you want? Well, you'll find him in school, sir. In school." The young officer began to laugh, and the Union dockhands, sweating in the heat, joined in.

General William Tecumseh Sherman had hopes for a break in the weather. A little rain to settle the dust devils in the street wouldn't hurt. He chucked his woolen frock coat and draped it over a nearby chair as his adjutant showed a dark-haired lieutenant into the schoolhouse. Swatting a fly from the corner of the headmaster's desk, the general scattered a stack of requisition orders that needed his authorization. The quick-tempered, feisty commanding officer scowled and muttered an oath. Second Lieutenant Jesse Redbow McQueen knelt to gather the pages and returned them to Sherman's desk, placing them near a worn leather-bound Bible and the general's navy Colt. Sherman gruffly nodded his thanks and settled back in his chair, folding his hands before him on the desk. Then he stood and sauntered across the schoolhouse that served as his headquarters. He helped himself to a cigar from a box stored on top of a wooden cabinet. He was a tall, redhaired man with a scraggly beard and hazel eyes that glittered passionately at the world. Sherman was a man made for war. It suited him.

Voices and the sound of approaching horses drifted in through the open window as a troop of cavalry rode down Main Street. Wagons creaking on their axles, shouted orders, faintly muffled gossip, and every so often, scattered derision from the city's unhappy inhabitants. Jesse shifted his stance and continued to suffer in silence, wearing the dusty blue uniform of a second lieutenant in the Union Army. General Sherman sized him up.

"So you're the one from New Orleans."

"Yes, sir."

"You supplied Farragut with some rather crucial information about the city's defenses."

"I managed to learn a few things while I pretended to set up my law practice. Luck had a lot to do with whatever I managed to accomplish."

"And nerve," Sherman conceded. He scratched at his beard. His bleak eyes, as befitting some Lazarus newly summoned from the tomb, peered intently at Jesse. "I like nerve in my officers. The Union will not be saved without it." Sherman stooped over and peered out the schoolhouse window as a detachment of troopers rode past. The general studied the returning patrol then returned his attention to the newly arrived officer. "What do I do with you, eh, until Major Abbot arrives?"

"Sir?"

"General Grant has envisioned you playing an intricate part in the campaign he's planning. But I am as much in the dark as you. I'm sure Major Abbot will make all things clear on his arrival." Sherman sat on the edge of his desk, propped one leg on his desk, and paused to light a cigar.

"Virginia tobacco, the very finest," Sherman mused, puffing on the cigar. "A gift from Earl Van Dorn, my Confederate counterpart, holed up with General Pemberton in Vicksburg. I look aside if the occasional luxury—a case of wine, a smoked ham, or some coffee—is smuggled out of Memphis, southward to my old friend. Van Dorn in turn ships me cigars. Yet a month or a year from now we may be trading barrages. War is madness played out on a grand scale."

Madness, thought Jesse recalling the fall of New Orleans. His mind reached further back to the McQueen farm along the Canadian River. Even the Choctaws and Cherokees, full-bloods or mixed like himself, were split into warring factions. As the government agent for the territory, Ben McQueen, Jesse's father, had seen the tranquil countryside become a battleground for night riders and vigilante groups owing allegiance either to the Union or the secessionist cause. Yes, war was indeed a madness that pitted father against son and brother against brother.

"You hail from the Indian Territory," Sherman matter-of-factly stated. "I recall seeing that in the dispatch I received from Grant."

"My grandmother was half-Irish, half-Choctaw, and practically raised me after the death of my mother." Jesse began to perspire in his woolen uniform. The schoolhouse was stifling in the still heat. And without a cross breeze to stir the air, it was only going to get worse.

"You might be pleased to know that some of your neighbors have arrived in the city. Two... no... three brothers brought in a herd of horses for my cavalry. Fine animals, I am told. As for the brothers, I believe they went by the name of Stark." The general noticed a change come over the second lieutenant; emotion seemed to drain from the young man's features, and his gaze became guarded. What was he concealing? the general wondered. "You know them?" he asked.

Jesse nodded. His left shoulder began to ache where the scar tissue ridged his flesh. The Starks were mixed-blood Cherokees who farmed and ranched in the good years and were suspected of thievery and worse in the lean times. Jesse would never forget one night in particular, a dark night, and a mare in foal and a knife thrown by a hidden assailant. The blade had narrowly missed Jesse's spine. Later on, Ben McQueen had found his thirteen-year-old son left for dead in the middle aisle of the stable. The mare had been killed and the foal stolen. There had been no proof the Starks were involved, but one of Elder Stark's own mares just happened to produce a foal that same night. At least that was their claim.

"Yes," said Jesse rubbing his shoulder. "I know the Starks." When he did not elaborate, General Sherman shrugged, exhaled a cloud of tobacco smoke, and returned to his place behind his desk. Behind him, covering part of the back wall of the schoolroom, hung a map tracing the serpentine course of the Mississippi River. Tennessee was depicted on the map, as well as Mississippi and a portion of Louisiana. There were blank spaces and a few penciled-in corrections. Memphis had been hand-circled in black, as had New Orleans. Vicksburg lay between them, a seemingly impregnable stronghold almost entirely surrounded by dense forests, swampland, steep hills, and deep ravines—in short, an inhospitable terrain protecting this last bastion.

Federal forces had been trying to figure out a way to approach and take the city for months, all to no avail. Now Grant had a new scheme, which involved clandestine as well as overt measures. Jesse didn't bother trying to guess his role in all this. No matter what scenario he devised, the truth always turned out to be twice as dangerous.

"Well now...tell me, are you really a second lieutenant?" Sherman asked.

Jesse actually held the rank of captain but he made no reply. Rather, he glanced at the door beyond which the general's adjutant, Sergeant Wallace, had been posted in a narrow foyer that served as the school's coatroom in winter. Wallace had been provided a desk and chair and there he remained throughout the middle hours of each day, screening the general's visitors. On this Monday alone the burly sergeant had refused admittance to a local planter, the town's indignant schoolmaster, and an irate tavern owner, furious at the improprieties of some overboisterous troopers.

None of that mattered to Jesse. He had arrived in Memphis under the guise of a newly commissioned second lieutenant, a young officer painfully innocent of the realities of war. The veteran soldiers stationed around the schoolhouse had immediately dismissed him as an untried recruit. General Sherman alone knew the truth behind Jesse's deception.

"Don't worry, we can speak freely here. Sergeant Wallace has been with me since Manassas," the general remarked. "I trust him completely. His loyalty is above question."

"Begging your pardon, General Sherman, but you aren't the one who risks a firing squad if you are captured in the line of duty. I cannot afford to be careless."

Sherman reddened. He had never been addressed in such a fashion by a junior officer, and he didn't like it one bit. However, the general was too good a soldier not to see that Jesse made sense. Sherman had an army to protect him. A man like McQueen had only his wits and a heightened sense of caution to keep himself alive.

"Yes...I see." Sherman clamped down on his cigar. The tip burned brightly as the general enjoyed his smoke. Clouds of smoke billowed toward an open window. "So be it," the commander added. "You'll find that junior officers are taking rooms at the Delta Hotel on Market Street. I will contact you when I have talked to Major Abbot."

"Thank you, sir," Jesse said, and saluted. Sherman acknowledged the gesture and returned the salute.

"By the way, Sergeant Wallace has a letter for you. It was forwarded to this command," Sherman said. He attacked the stack of requisitions on his desk, his weapons of choice a quill pen and brass inkwell.

Jesse's mood brightened at the general's information. Something from home was exactly what he needed right now.

He took leave of the general and hurried from the schoolroom. He found Sergeant Wallace dozing in the noonday heat, dreaming, no doubt, of Milford, Connecticut, picnics on the green, and pretty girls serving cool lemonade to thirsty soldiers.

Jesse helped himself to the letter bearing his name and left the sergeant undisturbed.

Chapter Four

Washington, D.C.
September 3, 1862

My Dear Son,

    I deeply regret that I missed seeing you in Washington. I have been appointed agent for the affairs in the Indian Territory. I will present the case for remunerations due the Civilized Tribes for the lands appropriated by the governments of Alabama and Georgia. I have spoken loud and long as to the rightness of such an action. In truth, justice demands a favorable decision from Congress. I fear anything less will only add fuel to the fire that already threatens to burn out of control in the territory. My failure will only convince more of our young men to cast their lot with Stand Watie and take arms against that which generations of our family have fought to uphold and defend, these United States. I am compelled to remain in the capital and do what needs to be done and say what needs to be said. I shall not desist but intend to approach Mr. Lincoln himself and personally apprise him of the situation in the territory. Quick action might well defuse this powder keg of divided loyalties. I pray you are safe and well. Peter Abbot has promised this letter would reach you. I trust he has kept his word. Take care of yourself, Jesse. God bless you. Keep your powder dry. And watch your back.

Your loving father,
Ben McQueen

P.S. I hope you will be able to talk some sense into your brother when next you see him.

Jesse glanced up from the letter and leaned on the balcony railing overlooking Market Street and the center of Memphis. The thoroughfare was crowded with wagons, men on horseback, and a number of citizens who went about their daily routine, seemingly oblivious of the occupying force. The inhabitants of Memphis, though devoted to the Confederate cause, appeared to be making the best of an onerous situation. Although the city had not suffered bombardment, Union gunboats docked in silence at the pier. Yankee soldiers hailing from Ohio, Michigan, Indiana, and Missouri formed a seemingly endless parade through the streets as the federals made camp and took up positions on the outskirts of the city.

The proprietor of the Delta Hotel, a diminutive man named Elmo Dern, had provided Jesse with lodgings in a front room on the corner above Market Street. A narrow alley ran along the south wall of the hotel and led to the stable at the rear of the building. Most of the room's furniture had been removed, replaced by an extra couple of cots. Jesse was sharing the room with two other officers, who evidently were out on patrol. An assortment of boots, clothing, and personal effects had been left in trunks at the foot of each cot. Jesse had yet to unpack his own carpetbag. His discarded coat and gunbelt were draped across the foot of the cot.

Jesse set the letter aside and unbuttoned his shirt. He filled a basin on the dresser with water from a china pitcher then splashed his face and hair. He straightened and studied his reflection in the mirror. When he cocked his head to one side, the rope burn was still faintly visible in a streak of discoloration along his neck. Save for that and the scar on his left shoulder blade Jesse showed little evidence of the life he had lived recently. Perhaps there was an extra worry line or two around his dark brown eyes. But then, war had a habit of stealing the youth from a man.

He considered hunting up some dinner and had noticed a promising place across Market Street bearing the name Petersen's. Elmo Dern had cheerfully recommended the establishment as setting a fine table. According to the hotel owner, no one fried a chicken or batter-dipped a catfish as well as Widow Petersen. Jesse intended to find out for himself. Right now, however, sleep took first priority. He stretched out on his cot and reread the letter from his father. He yawned and closed his eyes, the page fluttering to his chest. The sounds from the street blurred into an undifferentiated noise that lulled him to sleep. Dreams carried him from the stifling hotel room to a hard, yet beautiful landscape where the wind in the buffalo grass sang the wild free praises of home.

Jesse bolted awake and wondered why. Then he heard it again, a woman's muffled scream followed by a coarse male voice ordering her to be quiet. He glanced toward the window overlooking the alley. He'd left it open to allow for a cross breeze. The interior of the hotel room was not as oppressive as it had been at noon. But it was dark now; he'd slept away the afternoon. He had no idea of the time.

"C'mon, you little Reb darlin', just a kiss for me and Milo," the masculine voice chided from the alley below. "Yeoow."

"Keep your filthy paws to yourself," the woman protested.

"The bitch damn near bit my finger off," the first man exclaimed. "Catch her, Milo."

"No, you don't. Try for the street, will you? Come on back to the stable. I'll warrant you'll look a pretty sight spread out on the hay," a second man replied, his voice deeper than the first.

Jesse, still drugged from sleep, thought he recognized them both. He stood and ambled across the room to the window and peered down at the figures in the darkness, a woman and two men, one of whom was a hulking shadow who had his big arms wrapped around his female prey. The woman gamely continued her defiance in the face of his overwhelming strength. As of yet, no one on Market

Street seemed aware of her predicament. The lout clamped a hand over her mouth to silence her.

"Bite that, you she-devil, and I'll mark you permanent with my knife," the big man growled.

"We'll see about that, Milo Stark," Jesse called. When the brute turned his bearded, ugly features upward, the man above leaped from the window.

The lumbering brigand shoved the woman aside and raised his arms to protect himself. Jesse landed atop Milo Stark and knocked him to the ground. McQueen managed to roll clear and scrambled to his feet in time to face Milo's companion. The second man retreated toward Market Street and stepped into the pale amber glare of the lanterns hung to either side of the hotel's front door. Lantern light revealed a man of average height with a round, chubby physique and dark oily hair. His face paled with fear on seeing Milo fall.

"Emory Stark, I might have known," McQueen said. He advanced on the youngest of the Stark brothers. "Where there's Milo, there's Emory, standing in his brother's shadow. Well, you're not in his shadow anymore."

"Jesse McQueen," Emory blurted out. He didn't sound happy. "You leave me be. This ain't none of your concern."

Suddenly Emory's courage returned and he jabbed a finger in McQueen's direction. "Get him, Milo."

Jesse shook his head and grinned. "Won't work, Emory. You have to handle this alone."

"Watch out!" the woman in the alley shouted.

Jesse turned and instinctively ducked what appeared to be a ham-sized fist. Milo followed with a roundhouse left and missed again as Jesse retreated from his towering assailant into Market Street.

"Damn, doesn't anybody bluff anymore," he muttered, backing into the street. He noted a paneled freight wagon that had been left in front of the Collins Mercantile adjacent to the hotel. A pair of strong-looking geldings were hitched to the wagon. The horses calmly grazed upon a mound of hay left on the ground by their owner, who crossed the street to the Petersen House to satisfy his own hunger. Jesse veered toward the rear of the wagon, drawing big Milo Stark toward him.

"Break him up, Milo," Emory admonished from a safe distance.

McQueen continued to retreat. Looking past Milo, he could just make out the slim, girlish figure and frightened features of the young woman he was attempting to rescue. And doing a poor job of it so far, he thought. Jesse was no coward. But only a fool would trade blows with the likes of Milo Stark. He was broad as a barn and solid as granite. Mere brawn wouldn't take the measure of such a man, at least not without bruised and broken bones in the process. Jesse had other ideas. His shoulders struck the rear of the wagon. The oak panels rattled against the pickle barrels that had yet to be unloaded into the mercantile. Jesse darted to the right, then the left. Each time Milo cut him off, blocking his escape as he advanced relentlessly. The big man was grinning now. He'd cornered his prey; it was time for the fun part.

"Stand still now, Jesse," Milo said. "This is only gonna hurt all week."

"Go to hell, you yellow bag of guts," Jesse replied.

Milo growled, cocked his right arm, and loosed a pile-driving punch. The woman in the alley screamed. Jesse dropped. The wind from that iron fist fanned his forehead. Milo's fist shattered wood, plowed through the oak panel, and lodged knuckle-deep in a pickle barrel. Milo yelped in agony as splinters pierced his flesh and brine washed his lacerated knuckles. He tried to jerk his fist free, but fragments of wood dug into his wrists and held him fast. Jesse scrambled out from underneath the freight wagon, slapped loose the brake with a swipe of his hand. The geldings turned to stare at him, mirroring the man's reflection in their round, dark eyes.

"Say good night to the lady, Milo," Jesse remarked.

The big man's grizzled features paled beneath his bushy black beard. His mean glare lost some of its edge as he began to realize his predicament. Still he managed to work up one last threat.

"You stop right there, McQueen, or so help me, you'll pay. You hear me? Stop right there!"

It was one threat too many.

"Don't tell me," Jesse replied. He glanced at the geldings. "Tell them." He slapped the rump of the animal nearest him and both geldings lunged forward in a brisk trot.

"Oh, no!" Milo roared. He made a futile grab for McQueen as the wagon rolled along Market Street. The big man lumbered along in its wake, his forearm held securely by the shattered panel. "Whoa!" he shouted. "Hold up, you bastards." The geldings, sensing the drag at the rear of the wagon, quickened their pace. Emory Stark dashed after the wagon. "I'm comin', Milo. Hang on!"

Jesse watched them leave and sighed, muttering "Good riddance." He glanced at the alley. The young woman had sought the safety of the wooden walk in front of the hotel. The commotion had at last attracted an audience. A handful of merchants and peddlers, a few blue-clad soldiers, and several ragtag, black children had gathered to watch the fracas. A couple of the merchants even applauded Jesse's victory. But before long the audience broke ranks and continued on their way. The children scampered off in pursuit of the freight wagon. They were hoping to steal a pickle or two, making the most of Milo's miseries. Seventeen-year-old Ophelia Tyrone, on the other hand, chose to remain. She had auburn ringlets and cream-colored cheeks, a freckled nose, and the kind of flirtatious smile men fought duels over. She introduced herself and Jesse McQueen hurriedly tucked in his shirt.

"I did not associate such gallantry with that uniform," Ophelia said. Jesse noticed her parasol upon the ground. He presented it to the comely young woman with a courtly bow.

"I am in your debt, sir," Ophelia added.

"One that can be quickly settled by the pleasure of your company at dinner," Jesse quietly suggested. Looking up into her hazel eyes, he felt his knees weaken. "If you don't mind waiting while I fetch my coat..."

"I don't even know your name, sir."

"Lieutenant Jesse McQueen of the Indian Territory, ma'am, at your service. And you are...?"

"Your dinner companion, Mr. McQueen."

The Widow Petersen's chicken lived up to its reputation, as did her peas and corn bread and berry cobbler. The widow made no secret as to her allegiance. The walls of her restaurant were decorated with the stars and bars of the Confederacy. Interspersed between the Rebel flags were several of the widow's oil paintings depicting a handsome array of gray-clad soldiers marching off to war, leaving sweet-hearts and loved ones behind. The one above McQueen's table was entitled *Farewell to Alexandria*, and it featured an especially poignant rendering of sad-faced, cherubic children clinging to their mother's billowing skirt, their pudgy hands waving a last good-bye to the father they might never see again.

By the time Jesse finished the meal, he knew Ophelia's name and that her brother was the notorious Captain Bon Tyrone, a Confederate cavalryman and scourge of Yankee patrols. Ophelia had spoken longingly of Dunsinane, the Tyrone plantation northeast of Vicksburg. Jesse spoke of the family farm in the Indian Territory and how his grandfather had forsaken the comforts of his ancestral home outside Philadelphia for the plains of the territory. He spoke of his childhood and his Choctaw grandmother, Raven O'Keefe McQueen, and her magical ways, how she taught him of the spirit in all things, the wind, the earth, and the creatures of the plains.

Ophelia was a good listener and found herself liking the second lieutenant despite the color of his uniform. She kept him talking, and not just for interest's sake. She didn't want him asking questions about what had brought a young woman such as herself out into the Memphis streets at night and alone. She could always claim the lame excuse that her driver had run off and she had gone looking for him. But that was hardly the only reason, and the truth—a clandestine meeting with her cousin Elmo Dern—might well land her in a Yankee prison. So she smiled and led her companion on. Indeed, Ophelia found the stories of his youth fascinating. She recognized his loneliness. He was a man far from home and a stranger. She, on the other hand, was home, though equally a stranger. Memphis was occupied country now, peopled by enemies of which Jesse McQueen was one. By rights, Ophelia ought to hate him.

Instead, she ordered a second dessert and let the minutes flow by like the unceasing currents of the Mississippi. She wondered where they were carrying her.

Jesse leaned back in his chair and noticed the last occupied table had just emptied. Three middle-aged men, merchants all, filed across the lantern-lit room toward the front door. Constance Petersen waited for them, greeting each of the Southerners with an affectionate farewell. The widow was an attractive woman in her late thirties, doe-eyed and voluptuous in her saffron-colored dress and apron, her cheeks smudged with a trace of cornmeal. She had a knack for making each of the merchants feel important. The merchants had stared stonily at Ophelia and Jesse throughout the evening. They had made no attempt to hide their disapproval of the woman's actions, consorting with one of the Northern oppressors. But the merry widow of Memphis seemed to have melted the merchants' icy resolve with a whisper and teasing admonitions. The men left in better spirits. Jesse had the feeling the widow Petersen lived quite a colorful life. Obviously she was not about to pine away for her deceased husband. The widow turned from the door and, sensing Jesse's scrutiny, met his gaze. She flashed him a look of invitation and a lusty smile.

"Constance likes you," Ophelia said, noting the widow's interest.

"No doubt her husband died in bed," said McQueen. *With a smile on his face*, he silently added.

"Why, so he did. How did you know? The poor man, I am told, just wasted away."

"Drained," McQueen wryly commented.

Ophelia caught his meaning, blushed, and returned her attention to the last of the cobbler set before her in a stoneware bowl. Two bites and it was finished. Jesse gulped the last of his coffee. Being the last of the widow's customers made them both feel awkward. A young mulatto emerged from the kitchen and began collecting the plates and cups from the tables. The widow Petersen's was not a large place. No more than a dozen tables crowded the dining room. A kitchen dominated the rear of the building. Tonight a cross breeze from the river made the interior of the kitchen bearable and cooled the dining room. The flowered curtains fluttered over the open windows and a ship's horn wailed forlornly on the night air as someone bled steam from a boiler.

A Seth Thomas clock set on a shelf below crossed sabers began to toll the hour, ten bells. Ophelia Tyrone and her darkly handsome dinner companion exchanged glances, each reading the other's thoughts. It was time for a proper young woman to be escorted home. Jesse rose, slid back her chair, and taking her arm, led Ophelia to the door. He paid for their meal with Yankee dollars. Despite the restaurant's decorations and the widow's blatant allegiance to the Confederate cause, she was not too proud to accept the greenbacks. She thanked the couple and suggested Jesse might stop back "if he saw a light and felt hungry and needed something to take back to his room." Jesse blushed and thanked her.

Outside on the walkway, Ophelia made no attempt to hide her amusement.

"Your first day in Memphis and already you have made a conquest," she remarked, lifting the hem of her pale green cotton dress as she stepped over a snag in the boardwalk.

"Right town, wrong spoils," Jesse said. The widow Petersen was without a doubt more of a challenge than he had the stamina to meet. And besides, this Memphis belle had caught his attention. She was gracious and well-spoken and had certainly showed courage. They arrived all too quickly at the porch of Florence Bradley's Rooms for Ladies. The front windows were unshuttered and had been left open to catch the breeze. Jesse could look in on an empty sitting room with velvet-covered love seats, and chairs and japanned end tables. Lamplight caught the brass buttons on his blue tunic and played upon his features, highlighting his brown eyes with flecks of gold.

"Perhaps you'll allow me to call on you during your stay here in Memphis," Jesse said. She smelled of rose water and sugared berries. He liked that.

"What would people think of me?" Ophelia said, her eyes downcast, that flirting smile touching the corner of her red lips. The evening had begun, in part as a ruse to keep from answering any questions about what had brought her out unescorted onto Market Street at night. But she liked the officer. She found him colorful and exciting, this young soldier raised among the wild Indians of the western territory. Nor did he seem filled with the hostility that many of the other Northern soldiers exhibited as they swaggered through Memphis streets, contemptuous of the inhabitants who remained resolute in their sympathies for what seemed to some a lost cause.

"I have only known you these few hours, Miss

Tyrone. But I must say, you strike me as a person who doesn't give two hoots and a holler what other people think." Jesse touched the brim of his hat and opened the door for Ophelia. Her auburn curls brushed his cheek as she entered the boarding-house, and with one last, languid look in his direction she replied, "You're right" and closed the door.

Jesse whistled beneath his breath and muttered "Mmm-mmm, Jesse, what have you found?" He stepped off the porch, missed the top step, and stumbled forward into First Street. A flash of metal whirred through the space he'd have been filling if he hadn't tripped. He ducked after the fact and heard something thwack into the porch post behind him. He spied a fleeting shift in the shadows across the street near the corner of the First Congregational Church, a whitewashed wood-and-brick structure, its spire upthrust against a starlit sky.

McQueen reached down to his right boot and tugged free a Smith & Wesson .22-caliber pistol. Sporting an octagonal barrel a fraction over three inches in length, the seven-shot rimfire weapon made a perfect "hideout" gun. It was light and sturdy and, at close range, quite lethal. He'd bought the revolver from a Cairo gunsmith a few months after his experience with Colonel Baptiste's lynch mob during the fall of New Orleans. Its rosewood grip was a reassuring weight in the palm of his hand.

Jesse crouched behind the porch of Bradley's Rooms for Ladies. He looked up at the post closest to him. Lamplight glinted on the bone hilt of a knife sprouting from the wood. He focused again on the church, studying its front yard and steps leading up to paneled double doors. The front windows were shuttered. No threat there. Jesse judged the distance across the street and estimated it at better than thirty feet. Above him, on the second floor of the rooming house, a window began to flow as someone lit an oil lamp. No doubt, Ophelia Tyrone was preparing for bed. Jesse grinned, his thoughts turning lascivious. But the attempt on his life dulled his ardor. He stood and worked the knife free from the post. His assailant would have had to feel pretty sure of himself to try a knife at such a distance. He studied the carefully honed double-edged weapon in his hand. He knew of only one man that sure of his prowess, Titus Connolly, cousin to the Stark brothers. A lean cautious little man, a knifemaker by trade, Titus had carved his way through a number of tavern brawls. The Starks might be a rough and arrogant lot, but Titus Connolly...now there was bad blood.

Jesse returned the .22-caliber pistol to his boot and tucked the knife in his belt. He cast a wary glance toward the starkly sinister facade of the Congregational church and headed back toward Market Street and the Delta Hotel.

He kept to the shadows as best he could. Twice he was hailed by patrols and allowed to pass once his uniform and second lieutenant's rank were recognized. The dimly lit lobby of the Delta Hotel was empty save for Elmo Dern perched on a stool and hunched forward, his head cradled on his folded arms upon the front desk. The stairway behind the snoring proprietor led to the second-floor rooms. Men's voices and the clank of glasses drifted in from the adjoining tavern, and Jesse considered joining those unseen patrons for a drink then changed his mind and continued up the stairs. Dern remained impervious to his passing. The hall upstairs could have used an extra lamp. Jesse had good reason to be leery of shadows. He was thankful that his room was close to the top of the stairs. He felt a tightness in the center of his spine as he turned his back on the dark hall to unlock the door to his room. A turn of the key. The sound of the latch seemed ominously loud in the stillness of the hall. He stepped inside and closed the door behind him, breathed a sigh of relief, and relaxed, but not for long. The curtains were drawn, and Jesse's eyes struggled to adjust to the darkness. For a few seconds he was blind, vulnerable, and one thing more.

He was not alone in the room.

Peter Abbot might have passed for a schoolmaster but he was a major in the army of the United States. A bookish man of average height with a penchant for the classics, at forty-seven Abbot had caved a niche for himself in Washington among the military leadership directing the Union war effort. After Abbot created a network of agents that had directly aided in the capture of New Orleans, the War Department began to take him seriously and had handed him another mission. And like before, Jesse Redbow McQueen was Abbot's man.

Seated on one of the beds, Abbot struck a match and lit the oil lamp beside him on the end table. The glow played upon his snow-white hair, brushed forward to hide a receding hairline. Wire-rim spectacles precariously perched upon the bridge of his Roman nose. He had exchanged his uniform for a black frock coat and gray and black vest, white shirt, and black string tie. The right-side pocket of his coat bulged from the weight of the navy Colt .36 he always kept close at hand. This "schoolmaster" was a crack shot.

Jesse closed the door leading to the hallway and took a seat on the bed where he'd left his carpetbag and gunbelt.

"Bravo the dashing hero," Abbot quipped. "Rescuing the fair maid, the sister of Bon Tyrone no less. I couldn't have planned it better."

"I suspected your hand in it, Major," McQueen replied. Peter Abbot had been a close friend of Jesse's father. Ben McQueen and Peter Abbot had pulled each other out of some tough scrapes in Mexico, and Abbot had been a frequent guest at the McQueen farm in the territory. Jesse had grown up calling the man "Uncle," but this night "Major" seemed more appropriate. After all, such a clandestine visit could hardly be considered a social call: Abbot had stolen into the room and waited with curtains drawn for McQueen to return. His tone of voice was cordial, but his slate-colored eyes were hard as steel behind the round lenses of his spectacles.

"It was none of my doing. I was damn near tempted to buy the Starks a drink for their help. But Milo was in a 'pretty pickle,' and I didn't want to bother him." Abbot chuckled, enjoying his own cleverness. Then he became serious again. "I'd watch my back if I were you; the whole Stark family has brought a herd of horses up from—"

"I know," McQueen said, interrupting his friend. He held up the bone-handled knife. "They've already come calling."

Abbot frowned. He needed Jesse McQueen alive, not lying dead in some Memphis street, the victim of a private feud. Maybe he ought to step in and have Sherman toss Doc, Milo, Emory Stark, and their inbred cousin into the nearest prison stockade. Then again, they had proved useful once, and might again.

Jesse studied the older man seated across from him. He remembered Abbot's last visit to the Indian Territory shortly after the Confederates had fired on Fort Sumter, plunging the nation into war. Jesse had been eager to enter the fray. He was young and hungry for adventure. He had been reared on the exploits of his ancestors, a father, grandfather, and great-grandfather who had joined their fortunes with that of the country they loved. The Union was threatened and Jesse was determined to do his part. When "Uncle Peter" offered him a field commission, the young man jumped at the chance. But his experience in New Orleans had left him older and wiser. It had taught him something of the reality of war and shown him the dark side of Major Peter Abbot.

"Let me worry about the Starks," Jesse replied. "Why don't you tell me why I'm here in Memphis, demoted to a second lieutenant?" He removed his coat and shirt. He thanked the powers that be for the breeze stirring the curtains.

Abbot nodded. He stood and crossed the room and noticed the English coin dangling against McQueen's muscled chest.

"So the medal's yours now. When did Ben pass it along to you?"

"Before I left for New Orleans. I like to think it brought me luck."

"Maybe it did. You're alive."

"Were you worried for me, Uncle?"

Abbot met his gaze, quite frankly. He did not waver for an instant. "I never had the time," he said, his features impassive, even guarded. Jesse was unable to tell just how serious the major really was. The man with the spectacles coughed and reached inside his coat to remove a map of Mississippi and part of Tennessee. He spread the map on McQueen's cot, forcing him to slide to one end. His index finger traced a line to Memphis then south down to Jackson, Mississippi, and westward, a distance of about thirty miles to the undulating scribble denoting the Mississippi River.

"Do you know the *Iliad*, Jesse," Abbot asked, "how the Greeks besieged Troy in a war that cost the lives of many a gallant warrior?"

"Father read it to me," Jesse replied, puzzled.

The major placed the tip of his finger upon Vicksburg. "This is Troy. As long as it stands, we cannot control the river. Troy must be taken."

"And what am I do in all this?" Jesse pressed further. It was time to lay all the cards on the table.

"Why... Jesse, don't you see?" Abbot replied, shoving his wire-rims back upon his nose. "You are my Trojan horse."

Chapter Five

Titus Connolly dipped his head in the horse trough and straightened, brushing his stringy, shoulder-length black hair back from his face. He glanced around at Milo and Emory, who waited impatiently for their cousin to tell them what had happened. After all, he'd been gone all night and they had feared the worst.

Titus grimaced as he noticed the torn right elbow of his coat and cursed the fence that had snagged him as he raced past the Congregational church after hurling the knife at McQueen.

"Well, did you git him?" Milo blurted out. He'd wrapped the knuckles of his right hand with strips of cloth. Pain continued to etch his features and his eyes smoldered.

"No," Titus remarked offhandedly. "Bad luck, there. So I lit out and found Doc at the cathouse. We run us some whores." He shrugged. "Lost me a good knife, too," he added. Titus pulled on his short-brimmed hat and headed across the corral toward the barn. The horses they had brought up from the territory parted as the three men headed for the gate. Stallions and mares tossed their manes and nervously stamped their hooves, churning clouds of dust that billowed gold in the morning light.

Titus took the lead, but Milo, with his long stride, quickly pulled abreast of his cousin as they neared the barn. They followed the smell of the coffee Emory had started brewing at sunup.

"That's all you got to say. Bad luck?" Milo shook his head and raised a fist to the empty air.

"There'll be another time," Titus growled. "I didn't see you doin' any better." They entered the shadowy interior of the ramshackle barn. Days ago, they had found the place abandoned with a scrawled note tacked to the door. *Goddam the Union and Goddam you, Billy Yank. Look for me in Vicksburg.*

The Starks had understood the note to mean they ought to make themselves at home and had done just that while a Union purchasing agent dickered over the price for their herd. Most of the animals had yet to be saddle-broke, another of the Starks' responsibilities. Titus Connolly intended for Milo and Emory to bear the brunt of that work. Gambling and knives were his expertise, he thought as he ambled among the slanted beams of sunlight streaming through the weathered shingles.

Milo brushed past his cousin and headed straight for his saddle and bedroll. A Colt revolving rifle lay atop his saddlebags. Milo took up the weapon and checked the loads as best he could with his bandaged hand.

Emory had poured a cup of coffee for his cousin, but he changed his course and offered the coffee to the big man with the rifle.

"Calm down now, Milo. Drink this."

Milo slapped the cup from his brother's hand. The smaller man beat a hasty retreat, tripped over a blacksmith's hammer, lost his balance, crashed through the side of a stall, and landed on his ample backside amid the brittle hay and dried dung.

"Son of a bitch!" Emory exclaimed, his tailbone hurt, but his pride had suffered the worse damage.

"Put your gun down, Milo," Titus said, standing by the cook fire Emory had built in the blacksmith's forge. A skillet had been set next to a tin plate crowded with biscuits. Eight strips of thick bacon floated on a sheen of hot grease in the skillet.

"You had your chance, cousin, now butt out," Milo said, and headed toward daylight.

"Milo . . . when they were handing out dumb, you must've stood in line for a double share." Titus gambled he could knock the brute senseless with the skillet before the man swung his rifle to bear. "We come here to sell these horses to the army. What kind of deal can we expect after you shoot one of their own?"

"Go to hell, Titus. I mean to have my due and I ain't gonna wait. You had your chance, now I'll settle this my way." Milo started forward. Titus hefted the skillet in his right hand, prepared to cave in the big man's skull rather than allow him to pass. The two cousins squared off, facing each other across the straw-littered floor. Dust motes, whirring flies, and an air of pent-up violence swirled around them in the rising heat. Milo had bulk on his side; brick hard and nigh unstoppable when the black rage came over him. But Titus was a lean and hungry killer. He was older by five years and twice as experienced. He knew the dark side of men. He'd lived there most of his life. Now Milo was asking for a visit. Well, he had come to the right guide.

"Now, isn't this a pretty picture," a man said from the entrance. The barn faced east and sunlight silhouetted the broad shoulders and solid frame of Doc Stark. No physician, the eldest of the brothers had come by his name simply enough. His Cherokee mother had been so happy at having a traveling physician deliver her firstborn son that she named the infant Doc.

Upon the death of his father years ago, Doc Stark became the patriarch of the family. Now his burly presence in the doorway defused the confrontation in the barn. Doc was a roughhewn chunk of a man who seemed to carry an invisible mantle of authority wherever he went. Not as tall as Milo, the middle brother, Doc weighed about the same, apportioning his bulk on his shoulders, legs, and the gut that hung over his belt buckle like a bay window. His features were blunt and weathered by the elements. He looked at the world through a perpetual squint that masked the cunning in his eyes. His shadow stretched out before him and lay between Titus and Milo.

"Hope you aren't fixing to waste that bacon," Doc said in a conciliatory tone of voice. "I'm hungry. And so's my friend here." He gestured off to the side, and a wiry-looking black man clad in homespun cotton shirt, brown vest, canvas trousers, and black boots joined him in the open doorway. They entered together. The black man looked to be about thirty years old. His eyes were red-rimmed from lack of sleep and darted from side to side as he nervously checked out the barn.

"This is Cicero. He used to work on the Tyrone plantation and was a driver for Miss Ophelia Tyrone.

I believe brother Milo here has made her acquaintance." Doc glanced around at the youngest of the Starks, who emerged from the stall and proceeded to dust off his nankeen trousers. He wore an expression of innocence upon his round-cheeked face.

"Emory, you know her, too, I understand," Doc said, a kind of menace in his voice. Emory Stark gulped and assumed a hangdog look.

Cicero hurried to the forge and helped himself to a couple of biscuits from the tin plate. He deftly plucked a few pieces of bacon from Titus's skillet, while Titus himself stared at the black man in astonishment. Cicero nodded his thanks and, using an anvil for a stool, proceeded to wolf down his breakfast.

"What the hell is going on, Doc?" Titus said.

Cicero studied his four benefactors. Though mixed-blood Cherokees, there was nothing Indian-like in their appearance except perhaps for their long black hair. He found it curious when Doc told him they hailed from Indian Territory. Cicero had no formal schooling but he was a shrewd judge of character. At a glance he could tell these were four men who would do just about anything for a handsome profit. Right now he needed them to stay free. But soon they'd be needing him.

Doc turned to face Milo. His gaze dropped to the Colt revolving rifle.

"Jesse McQueen's in town. He did this to me." Milo held up his bandaged fist. "I aim to make him pay."

"Sometime—but not today," Doc said. He hooked a thumb in his gunbelt. A Colt dragoon rode high on his hip in a worn leather holster. "Let it lay. We don't need trouble with the army. Not now, when Cicero here is fixing to make us all rich."

His words had an almost magical effect on his two brothers and Titus. Suddenly all differences were set aside, animosity vanished, weapons were lowered as the Starks and their cousin came together in the center of the barn.

"That's how it should be." Doc nodded approvingly. "We're blood kin. If we turn against each other, we're no better'n animals."

"A pretty speech, Doc," Titus remarked. "I like how it began. Something about this darkie making us rich."

"The name is Cicero," the black man interjected.

"I found him hiding in the stable out back of Letitia's Sporting House down by the river. Seems he's a runaway."

"I'm free. I aims to stay that way," Cicero said, heading for the coffeepot.

"What's he got to do with us?" Milo asked.

"Gold. A strongbox full of Spanish gold," Doc replied. The men around him grew silent. The only sound came from the restless herd of half-wild horses in the pens. Sweat rolled down Doc's cheeks and lost itself in the black stubble. He shifted his gaze to the black man. "Tell them," he said.

"Spanish gold in a wood-and-iron chest, so big." Cicero held his hands about two feet apart.

"Where?"

"Hidden on Dunsinane, the plantation where I was born, just a long day's ride from Vicksburg," the ex-slave told them, nursing his coffee. It was the first time in his life Cicero had ever felt important, and he was enjoying himself.

"I don't know how old Marse Tyrone came by it. But before he died he done had my pa hide that chest on the plantation. Now only three people know its whereabouts. Bon Tyrone and Miss Ophelia is two. And I be the third. My pa told me where he put it for Marse.''

"On a plantation!" Titus said, ruefully shaking his head. "What are we supposed to do, fight our way to Vicksburg, us four, against the whole damn Rebel army? Cousin, I admire your notion of fair odds." He started to turn away, but Doc caught him by the arm and turned him back.

"We let Grant do the job for us. It's common talk that Sherman and Grant will be joining up to march on Vicksburg. No one's sure as to the course they'll take." Doc folded his arms across his barrel chest and looked from Milo to Emory to Titus. "I say we tag along. And when we're close to Cicero's plantation, we'll light out, get the gold, and head for Indian Territory."

"Taking me along," Cicero added.

"Of course," Doc told the black man. "We're partners. Equal shares and you'll ride with us out of this heathen land to freedom." He extended his arm. "And here's my hand on it, in front of my kin."

Cicero nodded and clasped Doc's outstretched hand. Then he returned to the biscuits and bacon, his appetite yet to be appeased.

Behind him, Doc Stark continued to smile warmly, though on closer look, his eyes betrayed him. They glittered with a different hunger. Spanish gold—now, there was a feast a man might live and die for—or kill for. It was all a matter of taste.

Chapter Six

Toad Bradley stood on the porch of his mother's Rooms for Ladies and stuck two fingers in a jar of dark brown honey then popped them in his mouth. He was eleven years old, fair-haired and sunburned. He wore woolen knee-length trousers, suspenders, an oversized shirt haphazardly tucked in his waistband. He sucked his fingers clean and pulled them from his mouth with a pop.

"I said she's gone, mister. And my ma ain't here, so I can't get her. But she'd tell you the same thing. Miss Tyrone up and left this morning." He jammed his fingers in the honey jar, then, as if remembering his manners, removed his hand and tilted the wide-mouth jar toward Jesse McQueen.

"Have some. Autumn honey's thick as molasses and sweeter. Some folks like the runny kind, when its yellow gold in the spring." Toad wagged his head. "Not me. Have some. I don't mind if you're a

Yank. My ma says just 'cause we hate you bluebellies don't mean we can't be Christian."

"No, thank you," Jesse replied, waving the jar aside. It was after ten o'clock and the city had come to life. A crowd had begun to gather at the First Congregational Church across the street. Jesse had questioned the purpose of such an assembly until he saw the hearse drawn by four black horses pull up to the white picket fence.

Jesse returned his attention to the youth in the doorway, who continued to watch him with interest. Soldiers in the streets and gunboats at the pier—it was all very exciting to the lad.

"Did Miss Ophelia leave word when she might be back?"

Toad pinched his lips and scrunched his brow and thought real hard. Then he shrugged. "I could ask my sister but she probably won't tell 'cause Mirabelle ain't said nary a word since she heard Lee Bucklin got hisself killed at Pea Ridge. You want I should fetch her?"

"No." Jesse handed the boy a couple of pennies for his trouble and stepped down off the porch.

"Thanks, Yankee," the boy called after him. Jesse didn't hear. He'd already shifted his attention to Major Peter Abbot, who came galloping toward him past the funeral procession lining the front of the First Congregational Church. Abbot's frock coat flapped like the wings of a blackbird as he bore down on Bradley's Rooms for Ladies. The major rode a brown gelding and held the reins of a roan mare, saddled and racing alongside him. The major reined to a halt in a billowing cloud of dust. Jesse fanned his hat before his face to keep the grit out of his eyes.

"C'mon. I'll explain later. We haven't a moment

to lose," Abbot said, tossing the reins of the mare into McQueen's outstretched hands.

Jesse vaulted astride the roan and took off after the departing figure of his friend. Thoughts of a fair, pretty Southern belle vanished at the urgency he heard in Abbot's voice.

Jesse leaned into the roan, becoming one with the animal's smooth sleek stride. He had not been born a horseman, but growing up among the Choctaws had bred the skills in him. In a matter of minutes he had caught up to Abbot. Wind rushed past the young lieutenant's face. The holster at his side slapped his thigh. He felt a rush of adrenaline, his heart pounding in his chest, and sensed that events were already in motion, bearing him into harm's way.

Colonel Bon Tyrone knelt among the sweet-gum trees and held a spyglass to his right eye. He cut quite a dashing figure in his gray breeches and tunic and knee-high black boots. Upon his head, a cocked-brim gray hat sported a black plume. A .42-caliber LeMat revolver was holstered at his side. The LeMat carried nine shots in its cylinder. Beneath its six-and-a-half-inch barrel, a second shorter barrel held a load of buckshot fired by the same hammer due to its pivoting striker. Boniface Tyrone, Bon to his friends, "the Gray Fox" to his enemies, was a husky, rawboned man of twenty-eight. He stood six feet tall and had auburn hair like his sister, Ophelia. A darker-hued mustache and goatee covered the lower portion of his face. One hazel eye squinted shut while the other peered through the spyglass at the federal soldiers encamped to either side of a winding road that followed the Mississippi Central Railroad line. With the fall of Memphis, no Confederate train would dare venture this far north of Vicksburg. Ten miles outside of Memphis, this troop of federal cavalry had been posted to track the comings and goings of civilians and put a halt to any contraband traffic that might still attempt to cross over into Mississippi. Patrols were a constant threat for any Rebel soldier brave or foolish enough to venture this close to Memphis. Bon figured both words aptly discribed him . . . and his bullheaded sister.

"I see the carriage. There is a wagon behind, but Cicero's not driving the team." Tyrone shifted his gaze back to his sister, garbed in a pale yellow dress and buttoned black boots.

Sergeant Spider Boudreaux doubled over and sneezed. The noise seemed as loud as a gunshot to Bon Tyrone, and he whirled around and fixed the round-bellied Cajun in place with an exasperated stare.

"Spider!" Tyrone peevishly whispered.

"Sorry," the sergeant muttered, wiping a fore-arm across his nose and snorting.

"Don't be sorry. Be quiet, man," Bon Tyrone testily replied.

"Hell, Bonnie, if we weren't all by ourselves, ass-deep in Yankees, a man wouldn't have to fret about sneezing," Spider pointedly reminded his commanding officer. His lack of respect for the colonel's rank did not pass unnoticed by Bon. He'd known Spider Boudreaux for the better part of a year. The Cajun had proved himself relentless in battle, a tireless campaigner. Although they came from different stations in life, war had made them equals, at least when alone. In such moments Boudreaux seldom deferred to Tyrone's rank.

"And I must add, if you'd only strapped some sense into your sister like I done mine, we wouldn't be here at all," Spider added. The Cajun was a heavyset man in his mid-thirties, bald as an eagle. He was brown-bearded, clad in a butternut uniform and short-brimmed cap. His rough, dirt-creased right hand clasped the walnut stock of his .44-caliber Walker Colt. Both men had left their rifled muskets in their saddle scabbards on the mounts they had ground-tethered a few yards to the rear.

"They've stopped her. Damn!" Bon drew his own revolver and checked the loads.

"Good lord, Bonnie, you ain't about to ride down there and take on them Yanks." Spider Boudreaux turned pale at the notion of charging a whole troop of Yankee cavalry. Yet if that was the case and Bon Tyrone saddled up, the Cajun didn't intend to let his friend die alone.

"Where's your breeding, my friend? I was told the French Acadians were men of valor," Bon muttered.

"It ain't them bluebellies I'm feard of, but you," the Cajun said, his feathers ruffled now. "A rich man's son like you never had to hunt his grub. I cut my teeth on my pa's long rifle and learned to shoot when I was a boy child, yes."

"Meaning what?" Tyrone asked, frowning.

"Meaning everyone knows you are the worst shot of all the First Mississippi Volunteers. A man has as good a chance gettin' hit by your lead ridin' with you as agin' you and that's the gospel fact, I warrant."

Tyrone colored. Of all the effrontery. The trouble was, he knew the damn Cajun spoke the truth. Brave, shrewd, careful, and daring, these were all qualities of Colonel Bon Tyrone. But in his hands, a revolver was about as useful as a club. Tyrone holstered the LeMat and returned his attention to a trio of blue-clad soldiers who had proceeded to block Ophelia's carriage while another couple of men proceeded to search the wagon behind her.

"Fool girl. Stubborn girl," Tyrone said softly, his voice thick with emotion. He glanced at Boudreaux. "Say, I met your sister when she visited Jackson. Biggest woman I ever saw. If anybody got a strapping, it was you."

Boudreaux scowled and his round cheeks reddened above his scruff beard. He didn't even try to deny it. Tyrone started to chide him further when a hue and cry sounded from the federals surrounding Ophelia's carriage. They'd discovered something. Tyrone's heart sank. His little sister was one step away from a firing squad. And he was damn near powerless to help her.

"You have no business stopping me. These papers are signed by General Sherman himself," Ophelia protested as the Union private pried open the trunk strapped to the rear of the carriage. The driver of the wagon began to shift nervously on the wagon seat. Joe Dobbs, a clerk from the Delta Hotel, had no desire to sacrifice his life for the Confederate or any other cause. Elmo Dern had instructed the clerk to drive Ophelia Tyrone's wagon thirty miles down the river road to a point where a locomotive would meet them and load the supplies, carriage, and the daring young sister of Colonel Bon Tyrone onto a freight car bound for Vicksburg. Dobbs was supposed to have returned to Memphis with the wagon. Now the timid little man feared he'd return in irons to await execution. A federal soldier lifted the tarpaulin covering the wagon bed and peered in at what appeared to be a brass bed frame and various boxes and barrels of fruit, salted meats, wine, and toiletries all destined for Major General Earl Van Dorn, compliments of his old comrade at arms, General Sherman. War was one thing, friendship another, and there seemed no reason why the two couldn't coexist.

But the courtesy between generals was the furthest thing from Ophelia's mind. Her own situation became more and more precarious with each blow from the stock of the soldier's musket as he battered the padlock until the catch released. Several of his friends had gathered around to see what treasures might be contained in the trunk.

"You have no right!" Ophelia continued to protest. She snatched up the buggy whip and stepped out of the carriage.

One of the soldiers slapped his sleeve. "The color of this here uniform gives us the right, missy."

"By heaven, here's a find," the first private exclaimed as he stared at twenty-four brown glass bottles of French brandy. He grinned. "Those generals sure are a thirsty bunch."

"No drier than I am right now," another of his friends mused.

The buggy whip cracked. One of the soldiers howled, clutched the seat of his pants, and hop-stepped out of the way. The others scattered as Ophelia attacked. The private by the trunk tried to take a bottle with him.

"Put that back," Ophelia warned, and nicked the tip of his ear with the whip.

"Yeow!" The private backstepped, lost his balance, and landed on his rump in the dirt. The bottle shattered on a rock.

"Dammit woman!" the private growled. "That's a waste of good..." His voice trailed off as the liquid's distinctively pungent fumes assailed his nostrils. "Brandy, my ass. That's chloroform! Sergeant Appleton!" The private scrambled to his feet and pointed at the woman. "Train your guns on her, boys. She's smuggling contraband to her Rebel friends."

The mood of the soldiers abruptly changed. They were no longer amused by the antics of a defiant young girl. Suddenly she was poison in their midst. Rifle muskets were leveled at her. A soldier caught up the reins to her carriage and kept the mare from wandering off.

Sergeant Appleton, an efficient-looking man with thick black sideburns and thinning hair, emerged from the cluster of tents set just off the road. He headed for the carriage, where the private quickly related his discovery. Sergeant Appleton looked at Ophelia, his features stern.

"Are all those bottles like the one Jones broke?" he asked. The woman remained silent. "I can smash 'em and find out for myself."

"They contain chloroform," Ophelia said, resigned to her fate. There was no point in seeing the medical supplies she had hoped to smuggle to Vicksburg needlessly destroyed. No doubt they would find the surgical instruments once the barrels of "salt pork" were opened.

"Then I'm afraid I must place you under arrest, ma'am," Appleton replied, touching the leather brim of his blue cap. "And I fear it'll go hard for you, no matter how pretty you be." The sergeant wagged his head and wiped the perspiration from his face with his forearm.

"Rider comin'," said Private Jones. Appleton shifted his gaze. Ophelia turned to look and recognized Jesse riding at an easy pace along the Memphis-to-Vicksburg road. Her heart sank. Now she was caught in another lie, pretending to the second lieutenant that she would be staying in Memphis when in truth she had surreptitiously left the city with the disguised load of supplies.

Her cheeks reddened as Jesse walked his lathered mount past the freight wagon and up to the Union sergeant. The rest of Appleton's men remained by their campfires.

Jesse remained impassive as he took in the surroundings. Ophelia thought it odd that he should pretend not to know her. Her own sheepish smile faded.

" 'Morning, sir," Sergeant Appleton said, saluting.

McQueen returned the gesture. He had left Peter Abbot back along the road, well out of sight of the Union cavalrymen. The major had provided him with crucial information about Ophelia Tyrone, and now Jesse knew what had to be done. Smuggling medical supplies out of a federal occupied city; McQueen admired the young woman's spunk. From what he knew of Ophelia and had heard of her brother, there was no lack of courage in the Tyrone family.

"What do we have here, Sergeant?"

"We caught this lady trying to sneak medical supplies to the Rebs," Appleton replied. "I'll dispatch a couple of men to drive the wagons back and lock her up." He held up the neck of the broken bottle. "Chloroform. She's got a trunk of it."

"And see her shot? Come now, Sergeant. There is precious little beauty in the world as it is. Why diminish it even further?"

"Sir?" Appleton frowned, trying to understand.

"A shipment of chloroform is not going to affect the outcome of this struggle one way or another," McQueen explained. He doffed his hat and bowed to Ophelia. "Let her pass."

"Sir? You ain't serious!"

"I gave you an order, Sergeant." McQueen slowly looked around and repeated his command in a threatening tone of voice.

"I aim to report this," Appleton said. He turned to the men around him. "You boys'll back me." They nodded, having little use for the sergeant but none at all for officers.

"My order stands."

Ophelia couldn't believe her ears. But she wasn't about to wait and give the Union officer time to reconsider. She returned to the carriage, took the reins from the soldier standing by the mare. At a flick of the reins the animal started forward. Ophelia heard the freight wagon creak on its axles as Dobbs gratefully released the brake and followed after the woman.

Jesse trotted up alongside the carriage as it left Appleton and his men behind. Now he was smiling, and his deep brown eyes seemed to flash and sparkle.

"I suppose this means you won't be joining me for dinner tonight," he said.

Ophelia glanced at him. Was he making fun of her? Her temper started to rise, then subsided.

"Why did you help me?"

"Because you needed help." McQueen shrugged. "And besides, who am I to deprive some poor wounded soul a modicum of comfort? Pain and suffering are color-blind. Should I be any less?"

"Will you be punished?"

"Probably."

"Then ride with me," Ophelia said. "Come south. Join us. My brother would welcome you."

"No...I don't know. Maybe someday. I have to think on it," Jesse said. He glanced over his shoulder. "For one thing, the sergeant will suspect me of being a Rebel spy and come after us." He tugged on the reins. Ophelia also stopped.

"If I go back now, he'll be afraid to disobey my orders," Jesse told her.

"Then all I can say, gallant sir, is thank you and farewell and—" Ophelia lowered her eyes then looked up at him with a smile full of flirtatious promises.

"And maybe someday..." She flicked the reins and the carriage rolled on past, leaving Jesse to whistle beneath his breath and wonder what kind of trouble he was getting himself into. Time would tell. If it didn't run out first.

Chapter Seven

On the day of his court-martial, as he was being drummed out of the service, Jesse Redbow McQueen had a dream—or maybe it was a vision. After all, he wasn't asleep. It happened without warning. The Union officers, the blue-clad soldiers drawn up into ranks, two solemn-faced drummer boys standing at attention, the cooling wind stirring the dust in front of the schoolhouse, the rhetoric and excoriation, everything seemed to blur into a disquieting haze as his sight turned inward. Suddenly he stood once again in the shadow of the bur oak on the McQueen farm and heard the sighing wind that carried the distant song of a meadowlark.

It was sunset, autumn, in the time of the harvest moon, and Jesse was fifteen years old. He had finished his chores, fed and watered the livestock, and secured the barn. He'd just started back to the house and the promise of a hearty supper by a warm fire when he chanced to glance up toward the hill that provided a windbreak north of the house. He spied the figure of his grandmother, Raven McQueen, standing at the summit. She seemed transfixed by the setting sun that painted the clouds gold and pink and bright vermilion against the rapidly darkening sky.

Jesse climbed the hill. Tired as he was from his chores, he felt drawn to his grandmother and could not deny the call. Coyotes had begun their mournful chorus. As a child he had thought the wild dogs were responsible for night, that they sang the sun down with their howling.

It was a fair-sized hill for this part of the country, a mound of earth rising a hundred feet from the rolling prairie floor. The short-stem grasses crunched beneath the fifteen-year-old's boots as he followed that quiet summons spoken in the stillness of his young soul. When he reached the hilltop, he found not only Grandmother Raven but his younger brother, Pacer.

At thirteen, Pacer Wolf McQueen was already showing the growth that had left him a head taller and a few inches broader than brother Jesse. And yet, in their roughhousing, Jesse had always managed to hold his own. Pacer Wolf had a long face with high cheekbones and straight red hair that hung to his shoulders. Though fair-skinned as Jesse McQueen, Pacer Wolf affected the ways of the Civilized Tribes. A one-eighth Choctaw was no different than a full-blood as far as young Pacer Wolf was concerned.

Even at fifteen, Jesse knew better. He loved his grandmother and his spirit was one with her people, but it was in the white man's world that he would make his home.

In the fading light Pacer Wolf could see his brother's accusing glare. Jesse McQueen had handled the chores for two because his brother had not arrived in the barn to share in the work.

"He has been with me," Raven told Jesse, reading his unspoken question. She smiled and placed her hand on the older brother's shoulder. "It was more important. Time is the swiftest rabbit, darting away through the grass. My days grow shorter. And when I am gone..." She shrugged. "There will still be stalls to clean, livestock to feed. There will still be rabbits."

Jesse's anger softened and he became alarmed at her words. Was she ill? "Raven?"

"Shh," she said, placing her fingers on his lips. In her fifties, with her black hair streaked with silver and windblown at dusk, she was still beautiful, still the same figure of kindness and love who had taken her two motherless grandchildren to her heart and shown them the world through different eyes, shown them wonderment and mystery.

"Give me your hand," she said, and placed it on Pacer's, until brother clasped brother.

Jesse and Pacer Wolf looked sheepishly at one another.

"The blood of the McQueens runs hot, pride is deep. But fire comes to divide, to tear apart the bond. If it is weak, the bond will break." She shook her head. Pity in her voice gradually turned to determination, and as the red sunset bathed her in its glow, she raised her arms to the horizon.

"I see a time of fire and sword. It will test you, yet you must remain strong. And the bond must not be broken though you walk different paths."

Pacer Wolf, already a strapping lad at thirteen, tightened his grip. He and Jesse had had their quarrels the same as any siblings, but they always stood united against enemies or threats from outside the family. There was nothing and no one the McQueen boys couldn't defeat.

Sensing the urgency in Raven's voice, the brothers locked hands and shared each other's strength while the blazing sun stained their clasped hands crimson.

Jesse faced the far horizon. Above the molten gold sun, a single cloud trailed its gossamer vapors like wings above the prairie, a plumage of fire and shadow, purple sky and iridescent streams of light. He wasn't sure what any of it meant, but it was important to his grandmother and Jesse could sense the power here, the presence of something beyond what he had ever experienced before. It frightened him a little, and left him awed, too. Then the light dimmed, colors died with the sun, and in the darkness the brothers released their handclasp.

Raven removed a small buckskin pouch from around her neck and placed it over Pacer Wolf's head. The thirteen-year-old boy looked puzzled. He started to open the pouch and Raven stopped him.

"You must never look inside," she said. "It is a medicine pouch, a spirit bag."

Pacer Wolf glanced down at the bag and cradled it in the palm of his hand. It certainly couldn't hold much.

"What is in it?"

"I will not tell," Raven said.

"Why, Grandmother?"

"So that your life will have mystery," she told him. Then she turned to Jesse. Even in the deepening dark, by the starlight, she could tell he felt awkward and left out. Raven smiled and embraced him, and the night flowed around them like raven's wings as she spoke softly, for him alone to hear.

"Your father will give to you that which you

must bear with honor and courage. It is powerful medicine and holds the history of your people, and it will make you one with all who have gone before." Raven stepped back and looked at the two boys and perhaps she wondered where the years had gone. At least that was what Jesse thought, watching her.

"You aren't going to be...uh...leaving us or anything, are you, Grandmother?" he asked, still uncertain.

"You mean am I dying," she said, and laughed. "No. It is only a sunset, not the last sunset." The wind swept over them, a night wind that howled with the coyotes and then was gone. "But do not worry, my young pups," she added. "Even when I am dead and my bones return to this good earth, I will never leave you."

A night of stars, the fading whisper of an autumn breeze, and mystery, the images shattered like broken glass as a drumroll brought Jesse back to the present. A soldier roughly stripped him of his brass-buttoned blue coat and his army-issue hat.

"Jesse McQueen," one of Sherman's officers, a major, droned on. Jesse braced himself. "You are hereby ordered out of this encampment. If you are found within the confines of a federal post or barracks, you will be arrested and summarily hanged." The major glanced over at a nearby captain standing before a rank of troopers, none of whom seemed to be enjoying these proceedings. "Captain Elys, start this civilian toward town."

"I know the way, you son of a bitch," Jesse retorted, and spun on his heels. He marched from the schoolhouse and past the soldiers ringing the front yard. One of the federals, a freckle-faced private, stuck out his musket stock and tripped Jesse as he walked by and sent him sprawling in the dirt.

Rough laughter followed by a chorus of cheers swept through the assembled soldiers. They considered this ex–second lieutenant a turncoat and were only too happy to show their contempt for him. Jesse stood and dusted himself off. A trickle of blood oozed from a scrape on his cheek where a jagged stone had cut him. He stared at the private. The young soldier tried to meet Jesse's eyes but lasted only a few seconds before averting his gaze. The men around him were veterans, though, seasoned at Wilson's Creek and a half a dozen nameless skirmishes that would never make their way into the history books.

"Get along, Reb lover," one of them growled. "We've buried many a friend since leaving Illinois and we ain't got no use for your kind."

"Seems he's been wearin' the wrong color uniform," another of the soldiers shouted from the ranks.

Jesse glared at the soldiers. Beyond them, he noticed several of the townspeople had also come to watch, and one of them appeared to be taking notes. McQueen had a feeling his court-martial would make the local newspaper.

"Maybe I have," he retorted, loud enough to be heard by everyone present.

A shove from behind sent him staggering out of the encampment and onto the wheel-rutted street that led toward the center of town. He looked around at Captain Elys, whose stern features appeared etched in stone. Jesse spat in the dirt and continued on his way, taking with him nothing but his gun and his shame.

"God, I hate to see that," General William Sherman muttered. Sunlight poured through the unshuttered window and turned the hardwood floor beneath his feet the color of butterscotch. He kept an unlit cigar firmly clenched between his teeth and looked more gaunt than usual as he watched what only he and Major Peter Abbot and the poor bastard outside knew to be a charade. The general turned to glare at his bespectacled visitor seated on a bench perusing a child's primer he'd discovered on the floor beneath a bookshelf. Peter Abbot sensed the general's stare and looked up.

"What do you want me to say, General Sherman?"

"I don't know," Sherman replied. His tall, rail-thin frame was bowed with the burden of command. "Maybe we should have told the men. They were pretty rough on McQueen."

"If we had told the men outside, then we might as well have posted broadsides throughout Memphis declaring the whole procedure to be a fraud, a fabrication concocted by myself to plant a Union agent in the midst of the enemy," Abbot flatly stated. He removed his wire-rim spectacles and wiped the lenses on a swath of cloth fished from his pocket. Abbot was dressed as a drummer now, a purveyor of women's undergarments and bolts of cloth. "General, with all due respect, in this business, the fewer people who know the truth, the better. The only reason I've told you is that I wanted to make sure you didn't have McQueen shot instead of court-martialed."

Sherman glanced up sharply, removed the cigar from his mouth, and tossed it in the nearest waste-basket. This black business had even ruined his taste for tobacco.

"It galls me to see an innocent man dishonored and humiliated as has been done this day. How do you stand it, Major?"

"I don't watch," Abbot matter-of-factly replied.

He set the primer aside and clasped his hands. "I sometimes wonder if it weren't better to be born a dog; to live, eat, sleep, to get by in ignorance. To die and be done with it. No decisions, no subterfuge, no right or wrong to worry about. Yes, I envy such an existence." Abbot stood and ambled over to another cabinet where Sherman kept a bottle of Kentucky bourbon and a couple of glasses. He poured a measure for himself after the general nodded his unspoken permission and then returned to his bench. He crossed his legs and leaned against the wall. "But I have been born a man in a time of war."

"And what sort of man is young McQueen?" the general wondered aloud.

"One who loves his country, General Sherman," Abbot replied. He sipped the bourbon, closed his eyes, and sighed. "Ben McQueen is just about the bravest and most honorable man I have ever met. His sons are cut from the same cloth." He raised his glass in salute to Jesse McQueen and gulped the last of the bourbon. It burned a fiery path down his gullet and he sucked in a lungful of air to temper the heat.

"So now what do we do?" Sherman gruffly inquired. He preferred his battles out in the open, both camps drawn up to either side of the battlefield. It was easier to order men to die when the way was clear and all parties were at risk. He wouldn't have traded places with McQueen for all the cigars in Virginia.

"We wait," Abbot told him, "for Johnny Reb to make the next move."

Chapter Eight

The court-martial was all the talk among the patrons of the Channel Cat Saloon down by the waterfront. And as most of the men lining the bar or slumped in chairs around the card tables wore blue uniforms, the conversation became louder and more threatening the longer Jesse remained in the room. He was seated in a corner with his back to the wall, and a bottle, three-quarters empty, rested on the table in front of him. The empty shot glass was like a challenge, daring the man to chance one more drink.

Jesse no longer wore his previous uniform. He had exchanged his blue trousers for a pair of faded brown canvas pants and a coarsely woven cotton shirt. Black boots, his leather gunbelt, and a worn-at-elbows brown frock coat completed his attire. He yawned and ran a hand through his shaggy black mane and wished he'd been able to talk the merchant of Evans's Mercantile into extending him credit for a hat. The merchant, however, was a shrewd Southerner who recognized a bad deal when it was offered him. He kept his hats and sent Jesse on his way bareheaded.

A chorus of ugly laughter erupted from along the bar. At a table nearest to McQueen's, five crewmen from the transport *Henry Clay* gambled for one another's pay. One of the cardplayers, a swarthy, pinched-face engineer, had lost all his money and was looking for someone to blame for his misfortune. Naturally, he found just the man responsible. Ignoring the protests of his associates, the engineer shoved clear of the table and lumbered unsteadily across the room toward the solitary ex-soldier in the corner. When he reached Jesse's table, the engineer leaned forward on his knuckles. Beads of sweat dripped from his jowls.

"Hey, turncoat, I heard all about you," he said. "Bad luck. You brung me bad luck is what."

Jesse poured himself a drink and, lifting the glass to his lips, surreptitiously surveyed the room. Yes, there they were, two men in civilian clothes standing near the door, trying not to call attention to themselves. They had been following him throughout much of the evening, from one waterfront tavern to another. The Channel Cat was the loudest, most crowded, and smoke-filled of the lot. The owner was a Union sympathizer and eager to serve the federals and take their money. For a mere dollar, one Yankee greenback, a man could even visit one of the girls in the rooms upstairs and have a *real* good time.

Jesse peered past the rim of the glass at his two "shadows." They were a mismatched pair. One sported a carefully trimmed goatee and mustache. He looked strong and, even in the ragged attire of a farmer, carried himself like an aristocrat. There was something decidedly familiar about him, but McQueen was certain he had never met the man before. His companion also wore the down-at-heel raiments of a dirt farmer, and a poor one at that. Yet from the look of his ruddy complexion and firm, round belly, the man had not missed too many meals.

The *Henry Clay*'s engineer shifted his stance to block Jesse's line of sight.

"I said what are you gonna do about it?" The engineer was drunk and looking for trouble.

"Leave the man be, Hank," another of the crewmen called out. "Come and take a dollar from the pot and spend it on a gal upstairs."

"Better listen to your friends, Hank," McQueen quietly added, his brown eyes hard as granite. He did not want trouble, but if it came...No. He swallowed his pride and began looking for a way out.

The engineer glanced around at his companions, who offered no encouragement. Suddenly a mustachioed corporal at the bar raised his whiskey bottle and shouted out, "Here's to President Lincoln! Here's to the United States! And down with Johnny Reb and them who turns their back on the Stars and Stripes!" Then he tilted the bottle to his lips and drank three times.

Several soldiers stood and shouted "Hurrah" and raised tankards and glasses in salute to the corporal's sentiments. The *Henry Clay*'s engineer grinned and wiped his nose on his forearm. He frowned, remembering the turncoat, and swung around. "Now as I was..." He was talking to an empty wall. He blinked and rubbed his eyes and stared at the empty seat as if half expecting a trail of blue mist to rise from the chair marking where Jesse had been. "What the hell?" the engineer muttered, shook his head, and decided to take his cohorts up on that dollar. He staggered past the open window to the right of the corner table. Like almost everyone else in the tavern he'd been so busy "hurrahing" the Union he hadn't noticed McQueen swing a leg over the sill and drop into the black alley outside.

But the two men by the door had seen McQueen make his escape, for they had ignored the boisterous throng. Bon Tyrone and Spider Boudreaux had no cheers for these blue-clad aggressors and what they represented. Tyrone nodded to the bald man beside him and started for the door. But the Cajun had a tankard of hard cider to finish and started to protest. Tyrone shrugged and, facing the room, wiped a hand to his mouth. "Here's to General Grant!" The soldiers were getting into the mood now and cheered wildly.

"Here's to General Sherman," Boudreaux called out, and took another swallow from the tankard. Again the soldiers in the Channel Cat responded.

"And three cheers for Jefferson Davis," Bon Tyrone called out. "Hip, hip, hooray!" And the tavern crowd, without realizing what had been said, raised their voices in a hearty hurrah for the president of the Confederacy. Spider Boudreaux gulped and set his tankard down and followed the Gray Fox out the door. On "hip hip" number three, the cheering died. "What the hell?" a voice called out, and the soldiers in the bar began looking around for the culprit who had instigated such a treasonous salute.

Jesse headed straight down River Street, leaving the taverns behind. He had spent half the night squandering the last of his money on bad whiskey and cheap conversation. To one bartender he had renounced any loyalty to the Union and in another saloon he had asserted that federal troops were without honor. On a street corner he had drunkenly voiced such sentiments as to rouse the ire of some passing soldiers, and only by the grace of their commanding officer did he escape a savage beating. But the Channel Cat had been his last stop. He had established his sentiments. Now it was time for action.

He left the tavern district and spied the drummer's wagon, its team of bay geldings ground-tethered in a vacant lot. With a furtive glance over his shoulder, Jesse veered toward the paneled wagon, shuffling and wavering just enough to give the impression of a man who'd reached his limits. He stepped up to the rear wheel, unbuttoned his fly, and proceeded to urinate against the hub.

"Goddammit, Jesse, I'm under here." Major Peter Abbot's harsh whisper drifted up from beneath the wagon.

"I know." McQueen chuckled. "Serves you right for putting me through that show this afternoon."

"Son of a bitch. All over my bedroll," Abbot muttered.

Jesse heard the sound of blankets and gunbelt and boots being pulled away from the spreading puddle. "Better stay under the wagon, I think I'm being followed."

"Oh, hell," Abbot groaned. "Think you're so smart . . . no respect for your elders . . . Ben didn't whip you enough when you were young. . . . Of course you're being followed. I've seen them. Dirt farmers, my ass. If one of them isn't a Confederate officer, I'll eat my hat. Well, no, I won't, seeing as you've pissed on it."

"Calm down, Uncle. My my, you do have a temper," Jesse said, buttoning his pants. He leaned on the wheel rim and scraped the bottom of his boots clean on a spoke. "I'm heading south," he added.

"Tonight?"

"Be safer than staying in Memphis what with half the army thinking I ought to be strung up and the other half shot."

"You don't have a horse."

"I'll steal one. I spied plenty of mounts in a corral yonder." McQueen glanced toward a barn and corral set well back from the bluffs midway between the town proper and the rowdy streets and alleys by the docks where Union gunboats and transports were moored along the banks of the Mississippi.

"That's Doc Stark's herd."

"Even better," McQueen replied. His boots were scraped clean. There was no reason to linger by the wagon any longer without arousing the suspicions of whoever might be watching. "I'll be seeing you, Uncle."

"Jesse. I promised your pa I wouldn't let you come to any harm. Don't make a liar out of me. The Starks are a mean bunch." The voice seemed to be coming from the front axle up near the singletree. The major had maneuvered to dry ground. Jesse was astonished. Damn if Abbot didn't sound almost worried. Uncle Peter must be getting softhearted in his old age.

"No problem," said Jesse. "The Starks will never know I've paid them a visit. Not till they count their tally. Remember, I'm part Indian." McQueen hitched up his trousers, stepped around the drummer's wagon, and headed toward the corral and the herd just waiting for him to make his pick.

* * *

A full moon bathed the restless herd in its silvery light. Wild mares and stallions circled the fencing and kept clear of Jesse as he opened the gate, leaving it unlatched. He trod steadily across the trampled earth. A roan stallion swung about to confront the intruder. The horse neighed and pawed the ground and shook his flowing mane as if it were a battle flag.

Jesse began to chant in a soft sibilant tone the words a Choctaw horse trader had taught him. It was a spirit song only a few men knew, for the ways of the Horse Clan were guarded and mysterious.

> "Be gentle, brave one,
> For you and I will be brothers.
> We will ride the wind.
> You will carry me and
> Sweet grasses shall be
> Yours to eat.
> Be gentle, brave one,
> For your brother is coming."

The blaze-faced roan gazed warily at the approaching human but held its ground as if spellbound by the chant. Jesse, pausing after each step, advanced on the stallion until he had drawn close enough to reach out and stroke its neck and muzzle. The stallion's hot breath fanned the man's knuckles, and the animal trembled as Jesse continued to run the flat of his hand over its flesh, all the while steadily repeating the spirit song. At last it was time for the moment of truth.

McQueen adjusted his belt, then gripped the stallion's bloodred mane. He checked the silent barn for a telltale movement. If the stallion fought him, the noise was bound to attract attention. The open doorway remained black and empty. Good. He'd caught the Starks sleeping. They'd never know. . . .

"I always said you had a way with horses, Jesse," Doc Stark's gravelly voice sounded behind him. McQueen's heart sank as he turned and saw the eldest of the Stark brothers step out from the shadows of a pole-framed shed at the far end of the corral. Hay had been piled beneath the shed's slanted roof, providing food for the herd and excellent concealment for Doc. Moonlight glinted off the long barrel of his Colt revolver. Stark was dressed as a Union soldier. He seemed to sense Jesse's astonishment.

"Yep," he said. "My brothers and I enlisted yesterday. Been assigned to saddle-break this stock here. Now the worm has turned, eh? We're soldiers and you—well—what are you? Let's see . . . a turncoat like your brother. And caught stealing army horses. Now that is sweeter than fresh cream skimmed from a pail." He took another stiff-legged step toward his captive. "Good judge of horseflesh, too. You picked the best of the bunch, charmed that roan proper. Reckon I'll keep him for myself. Now stand aside."

"And then what, Doc?" Jesse remarked, his muscles tense and ready to spring. He'd only get one chance. He had better do this right.

"Then we'll make Big Milo a happy man," Doc said. "I wouldn't be surprised if he beat you plumb to death." Doc cupped a hand to his mouth. "Milo! Hey, Milo!" He raised the gun and fired a shot into the air. The Colt thundered and spat a tongue of flame.

McQueen swung astride the roan stallion as it lunged forward. Doc tried to bring his revolver to bear on his captive, but Jesse crouched low on the stallion's back and Stark hesitated, unwilling to risk injury to the roan. Then he changed his mind and raised his revolver. Gunfire erupted from outside the corral. Two men on horseback blasted away at Doc, who spun on his heels and, despite his game leg, dived for the safety of the hay shed. He hit, rolling, and scrambled behind a water trough.

Jesse looked up in surprise at the actions of the two "dirt farmers" who had joined the foray. He didn't know who they were but he was grateful. Jesse started the roan toward the gate, then had a better idea and rode back through the corral, his gun drawn and a wild cry on his lips as he fired a shot. The panic-stricken herd fled before him. Flame blossomed in the barn doorway as Milo, Emory, and Cousin Titus staggered from their bedrolls, guns in hand. They opened fire as the startled herd barreled into the unlatched gate. It tried to swing open but the crush of horses shattered the wood and tore the hinges loose and the gate disappeared under the flashing hooves.

Jesse kept his knees locked on the stallion's belly as gunshots mingled with the thunder of the stampeding herd.

Doc Stark cursed and emptied his pistol at Jesse, veiled by the churning dust. "No!" he bellowed as his gun clicked on an empty cylinder. He'd fired the last of his loads. He hurled his curses after the stampeding herd.

Milo stood in the doorway and stared in disbelief as the horses crashed through the gate.

"C'mon!" he shouted to Emory and Titus before charging out the door.

Titus held back. He wasn't about to blunder outside into a hail of lead. He recognized Jesse and chanced a shot. He sensed movement behind him, whirled around, and came to within a fraction of an inch shooting Cicero between the eyes. The black man held out his empty hands.

"Don't ever sneak up behind me again," Titus growled, and turned once again to the escaping herd. The lean little man cursed and fired his Colt, and one of the mares lurched and crumpled to the ground, blood pumping from its side. That was one horse McQueen wouldn't steal. A lead slug splintered the wood a few inches from his skull and Titus jumped back, realizing for the first time that Jesse had help. He shifted his aim and traded shots with the two horsemen as they rode up to turn the herd and head it away from town.

"My God," Cicero said, standing alongside Connolly. The runaway slave peered through the moonlight at the men who had come to McQueen's aid. "Sweet Jesus, it be him. It's the Gray Fox hisself...Bon Tyrone." Cicero backed toward the nearest stall and his red-rimmed eyes were wide with fear. "Ain't no man can kill the ghost. Mebbe he come for me. Mebbee he heard how I aim to steal his daddy's gold. Mebbee..."

"I'll put a slug in you if you don't shut the hell up!" Titus said, already unnerved. How many Rebs were outside the barn? He stared ruefully down at the blue uniform he had recently acquired. Titus didn't intend to find out.

Milo Stark saw the horses and Jesse McQueen and wasn't about to let either of them escape. He thumbed back the hammer on his Colt revolving rifle and loosed a shot. Emory Stark, for the first time in his life, darted past his brother, eager to prove himself, tugging a short-barreled navy Colt from his belt.

"I'll get him, Milo," he shouted. But the noise of the stampede drowned him out. No matter, he thought, and let his cap-and-ball revolver talk for him.

It was no easy feat, riding bareback at a head-long gallop, crouched as low as possible. Still, if those damn Stark brothers didn't wing him with a lucky shot, he'd be all right. As Jesse cleared the wreckage of the trampled gate and raced past the barn, he spied Milo and Emory by the light of the moon. Their barking guns outlined them where they stood. For a few brief seconds McQueen and the Starks were opposite one another. Jesse heard the whine of bullets and emptied his own Colt revolver at the flashes from their guns. It could only have lasted a few seconds. Men fired point-blank at one another in the moonlight. Thunder and fire and death hung in the air like powder smoke, then Jesse was past the barn and rounding the corral. He tucked his smoking revolver back in his belt and held on with both hands. The stallion never broke stride. Up ahead, the two men who had joined the fray on Jesse's side took the lead and pointed the stampede toward the Vicksburg road as the barn and shattered corral receded into the night.

Doc Stark came lumbering out of the corral, making good time despite his game leg. His eyes were black with fury, and his chest heaved as he gulped in air. He looked from Emory, leaning against the wall of the barn, to Milo, standing barefoot, his bandaged fist cradling the rifle. Black smoke curled from the long barrel.

"What are you doing! Get your horses saddled!" Doc roared. He fished in his coat pocket and found an extra cylinder for his Colt revolver. He broke the weapon apart and reloaded.

"Nothin' we can do," Titus Connolly said from the door. "Cicero here says that was the Gray Fox himself, Bon Tyrone. No telling how many men are running with him. Besides, we got gold to worry about."

"I'll be damned if I'll let Jesse McQueen have these horses," Doc snapped. "Now, saddle your nags!" He glowered like an old bull looking for something to charge at.

Milo nodded. "We're with you. Right, Emory?"

The youngest of the three brothers merely groaned. It was all he could manage as his legs buckeled and he slid down the barn wall. Splinters snagged his shirt, tearing the cloth. His hands clutched at the red stain spreading across his belly. Numbness from the waist down. He saw his brothers rushing toward him and heard a sound like voices, but from far off. Someone was telling someone else to fetch a doctor. Emory stared at the blood seeping through his fingers. How could this be? No. It was a dream. He'd wake up—wake up any minute and be safe.

Jesse McQueen never quite saw it happen. One moment he was alone, riding drag on a galloping herd of wild horses, and the next, as if materializing from the shadows, Confederate cavalrymen appeared to either side of him. A mile later still more gray-clad riders took up positions flanking the herd, and by the time another few miles had passed the number of Rebels had swelled to forty, causing Jesse to ruefully consider the empty revolver in his belt. He had his hideout gun in his boot, but it would do precious little against such numbers.

When the men leading the herd signaled for the others to halt, Jesse felt his pulse quicken and he knew his hour was at hand. There'd be no escape. As the herd slowed, one of the two dirt farmers in the lead, the oddly familiar one, dropped back and brought his horse up alongside McQueen. The supposed farmer now sported a gray hat adorned with a black plume. He scratched at his bearded chin and watched Jesse with some bemusement.

"I reckon I owe you my thanks," Jesse said.

"Think of it as a debt repaid," the man replied.

"A debt?"

"My name is Captain Bon Tyrone."

Jesse nodded, catching the resemblance and fitting into place the piece of the mental puzzle he'd been struggling with. Ophelia's brother. The resemblance was strong. "Thank you, Mr. McQueen, for my sister's life. And for these fine horses," Tyrone added.

"My pleasure." Jesse glanced about at the hard-bitten cavalrymen who made up Tyrone's command. Each man carried a brace of pistols, a carbine, a big-bladed "Arkansas toothpick," and some sported a hand ax for felling trees or splitting skulls.

"Now what?" Jesse asked, prepared to run or fight, whatever it took to stay alive.

"Join us," Tyrone said. He chuckled softly. "I have a feeling my sister could find you the right color of uniform."

Jesse found himself liking this dashing Rebel officer. They could easily become friends. It would make betraying him even harder. And what about pert, pretty Ophelia Tyrone? *I'd like to see her again,* McQueen thought. The roan whinnied and shook its mane, eager to run.

"Well?" Bon said. "Join us. Or ride on back to Memphis, but Lord only knows what for."

Don't think. Don't feel. This is the war you must fight.

"I'll come along."

"Good." Bon grinned and clapped him on the shoulder. "Now relax. After all . . ." He gestured to the rough-looking bunch surrounding them, men who would have shot McQueen's heart out if they'd suspected the truth. "You're among friends."

Chapter Nine

"President Davis, may I present Captain Bon Tyrone of the First Mississippi Volunteers," said the diminutive Confederate general Joe Johnston, hero of Seven Pines and commander of the Army of the West.

Bon Tyrone saluted the president of the Confederacy, a hatchet-faced, sallow-skinned individual dressed simply in frock coat and trousers. Here was a quiet and unassuming man who bore the weight of his responsibility without complaint.

"Ah...the Gray Fox..." Davis extended his hand. "Tales of your exploits have resounded all the way to the capitol steps in Richmond along with the deeds of Jeb Stuart and Bedford Forrest."

"I am honored to have my name spoken in the same breath as those officers," Tyrone said humbly. "And may I present my sister, Ophelia, and her escort, Lieutenant Jesse McQueen."

Ophelia Tyrone, resplendent in a pale blue hoop

skirt trimmed with cream-colored lace at the hem and daringly low bodice, curtsied as if to royalty. All she knew of the Confederacy's beleaguered president was what she read in the *Daily Whig* and heard from the occasional officer who stayed the night as a guest at Dunsinane. But to meet the president in person left her speechless and in awe.

Davis bowed and kissed her proffered hand and, as she stepped past, shifted his intense gaze to the dark-haired man behind her.

"McQueen . . . the name is familiar to me. I knew your father. . . ." Davis stroked his chin.

General Johnston spoke up. "The lieutenant stole over a hundred horses destined for Sherman's own command. He is a remarkable horseman and has proven himself an invaluable courier between myself in Jackson and Pemberton here in Vicksburg. He is our best rider. I have never seen the like."

"Welcome, good fellow, and well done," Davis said, shaking the lieutenant's hand.

"It is an extreme pleasure to meet you, President Davis," Jesse said. His thoughts were a parade of possibilities. He could pull the Smith & Wesson from his boot and shoot President Davis dead, thus ending the butchery of war. But would it? Wars were made by more than one man. And Jefferson Davis, though the head of the Confederacy, was certainly not the heart. The suffering and bloodshed would continue until the resolve of one side or the other was crushed or until the nation as a whole, sickened by the loss of so many good men, halted the conflict out of exhaustion. No, shooting Davis would only result in Jesse's own death.

He continued on down the line, presenting his regards to the gray-clad officers and dignitaries of Vicksburg. Tall, humorless General John C. Pemberton, the Philadelphia-born commander of Vicksburg's defenses and the more than thirteen thousand soldiers garrisoned in the terraced city, was the last officer at the end of the presentation line. His perfunctory "good evening," repeated to each and every guest, did nothing to impede the flow of officers and their ladies as well as the select townspeople into the ballroom of this Greek Revival manor. Carriages lined the drive, while beyond the stone walls of the gardens out on Monroe Street, the curious waited for a glimpse of the president.

The house, ringed on all four sides by gardens of boxwood and magnolias, was the stately haunt of Judge Artemus Miller, whose daughter was Ophelia's contemporary and her closest friend.

Ophelia glanced at Jesse, placed her arm in his, and led him across the ballroom floor, removing him from the clutches of half a dozen young belles who'd swarmed like bees to honey the minute Captain Bon Tyrone entered the room.

"Shall I wait here and let you return for your brother?" Jesse chuckled.

"He can take care of himself. Rather those girls should beware," Ophelia said.

They had entered through the French doors opening onto the garden. Once inside, McQueen had to marvel at the ostentatious setting arranged for President Davis. The pianoforte, harp, violins, and woodwinds were still being tuned, the musicians struggling to hear the pitch of their instruments over the noisy conversations filling the ballroom.

A row of long heavy tables dominated one end of the room. Behind the tables a half-dozen red-coated servants plied the guests with platters of pork and roast beef, breasts of turkey ringed with dewberry jelly, loaves of piping hot bread, pecan pies, fig cakes, and bowls of Indian pudding with two sauces, a sugary-sweet one for the ladies, and for the gentlemen, one laced with enough brandy to curl the tongue. Bowls of wine punch had been placed at intervals and were refilled as quickly as they were drained.

"Judge Miller is determined to present the best possible face," Jesse observed. The walls of the room were festooned with red and gray banners, trailing gracefully out to the chandeliers above the heads of the festive crowd.

"Why shouldn't he? Just because some cowardly Yankee gunboats drop a shell in his garden from time to time is no reason not to be sociable," Ophelia replied with fire in her eye. Though Dunsinane, the Tyrone plantation, was eleven miles outside Vicksburg's fortifications, she spent enough time in this city of a hundred hills to consider herself one of its defenders. Like the majority of the townspeople, she was, above all else, stalwart. McQueen admired her spirit. She was as courageous as she was beautiful. In the two and a half months he'd spent in Mississippi, he had grown to care for Ophelia and her brave and noble brother. Yet he knew full well that such feelings could only place him in danger, for he had a job to do. A man playing the precarious role of a spy dare not risk dividing his loyalties. Jesse McQueen knew better, but it didn't make any difference.

"Where are we going?" Jesse asked as Ophelia guided him into the front hallway, the grand entrance to a grand house. The front doors were of mahogany, sturdy enough to withstand a battering ram, Jesse warranted, and there were narrow windows on either side to admit light and of course permit a furtive glance at whoever might be coming to call. A twelve-pound solid shot had landed smack in the middle of the front walk a couple of yards from the front doors during an earlier evening's bombardment from the river. Judge Miller had yet to have the shot removed. He allowed it to remain as if the projectile were a badge of honor to be displayed before his front porch. A black walnut hat rack stood beside the door, sprouting gray caps like so much foliage. The stairway itself was a graceful curve of white steps and a polished mahogany banister. This singular piece of sculpture captured the eye of the beholder and swept his gaze upward to the landing above.

"It's been a week since I've seen Elizabeth, and I simply refuse to enjoy myself until I visit with the poor dear." Ophelia tugged at Jesse's arm. "Do you mind terribly?"

"And if I did?" McQueen grinned.

"Then I would suspect you are not the same dashing, considerate, and valiant officer who rescued me in Memphis."

Jesse waved a hand toward the stairway. "Lead on."

The minute he entered the bedroom Jesse regretted coming. The stench of illness permeated the air despite the sunlight streaming in through the unshuttered windows and the merry sounds of the orchestra below that had finally begun to entertain the guests. Elizabeth Miller Greene, ten weeks pregnant, lay propped against a veritable bulwark of pillows in a canopied bed trimmed with sea-green silk. Ophelia's friend stirred and opened her weary eyes as the couple crossed the room to her side.

Jesse still carried childhood memories of a visit to his mother's bedside when he was seven and she was sick with pneumonia, her frail body racked by a savage cough that filled him with horror every time he witnessed it. His mother had died shortly after his visit and left Jesse with an emotional scar that time had yet to heal. He shifted his gaze from the sickbed to the fire in the hearth; noticing that the logs needed rearranging, he excused himself. Elizabeth was no doubt a pretty girl, but three weeks of nausea had left her eyes ringed with shadows, her complexion swallow, and her cheeks sunken.

She kept a porcelain basin beside her on the quilt. The bedroom door opened again and a young mulatto, one of the household servants, entered. Seeing that Elizabeth had guests, she immediately excused herself.

Elizabeth ran a hand through her oily brown tresses.

"I must look a fright," she weakly protested.

"Nonsense," Ophelia replied. She picked up a brush inlaid with mother-of-pearl and began to stroke Elizabeth's hair. The woman on the bed glanced across the room at Jesse, who was kneeling, stoking the fire.

"That must be the young man you have so often bragged on," Elizabeth said in a hoarse voice, loud enough for Jesse to hear. Elizabeth was a year older than Ophelia and forever hounding her friend about the joys of marriage.

Jesse looked up. Ophelia blushed right up to the freckles on her nose. He added another log to the fire and returned to Ophelia's side.

"Bragged on, eh?"

"Elizabeth, for one so ill, you do indeed prattle on," Ophelia gently scolded.

The woman in bed managed a weak smile, then held up a hand. "Listen." A woman's voice, singing a sweet lament, drifted up through the hardwood floor. The party was directly below.

"That must be Rosalie DuToit. She arrived in Vicksburg only a few days ago. Father said she is to appear at the Magnolia Theater later in the week for an evening of song and recitation." Elizabeth sighed and closed her eyes. "I wish I could attend. Still, isn't it grand that father hired her to sing for us. She has such a lovely voice." Her hand fluttered to her mouth, where she stifled a yawn. "Lieutenant McQueen appears to enjoy Mademoiselle DuToit."

Jesse was indeed listening intently to the muted tones of the woman below. He knew that voice, and it didn't belong to any Rosalie DuToit.

"Don't waste your time here," Elizabeth said, misinterpreting his interest. "Take the lieutenant downstairs. Parties are few enough these days." She closed her eyes, resisting the sickness that had left her bedridden. Ophelia grew pale and her features betrayed her concern.

"I'll be fine," Elizabeth managed, her brow furrowed with the effort. "This is supposed to pass. . . ." She shuddered, then continued. "Maybe I'll be well by the time Henry Lee returns from Port Gibson." Major Henry Lee Greene was an engineer charged with inspecting the redoubts and fortifications of Vicksburg and Port Gibson to the south.

"Elizabeth—"

"Please go, Ophelia dear. I love you, but please go. Maybe we can talk later. You'll be spending the night with us, won't you? Father will insist."

"Yes." Ophelia patted her hand and nodded to Jesse.

"A pleasure to meet you, ma'am," he said, and

bowed to the bedridden woman. Plagued by his own painful memories, he couldn't quit the room quickly enough. The servant, a slender young woman with a guarded gaze, brushed past them and hurried into the room as Elizabeth doubled up over the basin in her lap and began to retch.

It was, without a doubt, a happier house downstairs. There was sunlight and life, music, good food, merriment, dancing, and for Jesse McQueen, an old friend.

And an old enemy.

Chapter Ten

> *"Oh that this cruel war*
> *Would only end and free*
> *Sweet William from the battlefield*
> *And send him back to me."*

There was scarcely a dry eye in the ballroom. Jesse was the exception. Not that Rosalie DuToit didn't have a lovely voice. It was just that Miss DuToit was none other than Caitlin Brennan, the last person McQueen had expected to see in Vicksburg. *Well, Jesse, you've been wondering how Abbot would contact you,* he thought. *Now you know.* He was glad to see her, yet dreaded Caitlin's presence all the same. She was unpredictable and, unlike Ophelia Tyrone, left him on the defensive. As in New Orleans, one moment he'd wanted to make love to her, and the next to strangle her as she slept.

"Oh, Lord." He sighed beneath his breath.

"And should my darlin' boy
Be felled by shot or shell and
Ne'r return,
My love shall be a fire undimmed.
Forever may it burn,
Until that day when I by death will be
United with Sweet William
In eternity."

Ophelia dabbed at her eyes with a silk handkerchief she kept tucked up her sleeve, as did several other women standing nearby. The men shifted their stances, cleared their throats, and tried to hide their emotions behind sheepish glances and embarrassed silences. Then the room erupted into applause, and the tall, willowy woman clasped her hands and bowed. Ringlets of her thick, white-blond hair spilled forward. She glanced up and scanned the room with her emerald eyes and then settled on the sleek and powerful-looking Confederate lieutenant who watched her from the back of the room. She smiled. Then the orchestra began to play a Virginia reel and half a dozen unmarried officers in gray crowded forward, eager to have the honor of this first dance with the beautiful songstress.

That brief contact, even across the distance of the ballroom, had been enough for Jesse. Up until now, he'd lost himself in his role as a newly commissioned Confederate officer. He'd carried out his duties as a courier with the utmost efficiency. He had personally gentled many of the horses stolen from Doc Stark and his brothers, providing Bon Tyrone with much-needed mounts. McQueen had even joined the Gray Fox and his men on a raid into Tennessee to loot and capture a supply depot and rout the Yankee troops assigned to defend it. He'd done a lot of shooting but managed to keep from hitting anyone.

Caitlin's presence had certainly brought him back to reality. He wondered what message she carried from Abbot.

"Well, Mr. McQueen, shall we try the punch and then take our chances and join the dancers?"

Jesse turned to Bon Tyrone's fetching sister. Ophelia, for all her flirtatious ways, seemed innocent as spring. She waited for an answer, then tugged at his arm.

"Perhaps I should not have brought you downstairs after all," Ophelia remarked. "It would seem you've fallen prey to Mademoiselle's charms."

"Not in the least," Jesse protested a little too strongly, and turned toward the long, heavily laden tables. A crowd had already formed to sample the culinary delights Judge Miller had provided. Jesse found that all the Confederate uniforms tended to blur together, but managed to recognize a couple of officers he knew by name. Gentlemen and their ladies continued to approach the tables, the gathering of hungry guests gradually swelling. Jesse started forward and then froze as he glimpsed a shock of silver hair atop a stiff-necked, dapper officer. The Confederate finished sampling the wares and turned, balancing a plate of food in one hand, a crystal goblet of wine punch in the other. His sharply etched, hawkish features were split by a feral smile. Jesse felt an icy calm settle over him. And beneath his breath he muttered, "Colonel Henri Baptiste!"

"What?" Ophelia gestured toward the guests surrounding them with conversation. "Did you say something? Everyone is talking so."

Baptiste! Here! Jesse watched in horror as the Creole colonel lifted the wineglass to the light.

Baptiste was studying its color when he noticed McQueen. The Union agent maneuvered Ophelia away from the tables and toward the garden. There were two sets of doors heading out of the ballroom. President Davis's entourage blocked one, but the French doors nearest Jesse beckoned with freedom. Ophelia barely had time to pull her shawl up about her bare shoulders before McQueen steered her outside.

"Jesse, what on earth has come over you?" Ophelia sputtered, trying to catch her breath. The sky was deepening in hue and rays of golden light like the pillars of heaven lanced the clouds. The air was cool and especially bracing after the warm, crowded confines of the ballroom.

"A glass of wine did not seem so important," Jesse said. "After visiting your friend Elizabeth, I needed to breathe." He looked down into her hazel eyes, so open and trusting. He held her hand and momentarily checked the French doors. Colonel Henri Baptiste stood framed in the narrow panes. He was studying Jesse, trying to place the younger man. As yet he had not made the connection. McQueen was clean-shaven now and smartly attired in his lieutenant's uniform, a far cry from the lawyer he had pretended to be in New Orleans.

Just to be on the safe side, Jesse continued on into the garden until he paused beneath a trellis archway covered with honeysuckle vines. At last he was hidden from Baptiste's scrutinizing stare.

"You know, my brother has fought duels with men who have behaved improperly." Ophelia guessed this brash young officer wanted to get her alone for romantic reasons. Had desire simply overpowered Jesse and clouded his judgment? Now, there was an intriguing thought. He had never been anything but a perfect gentleman with her, and Ophelia was beginning to tire of it. She stepped closer to him and tilted her head just so, her lips moist and inviting.

"Why, Jesse, have you taken leave of your senses?"

"Maybe I'm just tired of waiting," he said.

"For what?"

"For this," he replied, and took his kiss. It was long and ardent. He made the most of the moment in case it was his last. Then, because her wine-red lips were willing, he chanced another. The shadows deepened. Music drifted out to serenade the setting sun and the couple hidden in the honeysuckles where time no longer mattered.

"Oh my, I beg your pardon," Caitlin Brennan said from the walkway, a bemused expression on her pretty face. Ophelia and Jesse bolted apart. Tyrone's sister blushed. McQueen merely glanced at Caitlin, as if daring her to make light of her discovery. "I picked a poor time to escape the crowd," she said. Jesse could read the wicked gleam in her green eyes and steeled himself for the worst. He'd seen that look before.

Caitlin, who wore no shawl, shivered as she stepped beneath the vine-covered latticework. "It's so much warmer in here," she observed dryly.

"It must be the honeysuckle," Jesse testily suggested.

"Miss DuToit, you have a lovely voice," Ophelia said. "I enjoyed you ever so much."

"Why thank you, Miss..."

"Tyrone—Ophelia Tyrone—and this is Lieutenant Jesse McQueen."

"Charmed, I'm sure." Caitlin pursed her lips and held out her hand for Jesse to kiss, a courtesy he performed in the most perfunctory manner. "And do you like my voice, Lieutenant?"

Jesse shrugged. "The voice—but not the song." He met her stare. "I think you need to sing a different tune."

"Maybe you could teach me. I can be found most days at the theater on Washington Street."

"If I think of one," Jesse said.

"Oh, try . . . do try." Caitlin patted Ophelia's arm, then returned to the walkway and started back to the ballroom. Jesse and Ophelia continued to stare awkwardly at one another, the moment they had shared irretrievably lost, courtesy of Caitlin Brennan's timely intrusion. Their discomfort was brought to a merciful end by the thunder of a distant explosion as Union mortar boats braved the Confederate batteries to lob shells into the terraced city.

"Perhaps we ought to go inside. It might be safer," Ophelia said, placing her slender white hand through the crook of Jesse's left arm.

McQueen nodded and led her out from under the honeysuckle and back to the ballroom, where Caitlin Brennan and Colonel Henri Baptiste prowled among the guests.

Safer? McQueen thought. *I doubt it.* He reentered the ballroom with all the enthusiasm of a man ascending a scaffold. Ophelia was immediately whisked from his arms by Bon Tyrone, who insisted on having at least one slow waltz with his sister, whom he claimed was the most beautiful woman in the room. Jesse wasn't, however, alone for long. Caitlin Brennan refused her way through a parade of disappointed officers to stand at McQueen's side.

"I believe you asked for my hand in this waltz," she mentioned.

Jesse started to refuse then considered how this might look and changed his mind.

"Good things come to those who wait," he

gallantly replied, and led her into the throng. He wasn't a good dancer, and to his profound gratitude, the orchestra kept up a slow steady rhythm.

"Smile," Caitlin whispered.

"What are you doing?" he asked.

"That was quite a scene in the garden. Please. Don't tell me—she loves you for your gallant self."

"You sound jealous," Jesse chided.

"And pigs have wings," she said. "Now hush and hear what I have to say." Bon Tyrone and his sister danced past. Ophelia seemed surprised at Jesse's choice of partners. As for Caitlin, she never missed an opportunity for mischief and changed her tone of voice, laughed aloud, and said, "Lieutenant, you *are* a rogue." As the Tyrones gracefully spun away Jesse closed his eyes, lost a step, and stumbled over himself, much to Caitlin's amusement.

"*Your* feet may be next," he threatened.

"There are rumors that construction has been completed on a Confederate ironclad to rival anything afloat. It is supposedly anchored somewhere on the Yazoo within striking distance of Porter's fleet. Grant needs to know if it exists and what sort of armament it carries. Abbot wants you to find out." Caitlin spoke swiftly, keeping her voice low and her features animated, as if she were flirting with her partner. She concluded her message with another merry laugh and, willing herself to blush on cue, gave the impression that Jesse had made the most scandalous of suggestions.

"How do I contact Abbot?" Jesse asked as the musicians finished playing and the guests heartily applauded. The bombardment had been brief and distant, and word had already spread through the crowd that Rebel gunners had driven the Yankee mortar boats back up the Mississippi. This good news immediately buoyed up the spirits of everyone present.

"I'll carry your report to Memphis," Caitlin said as President Davis led the guests in a rousing cheer for the Confederate artillerymen who were defending the city. "I'll meet you behind the theater by the alley door. No one will suspect me."

"Indeed?" Jesse said, the hairs rising on the back of his neck. He was being watched. He didn't have to guess by whom. "Tell that to my old friend Colonel Henri Baptiste. He's here in the room." He bowed and kissed Caitlin's hand and pretended to thank her for the dance. By the change in her expression he knew his words had struck home. Caitlin had never been formally introduced to the colonel, but they had traveled in the same social circles and he might remember her. If so, he might well be wondering what this cultured Confederate bride, who had supposedly been awaiting her husband's arrival in New Orleans, was doing here in Vicksburg with a new name and entertaining at the local theater. It was hardly the proper calling for a lady of breeding.

McQueen scanned the faces surrounding him, trying not to appear obvious. He discovered Baptiste in a corner, studying them both with a troubled expression. Jesse avoided eye contact with the diminutive Creole. Ophelia intercepted "her lieutenant" and flashed a look of defiance in Caitlin's direction as she bore him away from the clutches of this Mademoiselle DuToit.

Jesse was just as happy for Ophelia's company as she was for his and was about to tell her so when a shadow fell between them.

"Excuse me, Lieutenant."

Jesse's gaze grew cold and guarded and he

turned to find the silver-haired Creole standing at his side. Baptiste stroked his silvery goatee. "Ma'am," he said, acknowledging Ophelia.

"Yes?" Jesse felt a trickle of sweat trace a path behind his ear.

"I feel as if we've met. I've been trying to place you. I am Colonel Henri Baptiste, lately of New Orleans. Don't I know you?"

"A pleasure to meet you, sir. But rest assured, you do not know me."

"Lieutenant McQueen hails from the Indian Territory," Ophelia interjected.

"McQueen? No. Cannot place the name. And I have never been west of the Mississippi. Maybe it's just a resemblance . . . to someone else." Baptiste shrugged and bowed to the lady. "Pardon my intrusion." He backed off and headed out of the room to join several of the older men who had retired to the parlor to sample Judge Miller's brandy and cigars.

"An odd little man," Ophelia said, watching him depart. "Have you ever been to New Orleans, Jesse?"

Jesse ran his fingers beneath his gray collar and scratched at the rope scar on his neck, the legacy of his first encounter with Colonel Henri Baptiste. "Oh, I . . . hung around there once," he replied.

The musicians came to his rescue and struck up a lively Tennessee two-step. Jesse caught Ophelia by the arm and whirled her off into the dance before she could ask any more questions.

Chapter Eleven

The Rebel sentry never heard Jesse. He'd been gathering deadwood for a fire and came walking up out of a tangle of thorns and underbrush when the shadow of the intruder fell across him. As the sentry looked up, a gust of wind snatched his cap, revealing his matted, dirty brown hair plastered back from a high forehead.

"Damn!" the sentry muttered.

Jesse clubbed him on the skull with a red oak branch. The Rebel dropped his load of firewood and tumbled back down the ravine he'd just left. Jesse scrambled after the young soldier and pulled him undercover. A bruise the size of a goose egg began to swell on the unconscious man's scalp.

Jesse paused to check his surroundings, taking care to see if he'd attracted undue attention. The sentry might not be alone. He waited, pulling his greatcoat around him for warmth. It was the twentieth of December, a cold, damp day with the sun a ghostly orb masked by somber gray clouds pushed along by a gentle but insistent north wind.

Jesse had ridden out of Vicksburg before sunup, taking the Jackson road east of town. He was no stranger to the picket lines. They were accustomed to seeing the courier come and go. Once a couple of miles clear of the fortifications, he pointed his mare north to intercept the Yazoo at its juncture with the Mississippi a few miles above Vicksburg.

He'd spent the better part of the day skirting Confederate patrols while making his way along the south bank of the Yazoo. He'd cut inland, keeping to groves of red oaks, and stumbled upon the sentry quite by accident. The private's situation intrigued him. Cavalry patrols were fairly common, but a sentry posted this far from any town meant he was either on picket duty and there was an army encamped up ahead, or he was there to protect something the Confederates were attempting to conceal.

Jesse McQueen knew the only two Rebel forces of any merit were divided between Vicksburg and Jackson. He grinned and muttered, "I found it," and began to work his way along the ravine until the ground became too muddy. Then he climbed up the slope and followed a deer trail through the woods lining this bend of the river. He intercepted a bayou and began to wonder whether or not he ought to bring his horse up. But he could spy a patch of river through a stand of moss-hung cypress trees and the temptation was too great to resist.

The deer trail skirted the worst of the bayou. A water moccassin, a yard long and looking for all the world like a gray branch lying across the path, came alive and slithered off into the brackish waters of the bayou. Jesse kept his eyes peeled for more such "branches" as he worked his way up a gentle rise. The trees thinned there but the grass was waist-high, and Jesse walked crouched over in the feeble sunlight until he reached the bend in the river, a narrow little peninsula offering a view up- and downriver. The sluggish gray waters of the Yazoo flowed past on its ancient quest to merge with the Father of Waters and find the sea. Water splashed where a fish broke the surface of the river a few yards away. It would have been enjoyable to find a dry place to relax, to have a fishing pole, maybe smoke a pipe while catching a fat perch for dinner. But Jesse wasn't there for pleasure. The reason he had braved the elements and Rebel patrols was anchored about seventy-five yards upriver, a massive dreadnought, fully as large as the *Arkansas*, a Rebel ironclad that had chased the Union gunboats clear back to New Orleans before running aground and being destroyed by its crew.

"My God." McQueen whistled between his teeth and searched his coat pocket for his spyglass. "What a monster." Indeed, the warship was heavily armored and bristling with rifled cannons from firing ports on every side. Twin stacks trailed oily banners of smoke, residue from no doubt powerful engines that were the heart of the beast. The Union fleet that was keeping Vicksburg under such frequent bombardment was about to find itself in a hell of a lot of trouble when this formidable-looking vessel made its way into battle.

Now, there was a puzzle. Evidently the ship had been sighted at night and chased a column of federal steamers back toward Cairo. But why hadn't it come to the aid of Vicksburg's inhabitants? Such a war vessel backed up by Vicksburg's batteries could drive off Porter's gunships once and for all. What were the Rebels waiting for?

He lifted the spyglass to his eye, adjusted the focus, and the flag flying from the bow of the dreadnought went from a blur to the defiant stars and bars of the Confederate Navy. McQueen rose up on his knees and parted the tall grass and managed to make out the name *Glen Allen* burned into the hull.

Moisture was seeping through his woolen trousers, soaking his knees. It was too damn cold for such carrying on. Abbot was most definitely having his revenge. Well then, get it over with. "All right *Glen Allen*, tell me your secrets."

He scanned the ironclad's sloped sides, taking a quick stock of the vessel's guns and armor. He frowned, shifted his spyglass, tried to make sense out of what he was looking at. "What the hell ..." Then Jesse grinned. "Well, I'll be damned."

The *Glen Allen's* wooden hull had been painted to resemble iron plating. Its impressive array of cannons was no more than logs painted black to resemble nine-pounder cannons and Dahlgren guns.

"Quaker guns," McQueen muttered. Utterly harmless. Merely a ruse the undersupplied Confederate Army had tried before with success. Jesse lowered the spyglass and tucked it in his coat pocket. Then he sat back on his heels, taking a moment to digest his discovery. The Rebel dreadnought was about as dangerous as a toothless, clawless panther.

He shivered. It was going to be a tedious and miserable ride back to Vicksburg. But the darkness would hide him from patrols. With some luck, he'd be in Vicksburg sometime after midnight. Out of the frying pan and back into the fire.

*   *   *

It was two o'clock in the morning when the bone-weary rider slipped past the northernmost redoubt, following the twisting, winding course of a steep ravine. Jesse heard the hammering of artillery in the distance, the thud of mortars, the crisp, savage bark of the Napoleans and the deep-throated boom of a Parrot gun. The bombardment kept the attention of the sentries riveted on the beleaguered stronghold.

Once within the Confederate defenses on the outskirts of the city, Jesse walked his mount upslope to stand atop a ridge. The view was spectacular. With its series of bluffs rising two hundred feet above the river, Vicksburg looked for all the world like some impregnable castle. Its buildings clung to every ridge and hillside, its streets rising and falling with the lay of the land, so townsmen seldom stood on level ground, at least outdoors. There were fires in the streets this night and shells bursting overhead like exploding stars. Half a dozen gunboats had entered the bend of the Mississippi and steamed downriver opposite the bluffs, where they kept up a blistering bombardment of the city in a vain attempt to wear down the defenders. The shore batteries returned the fire with ferocious intensity. One of the gunboats, a paddle wheeler converted into a military ship, was already ablaze, and another had had one of its smokestacks shot away. The gunboats had paid a price for their trip downriver. And so had Vicksburg.

Jesse started down the road, a thoroughfare of hard-packed earth bordered by towering red oaks whose branches intersected to form a tunnel above the road. Twenty minutes later he entered the city.

The streets were for the most part deserted. The townspeople had retired to their basements and root cellars or the caves that many of Vicksburg's inhabitants had dug into the hillsides. From time to time Jesse passed several bucket brigades hurrying from one fire to the next. They paid no attention to the weary gray rider making his way through the cold streets. A patch of the night sky was aglow from the burning wreckage of the Presbyterian church, into the steeple of which an explosive shell had lodged. Jesse watched the burning church from a distance then continued uphill for another couple of blocks until he reached the narrow alleyway that ran behind the Magnolia Theater. Here was a pitch-black corridor lined with discarded crates and barrels. The mouth of the alley opened like the jaws of a trap. All he had to do was deliver his report to Caitlin and leave, and yet some inner sense told him to ride on. With his hat pulled low and his collar turned up against the chill night air, his features were well concealed. What was he worried about? He stared at the alley. The bombardment was lessening in intensity and he imagined the Yankee gunboats were withdrawing back upriver. They'd pummeled the city, disturbed its inhabitants, and taken enough damage from the batteries for one night.

They were pulling out. And so was he. Caitlin Brennan, Peter Abbot, and Sherman and Grant and the whole blessed Union Army could wait one night. He had nothing to base his suspicions on but instinct. No matter. Death waited for him in that alley. He was certain of it.

To all appearances Jesse was only another Johnny Reb, pausing to fasten the buttons of his coat and tug his hat lower on his head for protection against the cold. A rider who tarried a moment but had business elsewhere.

The ground trembled as the shore batteries several streets below fired a final volley after the retreating steamers. The roan was too tired to be skittish. The animal usually kept its head around the rattle of pistol and musket, but artillery was another matter entirely. The stallion was never comfortable around the field pieces and quite often fought its owner's steady hand, shying and pawing the street whenever the cannons opened up.

Tonight the stallion plodded along, seemingly impervious to the roar of the guns or the smell of powder smoke that drifted like a pallor over the darkened city. Jesse took the shortest route possible, skirting the block where the Presbyterian church had become a funeral pyre of collapsed timbers. A gentle, cold rain began to fall. Droplets collected on the brim of his gray felt hat and poured off every time he lowered his head. He found Monroe Street and pointed the stallion up the steep hill toward the two-story Greek Revival manor crowning the summit. Judge Miller had proved himself a hospitable Southern gentleman. After meeting the Union agent at his party, the judge had insisted McQueen stay in one of the guest rooms.

Jesse didn't plan to try to sneak into the house at this late hour. The stables offered a bed of hay in a dry stall out of the rain. McQueen had slept in worse places. On such a damp wintry night a stable would do just fine.

Jesse unlatched the gate without dismounting. He walked the stallion to the drive and, keeping to the right near the garden wall, skirted the house and headed straight for the stable set off from the house and far enough back so as not to be obtrusive.

Jesse dismounted and led the stallion to the stable doors. Lamplight spilled through one of the windows. Someone was up and about. The Union agent thought up a reason for his untimely arrival, then opened the door and brought the stallion inside.

The air was thick with the smell of leather and decaying hay, horseflesh, and brewed coffee. Bon Tyrone stood before a cast-iron woodstove, adding tinder to the firebox. A blue enamel coffeepot rested on one of the burners, steam curling from the spout. Tyrone had stripped down to his flannel undershirt, gray pants, and mud-spattered boots. His gunbelt hung from a wall peg along with his campaign hat, gray shirt, coat, and rain-soaked greatcoat. From the look of his uniform, Tyrone hadn't been there long himself.

The Confederate officer looked around as Jesse entered and unsaddled the stallion in the nearest vacant stall. Tyrone lifted his coffee cup in salute.

"'Oh, Young Lochinvar is come out of the West,'" he said.

Jesse glanced over at the captain. "'So faithful in love, so dauntless in war, there never was knight like the young Lochinvar.'" He finished with the stallion, dumped a mound of hay in the stall. There was already water in the trough.

"So you've read Sir Walter Scott?" Tyrone said, folding his arms across his chest. "Even in the Indian Territory."

"My father and grandfather were educated. They taught my brother and me the classics." He glanced up at the rafters, where shadows flickered like dark wings. "And my grandmother taught us of mysteries."

Tyrone stroked his goatee while he considered the man's reply. *This McQueen is a most intriguing fellow,* he thought. *I have never known his like.* Tyrone handed him a heavy tin cup and gingerly lifted the coffeepot, using a piece of burlap to keep from burning his hand.

"Real coffee?" McQueen noted aloud, inhaling the aroma.

"Took it off a bluecoat last week," Tyrone replied. "He wasn't going to be needing it anymore." The implication was clear.

Jesse studied the man filling his cup. Bon Tyrone was as good as they came—brave and honorable to a fault. But he was a killer, as war made all good men killers. And he would continue to be until the Confederacy was defeated. Jesse couldn't help but wonder what might happen if he and the Gray Fox had to confront each other. He did not relish the prospect.

"A bad night for riding," Tyrone said. He was curious about Jesse's whereabouts but too much of a gentleman to ask outright.

"A *miserable* night," Jesse pointedly corrected. "But Pemberton figured the boys in the redoubts deserved to hear the message President Davis had prepared for them. He asked me to deliver it rather than risk Davis's life unduly." He sipped the coffee and sighed as the steaming bitter liquid returned life to his veins. "You brewed this strong enough to float a horseshoe," he added, sloshing the contents of his cup.

"It will get me through till morning," Tyrone said, growing serious. "Which is what I need after this night's black business."

"What business is that?" Jesse asked.

"I was given the unpleasant task of arresting Rosalie DuToit. She was accused of being a spy by Colonel Henri Baptiste. He claims to have met her in New Orleans. Only she had a different name then."

Jesse shrugged and tossed the dregs of his coffee cup into the stove; the liquid sizzled on contact with the flames. He struggled to keep his voice free of emotion. The news of Caitlin's arrest had shaken him. Damn Baptiste. And what else had the damn Creole told the authorities?

"So she changed her name. That hardly makes her a spy for Lincoln."

"Spider found a tintype at the bottom of her trunk. It showed her in a chair, and behind her, a Union officer with his hand on her shoulder." Tyrone sat on a three-legged stool by the stove. "Perhaps it's a lover, or her husband, of maybe just her brother. Either way, Miss DuToit, or whoever she is, will be taken to Jackson on Davis's train and held under guard until General Johnston learns the truth." The Confederate captain shook his head. "I dislike making war on women."

Jesse nodded, sharing the captain's sentiments. He ambled over to an empty stall and used the pitchfork to pull together enough dry grass for bedding. He unfurled a woolen blanket and spread it over the hay, then unbuckled his gunbelt, draped it across the wooden siding, and stretched out upon his makeshift bed. A second stove, set against the wall in the center of the stable, gave off enough warmth for the horses, but Jesse was grateful for the extra warmth the straw provided.

Up at the front of the barn, Bon Tyrone blew out the lamp, plunging the stable into what seemed at first total darkness. Once McQueen's eyes grew accustomed to the dark, he noticed the stoves also cast a feeble glow that the rafters swallowed up. He heard Tyrone stretch out in another stall.

"It would be a shame to have to drop a hangman's noose around such a pretty throat," Tyrone muttered.

"Yes, what a waste," Jesse agreed. Caitlin had saved his life once. Now he would have to return the favor—somehow, someway—or die trying. "More's the pity."

Chapter Twelve

Caitlin spent the morning of her arrest toying with her breakfast, cornmeal mush flavored with molasses, honey cakes, and a pot of English tea. She had been apprehended, her room at the Magnolia searched, and then brought to an unassuming little cave set in a hillside overlooking Clay Street. There were many such caves, all furnished as comfortably as possible with furniture salvaged from homes that had been seriously damaged by shells from Union gunboats.

Caitlin's prison sported a four-poster bed, a woodstove, a rolltop desk and chair, a washstand, and a whatnot—a triangular stack of shelves carved of black walnut and displaying an assortment of porcelain cups and tiny bells shaped like tulips. The owner of the cave, Letitia Denard, had spent time between her poor battered house and the cave until she was injured when the porch of the former collapsed. She was convalescing at her sister's home only a couple of blocks away, leaving her servant, a buxom black woman named Arabelle, to look after the house, cave, and all of Letitia's belongings.

Arabelle had brought Caitlin her breakfast an hour after sunrise. With the guards outside listening through the open doorway, the black woman made no attempt at conversation.

On her return, Arabelle closed the door behind her. She lifted the hem of her brown woolen dress and waddled across the room.

"Honey chile, you ain't touched a lick a' breakfast. And you gots visitors comin' up the street. I seen 'em from the porch."

"I'm not hungry," Caitlin said.

"Can I get you somethin' else? There ain't much. . . ."

"A way out of here would be nice," Caitlin dryly suggested. The black woman grinned broadly.

"Sure 'nuff and I would give it to you, but the only way out of here, dear one, is right through the door and past them guards outside." Her work-roughened hands pulled a kerchief from her apron and wiped the perspiration from her shiny black forehead. She was a pretty woman for all her great bulk. Her oval features were devoid of artiface.

"Folks says you a spy. That you works for Mistuh Lincoln. I say, God bless you and Mistuh Lincoln. Yes, ma'am. He gonna put an end to the buyin' and sellin' of chillen and poor black folk, and I don't care who hears me." Her brave words, though well meant, were not quite true. Despite the Emancipation Proclamation, Arabelle was still a slave, and in fact, she cared most certainly who heard her. A look of horror crossed her face as the door behind her opened and Colonel Henri Baptiste swaggered into the room. He had brought a couple of soldiers to relieve the guards posted by the door. Arabelle clamped her mouth shut, picked up the breakfast tray she had left on the table, and hurried from the room. The Creole frightened her. A man like Baptiste could cause her a lot of grief.

Baptiste waited for the servant to leave and then closed the door after her. He walked across the cave and took a seat at the table. He removed his hat and placed it in front of him. Lamplight played upon his silver hair. His eyebrows arched as he stared at his prisoner. He scratched at his bushy white sideburns and smiled. He pulled a silver hair from his goatee, examined it a moment, then blew it away.

"Comfortable, Mrs. Windthorst? That was the name you used in New Orleans wasn't it? Amanda Windthorst. The patient and faithful wife. Yes, I remember now." He reached in the pocket of his greatcoat and removed a silver flask, his ration of bourbon for the day.

"I don't know what you're talking about," Caitlin said in the brassy voice she had adopted for Rosalie DuToit.

Amanda Windthorst had been quiet, almost shy, and very ladylike and proper.

"You are most clever. But you overlooked one important part of the pretense. You are a very attractive woman. I wasn't the only man in New Orleans who noticed, either. With your husband supposedly gone, and the thought of you sleeping alone every night . . . yes, indeed, I was quite enamored of you. I never dreamed it was all a performance for our benefit. So that we wouldn't suspect you were a spy sent to betray us."

"I've never been in New Orleans," Caitlin retorted. "However, I have performed in theaters in Philadelphia, New York, Baltimore, and up and down the coast. You have mistaken me—" She never finished. Colonel Baptiste slammed his fist down on the table, half rose from the chair, then settled back.

"Lies! Just hear them, pouring out of your mouth." He wiped a hand across his mouth. "Do not take me for a fool."

"It is hard not to," Caitlin said. She combed her fingers through her pale hair and sighed. "But I assume you'll come to your senses and allow me to return to the theater." She straightened a landscape painting that Letitia had hung from the sod walls to give the cave a more homelike feeling.

"I wouldn't count on it," Baptiste said, frowning. He folded his arms, a smug expression on his face. "Johnston has ordered me to find out the truth from you." He smiled without a trace of humor, his eyes narrow and wicked looking. "I won't fail."

"You already have, Colonel. You believe I'm someone I'm not. Why, I wouldn't have the courage to be a spy." As she spoke Caitlin noticed the Creole remove the tintype that had been discovered in her trunk. She had been a sentimental fool to bring it with her. John Brennan had fallen on the blood-soaked fields of Bull Run. Everyone had expected the battle to be like a picnic. No one was supposed to get killed. But Rebel troops had chased the Union soldiers back to Washington.

Baptiste held the image of her husband in his hand with such casual disregard, it was all the woman could do to restrain herself. She wanted to rip the tintype from his grasp and attack her arrogant captor. Caitlin figured she could at least blind him before the guards burst into the room to drag her off to the gallows.

Henri Baptiste thought he glimpsed a slight quiver in her expression, and his smile broadened.

"I lost everything in New Orleans. My estate, slaves, my family wealth." His hate-filled eyes narrowed. "Someone is going to pay. It might as well be you."

He tucked the tintype back in his pocket and stood, walked around the table, and moved in close to the woman. She was physically bigger than he, but he was definitely in control. He liked that.

"Of course, I might be persuaded to change my mind. I might even forget I saw you in New Orleans. You could help me forget." He reached up to stroke her hair. His voice was deep and resonant, like the purr of a big cat. He had an orator's voice and a politician's shallow charm, as shifting as the sands. "I think you know how."

Caitlin caught him by the wrist and batted his hand away.

"I'd sooner drink spit," she remarked.

A shadow seemed to fall across the face of the colonel, stripping away the mask of false civility. He retreated a step as if she had physically assaulted him.

"I warrant you'll sing a different tune when you sleep in the shadow of the gallows."

He retrieved his hat from the table and without another word left the cave. Caitlin sighed and sat down on the bed, the mattress creaking beneath her. No one really had any proof she was a spy, only the tintype and Colonel Baptiste's word. But in the hysteria of war, with Grant poised to strike at the heart of the Confederacy, reason might not prevail. As for the quality of mercy, it had been strained to the breaking point at Shiloh and Chancellorsville and Antietam.

There came the sickening realization that she might not be able to bluff her way out of this predicament. As for Jesse, what could he do? He was brave enough but how capable was he? Baptiste was taking her to Jackson on the same well-protected train that Jefferson Davis would be riding. One man wouldn't stand a chance against the troops guarding the president. In the silence of the room, in these desperate hours, Caitlin Brennan had never felt so alone in her young life.

She cupped her face in her hands and lay back upon the feather mattress. But she did not cry.

"Colonel Henri Baptiste certainly cuts a dashing figure," Ophelia commented. The smartly dressed Creole was preparing to spur his charger down a well-trod path that led between two rows of posts. Each post stood about six feet tall and was topped by a sackcloth pillow roughly the size of a man's head. She glanced at Jesse, beside her in the carriage, to see if she had aroused a little jealousy in him. He seemed preoccupied. She nudged him. Jesse looked at her. "What . . . oh yes . . . the very thing." Ophelia frowned. Where exactly were his thoughts?

That afternoon Captain Bon Tyrone had arranged a demonstration for Jefferson Davis and his staff of generals, to amuse the president while waiting for last-minute repairs to be concluded on the train to Jackson. Last night's bombardment had damaged the locomotive, but the engineers had assured the president he would still be able to continue his rail tour by evening.

It was a cold, somber afternoon and a challenge to Vicksburg's inhabitants to make the best out of a bad situation. They had brought picnic lunches to this meadow on the Warrenton road near the railyard. Davis and Generals Johnston and Pemberton sat in the shade of a white canvas tent. Storm clouds continued to build to the north. The sky overhead was threatening, and most of the spectators kept to their carriages, with blankets on their laps and baskets of fried chicken, hot bread, and flasks of brandy to keep their bellies full and warm.

Jesse and Ophelia had watched from her carriage as the Gray Fox led his raiders through an intricate drill designed to show off their horsemanship and their fighting ability. Tyrone's cavalry had concluded the demonstration with a headlong charge at full gallop. Rebel yells filled the air as they swept past the president's party. The townspeople clapped and cheered and President Davis personally congratulated the horsemen, delivering a brief impromptu speech about the quality and dedication of these knights of the Confederacy.

Now Colonel Henri Baptiste presented himself. He rode a chestnut stallion and brandished a gleaming saber in his right hand. Sunlight glinted off the thirty-six-inch curved steel blade and the brass hilt protecting the swordsman's fist.

"The sword is a gentleman's weapon. In New Orleans, a lad of breeding practices swordsmanship from the day he walks," he loudly explained, striving to be heard. He raised and lowered the saber in salute to President Davis and the generals in the tent, then bowed graciously to the carriages, right and left. Many of them contained young ladies who obviously had fallen under his spell. He held the chestnut to a brisk trot and continued around the twin rows of posts until he neared the far end. Then he angled out across the meadow for a dozen yards, whirled, and charged the spectators. He guided the

chestnut down the path between the posts. His
saber flashed, became a blue of bright motion cutting left and right, left and right. The sackcloth
pillows exploded in a flurry of goose feathers. A
murmur of approval rose from the spectators. Not to
be outdone by the man from New Orleans, Bon
Tyrone drew his saber, as did the men in his command. Tyrone galloped out into the field once more
and led his men along the same path between the
poles. Black servants hurried to replace the sackcloth pillows as the Gray Fox and his men charged
past with their sabers flashing in the sunlight. They
kept the feathers flying to the delight of the audience, whose hearts swelled with pride.

Jesse sensed he was being watched and looked
up as Baptiste approached him. The Creole saluted
and bowed to Ophelia.

"Well done, sir," she said.

"Thank you, ma'am. A compliment from beauty
is always the highest honor." He shifted his gaze to
Jesse. "I am told you are a horseman. Can you
handle a saber? It is a gentleman's weapon, as I have
said."

"But of course," Jesse replied. "Whenever I am
attacked by pillows, it is the first thing I reach for."

Bon Tyrone, riding up on his black charger,
overheard the conversation and had to look away
immediately to hide his amusement. Ophelia lacked
her brother's subtlety and laughed aloud, then brought
a hand up to her mouth when she saw the anger
flash in the colonel's eyes. Baptiste whirled his
horse about and rode back to the poles. This time
he ordered the Negroes to place candles on the
tops of the poles. When one of the servants moved
too slowly, the colonel swatted him with the flat of
the blade and exhorted him to hurry. Jesse scowled

at the man's conduct. His dislike for Henri Baptiste increased the more he came in contact with him.

"He is a proud man. And proud men can be dangerous," Bon Tyrone advised.

"Pride goeth before a fall," Jesse replied.

"Perhaps." Tyrone steadied his charger and turned to watch with professional interest Colonel Baptiste's latest display. "Depends on the man, I'd say."

Jesse dropped the conversation. His thoughts were on Caitlin, held prisoner and waiting to be taken to Jackson. He had even heard a rumor from Spider Boudreaux that Baptiste intended to continue on to Richmond with her. There'd be no rescuing her from the capital of the Confederacy. He'd have to do something before that happened. He began to formulate a plan.

"Why, Jesse McQueen . . . your thoughts are miles away." Ophelia playfully pouted. "I hope I can blame your disinterest on lack of sleep and not on the company you're keeping."

"What . . . yes, I mean no," Jesse stammered. Then he patted her hand. "Please excuse me." He climbed out of the carriage and, circling Tyrone on his mount, cut straight in front of the carriages on a course for General Johnston in the president's entourage.

"Well, I never." Ophelia stared after her departed escort in disbelief. Bon Tyrone chuckled good-naturedly, dismounted, and joined his sister in the carriage.

"Never fear, sister. I'll be happy to help eat your chicken."

Ophelia "harumphed" in disgust. *Of all the unmitigated nerve,* she thought, trying to work up anger at the dark-haired lieutenant who'd abandoned her.

"I never thought I'd see the day when a man

didn't fall under your spell and obey your every whim like a well-trained pup. Yes, sir. There goes a man with character." Bon Tyrone was definitely enjoying this. After all, a brother had a sacred duty to torment his sister.

Ophelia turned on him, her temper flaring. "You can choke on that chicken for all I care, Mr. Boniface Tyrone."

Tyrone grinned. "Whew. You're still quite the firebrand when your dander's up." He noticed Spider Boudreaux standing a few yards off to the side of the carriage. The gruff-looking Cajun had ground-tethered his horse and couldn't take his eyes off the picnic basket on the floor of the carriage. Tyrone motioned to the sergeant to join him. Spider virtually beamed as he hurried over to the carriage, delighted at sharing in his captain's good fortune. He doffed his hat, bowed to Ophelia, and glanced from the picnic basket to the woman who had prepared the meal.

"If'n you don't mind, Miss Ophelia?"

"By all means," the woman replied, cold as the chicken she had packed with care. "Help yourself."

Jesse was halfway to the president's tent when a chorus of cheers erupted from the crowd. The loudest came from a cluster of carriages occupied by a bevy of young unmarried ladies. Another carriage held an older but singularly attractive widow who made no attempt to hide her interest in the colonel from New Orleans. Baptiste charged pell-mell past the posts, topped with the candles the servants had just lit. The colonel, wielding his saber, attempted to trim each burning wick, a feat requiring a delicate touch and expertise with the blade. Jesse looked around as Baptiste cleared the posts, leaving about half the candles untouched but the other half trailing smoke. There was no doubting the Creole's skill. But that didn't make him any less a murderous bastard as far as Jesse was concerned. He continued on toward Davis's tent, ignoring Baptiste until the Creole called him by name.

"McQueen!"

Jesse faced the colonel. He was weary of Baptiste's games and his arrogance. "What do you want, Colonel Baptiste?"

The man on horseback walked his mount toward the president's tent. He made certain to bow to the ladies and saluted them with a sweep of the saber. He stopped his horse about fifteen feet from Jesse.

"Perhaps you'll give us all a demonstration how a gentleman of mixed blood fights." Baptiste glanced over at the young ladies who'd begun to titter among themselves. His skill and bearing had certainly won them over. "I mean, if a gentleman were to challenge you. How would you defend yourself?" He sliced the air with a series of savage cuts. The steel blade whistled as it described each arc, each brutal slash. Then he froze, holding himself steady, saber poised, prepared to strike. "All in fun, of course," he finished, grinning.

A gunshot cut short the ladies' applause. One moment Jesse was standing motionless, his arms at his side, the next his right hand brushed his side, the navy Colt filled his hand. The gun barked once, blasting the saber's blade off at the hilt. The yard of curved, sharpened steel spun off through the air, striking the stallion. Baptiste had only a second to blink in disbelief and stare dumbfounded at the useless weapon in his hand before his frightened mount leaped and bucked.

"Looks like that New Orleans gator's been defanged," Spider called out. Several of the First Mississippi Volunteers made catcalls, only adding to the colonel's humiliation.

Jesse holstered his revolver, but kept a wary eye on the Creole. Black powder smoke drifted between them while the colonel struggled to stay in the saddle. He was forced, at last, to dismount. He leaped clear as the chestnut stallion raced past the carriages and down the Warrenton road toward Vicksburg. The shattered sword had left a bloody patch on the animal's rump.

Colonel Henri Baptiste dropped a hand to his revolver as he glared at McQueen, who had turned his back to him. The colonel started to draw his gun.

"Let it drop, Colonel," said Bon Tyrone, climbing out of Ophelia's carriage and approaching the colonel. "No reason to take offense. We're all wearing the same color uniform."

Baptiste appraised Tyrone with the same shrewd gaze that had served him so well as a slave broker in the crescent city. The Union occupation had put an end to what had been a thriving trade. It was a loss he keenly felt.

But something in Tyrone's voice overrode his anger and his wounded pride. "The same color, sir. I wonder." He lowered his holster flap. "You may champion this red nigger, Captain Tyrone, but I surely don't need to stand here and watch." He spun on his heel and left the meadow. He marched at a crisp pace but had only covered a dozen yards or so when one of the widows quit the field and drove her carriage up alongside him. Though he'd be leaving when the repairs were concluded, the widow saw no reason why she shouldn't give Baptiste a farewell to remember.

"A most interesting display, Lieutenant McQueen. And fine shooting," President Jefferson Davis remarked as Jesse entered the tent. The officers were sharing a bottle of sherry. The president of the Confederacy was gnawing on a chicken leg.

Jesse saluted the officers. "Thank you, Mr. President," he said, then shifted his attention to General Johnston. "May I take a moment of your time, General Johnston?"

"Any man who can shoot like that can have all afternoon," Johnston replied, chuckling. "Colonel Baptiste can be somewhat of a bore. I didn't mind seeing him taken down a notch."

"Sir, I was thinking perhaps I might ride on to Jackson. As the train won't be ready until tonight, I ought to be able to check most of the tracks. If I find any trouble, I'll have the train flagged down and the engineers aboard can see to repairs. And there'll be soldiers to help them."

Johnston stroked his chin, rubbed his neck, and slowly nodded. "Very well, Lieutenant. President Davis and I prefer to finish this journey in the comfort of his railroad car. But I'd feel happier with the tracks inspected against the acts of Yankee sympathizers."

The dour-looking General Pemberton spoke up. "Perhaps you ought to take someone with you." He did not think he had enough troops to defend the city. Johnston had spent the entire morning telling the Philadelphian he had all the troops that could be spared.

"No," Jesse retorted a bit too quickly, then

caught himself. "I can cover more ground on my own." Another man tagging along would ruin his plans. He had to be alone.

"Have it your way, Lieutenant," Johnston said. Jesse breathed a sigh of relief. He bid the generals a good afternoon and ran back toward Ophelia's carriage. No matter that she was furious with him. He needed to ride back to Judge Miller's house, where he had stabled the roan stallion. And he'd have to borrow another mount from the judge's own stock. Fortunately, Miller prided himself on raising prime horseflesh. His stallions were bred for speed, which was all well and good. For tonight, Jesse McQueen wouldn't have a moment to spare.

Chapter Thirteen

The front barreled out of the north a couple of hours after sundown. Strong gusting winds laced with icy rain stung Jesse's cheeks and hands. The night, black as Mississippi mud, hid his huddled form as he crouched over the railroad track and stuffed a makeshift fuse into the powder keg he'd wedged beneath the rail irons.

Jesse had left Vicksburg late in the afternoon, leading an extra horse with the express purpose of making a hard, fast run to Jackson. As he'd be following the tracks across rough terrain at night instead of keeping to the well-traveled road, the second horse made sense. An animal could throw a shoe or cripple itself on such a night. He had ridden unchallenged through the breastworks, halting only once atop a wooded rise to watch the setting sun poke out from behind the lowering clouds and bathe the sky in crimson and gold. The Warren County Courthouse with its pillared verandas and gleaming cupola dominated the horizon. And at that moment Jesse had recalled Major Abbot's analogy between the Civil War and the Trojan War. Indeed, the Greeks must have felt these same emotions that even now coursed through his mind as he beheld the fabled fortress city among whose warriors Jesse McQueen kept perilous company, like a man dancing on a gallows door with his neck in the noose.

He shivered and blew into his hands and returned his attention to the dangerous task before him. With trembling hands, he fished a tin of sulfur matches from his coat pocket. Two strikes and he cupped a flame, shielding it from the wind as he lit the fuse. He tossed the match aside and scrambled across the tracks. His boot toe caught on the iron and he tumbled down the embankment. Jesse scrambled to his feet and, glancing back over his shoulder, ran headlong into a menacing night-shrouded figure.

It was a big man, fully six feet tall, broad-shouldered, wide-chested, with an enormous gut straining the buttons of his wolfskin coat. Jesse rebounded off the man, staggered back, and reached for his revolver. The big man lowered a shotgun at his midsection.

"That'd be a fool thing to do," he growled, thumbing the twin hammers of his shotgun. "I loaded me this with nails. They can ruin a man plumb awful."

Jesse lifted his hands and showed the man his empty palms. "No call for trouble. You startled me, coming up so quiet." His mind was racing. Had the wind blown out the fuse? A droplet of sleet doused the flame? And this blasted stranger... "Who are you?" he demanded.

"Jed Burlock," the man growled. "I run slaves over to Nachitoches. Lost me a couple of niggers I was bringing over to a man in Edwards. I was too kind to the little bastards. I treated 'em square and they repaid me by runnin' off." Burlock held the shotgun with one hand and patted a black-handled whip, its leather grip capped with a silver knob. He kept the whip in easy reach. "I'll peel their flesh when I run 'em down."

As Burlock brushed by, Jesse could make out the man's pasty-white features and bushy black brows now furrowed in a frown. He smelled of raw liquor and strong tobacco.

"I found your horse tethered yonder. What the hell you doin' up there on the track?" The slaver spat a stream of tobacco in the dirt.

"I've been inspecting the rails. A train's due here on the Jackson run."

"You ain't no lineman," Burlock muttered, keeping the shotgun trained on McQueen. "Lie to me, boy, and I'll cut you in half and I don't give a shit about what color uniform you're wearin'."

"I'm riding the line," Jesse repeated. He hooked his thumbs in his belt. "I was making good time until I saw these darkies—"

"Two of 'em. Young 'uns. One's a buck, about eleven. The other's a pretty little gal, ripe as a cherry." The burly slaver had forgotten his suspicions. He'd lost his property and was bound and determined to get them back if it took all night. "You seen 'em?"

"The very same!" Jesse blurted out. "I just now chased them off." He pointed toward the tracks and tried to sound convincing. "I had a feeling they were runaways."

The slaver swung around and lumbered up the rise to the rail irons, where he stood bracing the north wind, his bleak eyes searching up track and down, then straight ahead to the cotton field, fallow in winter. "Which way did they head, goddammit?"

He turned, expecting the lieutenant to be at his side or at least back down the rise. Where the hell had the grayback run off to?

"Reb!" The north wind carried away his voice. "Hey!" The big man muttered a curse. A yard from his mud-spattered boots, a tongue of fire leaped into the air, sputtered, spewed a tendril of acrid smoke and then a geyser of sparks. In the light of the flickering fuse, seconds before the powder keg ignited in a blinding flash, Jed Burlock, slaver, spied the danger and knew he'd been tricked.

"Well, I'll be..." A blinding flash, a deafening roar, and then he was—

"Gawddammed!"

Chapter Fourteen

An abruptly opened door followed by a chill wind that swept into the bedroom roused Tom and Obedience Spivey from their sleep. Obedience, in her nightcap and bedclothes, was the first to notice the stranger standing in the bedroom doorway.

"Heaven protect us," the woman exclaimed as she pulled the comforter up to her double chin. Her eyes grew wide and her breath fluttered as she struggled to regain her composure. Her husband rubbed the sleep from his eyes and finally managed to focus on the man in the greatcoat looming over them, a lamp in his hand. The yellow glare set Jesse's chiseled features in stark relief. The interior of the mercantile was warm, thanks to a Franklin stove still glowing with red oak logs. Tendrils of steam began to rise from Jesse's rain-soaked coat. Water dripped from the hem and left a puddle on the bedroom floor.

Edwards, Mississippi, consisted of a mercantile

and a one-room train depot. Spivey's mercantile furnished necessities for the plantation owners and for the farmers who populated the land between Vicksburg and Jackson. And when there were passengers for the railroad, Spivey hung a red lantern on a post by the tracks.

"Get the gun, Tom, get the gun!"

"Be quiet, woman, you'll see me killed," Tom snapped. He scratched at the white fringe of hair circling his bald pate like a snowy wreath. "I don't have no money, mister. But take what you need from the shelves and leave us be."

"I haven't come to rob you," Jesse explained. "It's me, Tom. Jesse McQueen. I've stopped here often enough on my way to Vicksburg and back to Jackson."

"Take what you need?" Obedience sat upright and glared at her husband. "And we have not one thing to spare. Hard as times are? I'm married to a coward."

"Cease your jawing, woman. By gum, you carry on more'n a cat in heat." Tom Spivey put on his spectacles and crawled out from under the comforter. A thin wiry man with a bandy-legged stance, he reached for his trousers and tucked his nightshirt into them as he buttoned them up. "Didn't you hear the lad? He ain't come to rob us. Why, it's that nice lieutenant, the one who brung us them dried apples when you took sick."

"Oh my," Obedience exclaimed.

Tom Spivey glanced up to heaven and wagged his head, a long-suffering expression on his face, as he followed Jesse down the short narrow hall that opened onto the general store. The room smelled of leather and tobacco and chicory coffee brewing on the stove. Many of the shelves were bare, thanks to the Union blockade that had bottled up Confederate ports. But there were still some leather goods and bolts of cloth and nankeen pants and a few tins of meat and jars of canned fruits and sacks of flour. The pickle barrel was still half-full. And only a few days ago Tom had come by a packet of needles that the merchant considered more precious than gold. He intended to sell them individually and make a tidy profit.

"Lordy, you are a sight, boy," Tom said. At fifty-nine, he called everyone not older than himself "boy." He grabbed up the coffeepot and sloshed the bitter brown liquid into a tin cup that he had to hold by the rim because the metal handle was too hot. He took a sip and grimaced.

"Damn them Yankees. Keepin' a man from his coffee ain't no civilized way to fight a war." He looked up as McQueen helped himself to a worn, woolen black cape and an empty flour sack.

"There'll be a train coming through. I don't know when exactly, but it'll be Jackson bound. You'll have to flag it down."

"What for? Awful late for a train..." Tom scratched at the salt-and-pepper stubble shading his chin. "You been samplin' my muscadine wine afore you waked me?"

"Jefferson Davis is on that train."

"Glory be!" Tom Spivey snapped to attention as if the president of the Confederacy were already standing over by the molasses candies.

"Northern agents have blown the track about a mile east of here." Jesse placed a hand on the old man's knobby shoulder. "Stop that train. Davis can wait here while the track is being repaired. They can tear up a section back here and swap it for what's been damaged."

"President Davis himself, stayin' right here," Tom Spivey recited, as if repetition would guarantee his good fortune. "President Davis comin' here."

"Just see that you stop the train. Tell them I've gone on ahead."

"By gum, for President Davis I'll hang both lanterns. I'll stop that train, never you mind." The merchant had become flush with excitement. He hurried behind the counter and pulled his coat from a wall peg. He kept an extra red-tinted lantern on one of the lower shelves. He picked it up along with a couple of matches.

"Mama! Get yourself dressed. We're fixin' to have President Davis stayin' right here at Edwards."

Obedience loosed a panic-stricken screech as she fought her way out of a tangle of blankets and comforter, excited and appalled by her husband's announcement.

Tom Spivey turned to ask Jesse for more facts about the Union agents, but the gray-clad lieutenant had vanished into the cold and dark. The merchant scratched again at his stubbled chin and pondered the lieutenant's strange behavior and sudden departure.

"He took my cape and that flour sack," Tom Spivey muttered. "I wonder what for."

Twenty-nine tons of iron and steel came driving through the snow flurries in a night as dark as a witch's heart. The locomotive, affectionately called the *Bull Run Belle* by those it served, pulled a coal car, two troop cars (whose occupants were for the most part sleeping), the president's private car, a freight car containing the president's carriage and mare, and the mail car in which Colonel Henri

Baptiste and two Confederate privates kept uneasy watch over Caitlin Brennan.

The steam whistle on the locomotive howled like a demon, and black smoke laced with sparks streamed from the iron smokestack as the train skirted the banks of Black Bayou a few miles west of Edwards. There were always plenty of deer on the fringe of the bayou and the engineer loosed another whistle blast to chase off any that might be on the tracks.

"What was that?" Bill Pike said, roused from sleep by the whistle. He was a young man of average height, with the lean solid build of a farmer. Tobit Bascomb, Pike's companion and older by a year, grinned, showing a row of buckteeth.

"Just the devil gathering up his souls like a man picking cotton, only thing is, the devil does his ginning in hell." Tobit Bascomb reached out and tugged Pike's gray cap down over his eyes.

"Cut it out, Toby. It ain't funny," Pike complained. "You shouldn't talk like that. Ol' Scratch is liable to hear and come a-flying."

"Why not? I ain't got nothing to fear." Bascomb chuckled. "I read the Good Book twiced a day and don't curse or drink none." He leaned forward, propped on the barrel of his rifle. "Pity the same cain't be said for you."

"Hogwash is what you're saying." Pike leaned back in his chair. He was satisfied he'd won the argument. But Bascomb continued to grin and stare at him. This was a warm place here by the stove, but Pike thought if he stayed much longer, he'd just have to up and wallop the bejesus out of Tobit Bascomb and that was a sure bet. No telling how such a commotion would set with the colonel. Better to back off and cool down, the private told himself. And with that in mind he stood and pulled his coat around himself and headed for the door.

"Where the hell are you going, Private Pike?" Henri Baptiste said, sitting on the edge of a narrow cot at the opposite end of the mail car. Across from him, her wrists joined by shackle irons, Caitlin Brennan pretended to sleep, bowed forward over a desk, her head cradled on her folded arms.

"That chicory coffee's gone right through me, Colonel. I need to..." The soldier glanced at the woman and then crooked a thumb toward the door. The tail end of the mail car sported a narrow, railed platform. A man could stand there out of the wind and empty his bladder.

"Go on," Baptiste grumbled.

"Thankee, Colonel." Pike made his way to the rear of the car, unlatched the door, and stepped outside, closing the door behind him. The noise of the engine, the rattle of iron wheels upon the iron rails, the droning of the wind immediately surrounded him. He gasped as the cold started to sink into his bones. The night hung black and ominous about him. For one brief second Pike thought he saw a riderless horse racing alongside the mail car. He rubbed his eyes, peered once more, and saw nothing. The young man began to question the wisdom of unbuttoning his fly. Finally he decided to wait. Maybe he could hold out till the train rolled into Jackson. The issue resolved, Pike turned to reenter the car and gasped in horror. A monstrous apparition had materialized between him and the door. The frightened soldier staggered against the rail guard and started to cry out, but a solid right fist clipped him on the jaw and knocked him backward over the rail. Pike struck the tracks, was knocked senseless, rolled down the embankment, and was lost to the night.

Jesse straightened the flour sack covering his head, adjusting the eyeholes so he could see properly. His hands were numb from the cold and there was still much to be accomplished. He tucked his hands under his arms for warmth. He had to be able to handle a gun if he wanted to rescue Caitlin. Baptiste wasn't about to hand her over without a fight. Jesse had no way of telling how many men were guarding Caitlin, but he counted on the element of surprise and hoped his plan didn't backfire in his face.

"I know you are not asleep," Baptiste muttered in the ear of the woman slouched over the brakeman's desk. He placed a hand on the back of her head and stroked her hair. Caitlin bolted upright. Her sudden movement caught the Creole by surprise and he jumped back and pulled a revolver from his belt. Caitlin smiled into the barrel of the navy Colt and took pleasure in having startled him.

"You'll be laughing out of the other side of your mouth when I bring you to Richmond." Baptiste kept the revolver trained on the woman. Looking into his wild eyes, Caitlin Brennan thought he might actually shoot her dead. "Yes, to Richmond. Folks there have no patience for spies. You'll make a pretty corpse." He was no longer the dashing Creole. His uniform was rumpled, the coat unbuttoned. His white hair needed brushing. The odor of brandy clung to his breath.

"Someone needs to talk some sense into you, darlin'," Caitlin told him in her best Rosalie DuToit drawl. "Maybe it ought to be me." She shrugged and gave him an inviting grin. It was time to stop waiting for a rescue and help herself. She might not have another opportunity. A change of tactics was called for. If she could lay a hand on his gun, only two men stood between her and freedom. "I've fought it long enough. If a girl's got to surrender her honor, it might as well be to someone worthwhile."

Baptiste noticed the difference in her tone of voice. And he liked it. The Creole, in his liquor-clouded judgment, did not have enough sense to be suspicious. Her sudden capitulation made perfect sense. She was a woman and by nature weak. Faced with the prospect of execution, she had broken like a twig. He reached in his coat pocket and removed a silver flask, unscrewed its top, and drew closer to his prisoner. The iron links chaining Caitlin's wrists clinked when she reached up to place her hand over Baptiste's. The colonel tilted the flask to her lips and poured a measure of brandy into her mouth. Her eyes were pools of invitation.

"Bascomb," the Creole officer said. "John Pike outside. You'll be warm enough. The platform's out of the wind."

"But, Colonel . . ." the Rebel protested.

"This won't take long," Baptiste said.

"Oooh, I hope it will, darlin'," Caitlin whispered. A droplet of brandy spilled from the flask onto his knuckles. She ran her tongue along his finger, licking the brandy trail from the back of the colonel's hand. Baptiste gulped and glanced sharply at Bascomb, who withered before his stare.

"I gave you an order, Private, now get the hell out!"

Bascomb grumbled a halfhearted "yes, sir" and beat a hasty retreat toward the backdoor. He grabbed the latch and angrily yanked. At the same instant

Jesse McQueen, on the platform outside, gave the door a mighty shove. The door flew open and crashed against the back wall. Jesse barreled off balance into the car, black cape fluttering and gun in hand. He slammed into Bascomb and both men crashed into the Franklin stove and went down.

Baptiste stared with his mouth agape at this strange apparition, momentarily dumbfounded. Caitlin was as shocked as her captor.

Bascomb smacked against the cast-iron stove with the back of his head and went limp. Jesse struggled to untangle himself. He was blind! The damn mask had been twisted off center as he fell. Through a corner of an eyehole he glimpsed Henri Baptiste, galvanized into action. The colonel leveled his Colt revolver at this would-be rescuer. Caitlin lunged forward, caught Baptiste's wrist, and chomped down, burying her teeth into the flesh at the base of his thumb.

Henri Baptiste howled and fired. The gun thundered in the confines of the rail car. A bullet ricocheted off the stove and burrowed into the ceiling. Jesse pulled off the cumbersome flour-sack mask and rolled out from behind the stove in time to see the colonel wrench free of Caitlin. Blood oozing from his hand, he turned the weapon on her.

"Baptiste!" Jesse shouted, and fired through the billowing powder smoke. Baptiste staggered against the door that opened onto the coupling between the cars. He steadied himself and snapped off a shot as Jesse fired again. The two guns, both .36-caliber navy Colts, roared simultaneously. Jesse felt death fan his cheek. The Creole jerked to the left, taking a second slug in the chest. He raised his hand, determined to kill his attacker, but he no longer held a gun. He shoved clear of the door and staggered toward Caitlin, dropped to his knees, and steadied himself against the desk. Blood pumped from two black holes in his chest. A shadow fell across him. He looked up into the solemn features of Jesse McQueen. The man from the Indian Territory opened his shirt at the neck to reveal the white-puckered ridge of scar tissue around his neck.

"The next time you hang a man, Colonel, you'd better be sure the job gets done," Jesse said through clenched teeth.

A look of recognition swept over Baptiste's features.

"You..." he said weakly. "You." Fainter still. There wouldn't be a next time. His eyes glazed over as the life ebbed from him. Jesse took the key from the dead man's pocket and tossed it to Caitlin where she lay, sprawled on the hardwood floor.

"Free yourself. I'll uncouple the car."

Without further ado, Jesse holstered his gun and opened the door now marked by a smear of blood and a lead slug buried in the wood panel. He stepped out on the coupling. The roar of the locomotive and the rush of the wind filled the mail car.

Caitlin unlocked her iron bracelets and, as an afterthought, fished through the pockets of the dead man until she found the tintype. She heard a loud clank and felt the car immediately slow down, the noise of the train gradually diminishing. Jesse stepped inside and closed the door.

"They won't notice the car's missing until the train pulls into Edwards," he explained, blowing into his hands.

"You bastard, look what you did to my picture." Caitlin held up the tintype—or what was left of it after Jesse's first shot blew half of it away while mortally wounding Colonel Henri Baptiste.

"You're welcome. Don't bother to thank me. Just stay here till Johnston sends some soldiers back from Edwards." He crossed to the side door of the mail car and slid it open. "It's slowed enough to jump. You coming?"

"Wait," Caitlin grumbled. She hurried across to the Franklin stove and tossed the tintype into the firebox. Then she scooped her dress up over her head and helped herself to Bascomb's coat and pants. The unconscious Rebel never stirred as she undressed him. As an act of kindness she covered him with her dress and then pulled his gray trousers on over her pantaloons. Dressed for travel, or for that matter, leaping from trains, she joined Jesse at the door.

"Thank you," she grudgingly managed.

"You're welcome." Jesse grinned.

"That was quite an entrance," she added.

"It's the exit that counts." They leaped from the freight car and hit the embankment running. Bascomb's boots were too big for Caitlin and caused her to stumble and scrape her hands and knees. She cursed her clumsiness in a most unladylike fashion.

"Why, Miss Brennan . . . I'm shocked," Jesse said, helping her to stand. The mail car continued on past them and vanished in the moonless night. Icy rain stung the woman's face and hands, and she pulled her stolen coat around her ample bosom. McQueen draped his cape over her shoulders. He had worn his woolen greatcoat underneath.

"Now what? We'll freeze before we've walked a mile," Caitlin complained.

"We aren't walking. We'll ride to a barn where I've hid out provisions and a horse to carry you to Memphis." Jesse raised his hands to his mouth, cupped them, and whistled, softly at first, then louder. Three times he whistled, waited, blew three more notes. Caitlin looked at him askance. She was thinking he'd no doubt taken leave of his senses when a roan stallion materialized out of the gloom and obediently approached Jesse, who caught up the animal's reins.

Caitlin watched him with newfound respect. He leaped aboard trains, engaged in fisticuffs and gunfights, rescued fair maidens, and now summoned a saddled mount out of thin air.

"How did you do that?" she asked.

"Something my grandmother taught me," Jesse said. He climbed into the saddle and reached down for the woman in the cape.

"And my granny only taught me to bake custards," Caitlin wistfully added. She caught his hand, swung up behind him, and wrapped her hands about his waist.

Jesse walked the stallion across the tracks and down the embankment. He headed north toward a gap in the trees barely visible in the dark.

"Are you sure you know where you're going?" Caitlin said, her breath tickling the back of his neck.

"Hell no," he answered. Then he added with a morose laugh, "Do you?"

Caitlin fell silent.

Chapter Fifteen

The barn stood like a lonely sentinel on the edge of an abandoned cotton field. Its boards were weathered and gray and the structure leaned to the left as it waited for owners who would never return. The front doors were propped shut but the loft door hung from one worn leather hinge, leaving a gaping hole that looked for all the world like an empty eye socket. Despite its sinister appearance, the ramshackle structure seemed a work of art to Jesse and Caitlin as they walked the stallion across a patch of blackened earth where a dogtrot cabin had once stood. Snow had begun to settle on the two riders and the weary roan, but the wind had died down, and save for the crunch of the stallion's hooves on the soot-blackened remains underfoot, the world had become a place of peace and serenity. Jesse wondered how long it would last. The answer came all too soon.

"You hold it right there," a youthful voice called

from the barn loft. "This shotgun I's holdin' gotta smooth trigger, filed off real fine. Y'all even breathe wrong and I'll shoot your lights out." What looked like a gun barrel poked out of the black loft.

Caitlin stiffened as Jesse reined in his horse. "Now what?" she muttered.

Jesse didn't know. But a night full of close calls, quick timing, and desperate plans had taken its toll. Just ahead was a haven from the bitter cold and no one was going to keep him from it. He had left provisions in the stalls and two horses, the extra mount he had taken from Vicksburg and the solid-looking gelding that had belonged to Jed Burlock, the slaver.

Burlock! Of course, Jesse thought. He felt Caitlin reaching for her gun.

"No," he told her. Then he called to the youngster in the barn: "I aim to come on in. There's bacon and I figure on cooking it up and some biscuits, too, and boiling a little chicory coffee. I packed a jar of plum preserves that ought to go mighty good with those biscuits." Jesse started the roan forward, taking his time, giving the youth inside the chance to consider his options. "Talk it over with the girl. I'll bet she's hungry."

"How'd you know...uh...there ain't no gal hereabouts."

"Sure, and that shotgun isn't a piece of that firewood I gathered all on my lonesome not two hours ago."

Jesse thought he heard a girl's muffled cry of alarm, and the make-believe gun was pulled inside the loft. Jesse rode up to the front door. He and Caitlin dismounted and tugged open the doors. The bottom of the doors scraped the ground and the brittle leather hinges threatened to split. Jesse led the stallion out of what had become settling snow. Caitlin, still suspicious, kept to the side nearest the first stall. She took comfort in the Colt revolver tucked in her belt.

Jesse maneuvered through the darkness until he found the carpetbag he had left just inside the door, buried under a mound of brittle grass and decaying hay. He removed a thick beeswax candle from the bag, lit it, and walked into the center of the barn. There wasn't much to the structure, just four stalls, a narrow loft whose floor was missing several planks. A bin for oats at the rear of the stall looked as if it hadn't been opened in years. Jesse spied a field mouse scurrying out through a hole in the wall near the bin. No doubt the tiny rodent was only one of many. Spiderwebs hung from beams supporting the loft. A dust-covered cast-iron stove set between two stalls off to the right offered the only chance at surviving the night. Jesse had already filled the firebox with kindling. Using the candle, he lit the dried wood, and in a matter of minutes the flames from the stove cast a cheery glow into the center of the barn.

"Jesse . . ." Caitlin spoke his name as a warning. He turned and saw what had alarmed her—bits and pieces of straw showered down from the gaps in the loft flooring. A board creaked, then two dark-skinned faces peered over the edge of the hayloft. The boy might have been eleven, the girl a couple of years older, her homespun garments spattered with snow and clinging to her budding figure. They were cold and frightened. But the boy still held the red oak limb he'd tried to pass off as a shotgun.

Jesse noted that the back stalls still held the horses he'd left for Caitlin. Evidently the runaways had themselves just arrived, else his provisions would have been ransacked and the horses stolen. He couldn't blame them.

"Don't be afraid. You can come down," Jesse said.

"Stay where you are, Beckah," the boy said, placing a hand on the girl's arm. But the fire in the stove was mighty inviting.

"It's all right," Jesse said. "Mr. Burlock is dead."

He could have fired a shot at them and had the same reaction. Both youngsters flinched. The girl stifled a scream of terror. The boy's eyes widened in his ebony face, and though he tightened the grip on the branch, his eyes grew moist.

"Tommy Lee, you hear what he done said," Beckah whispered hoarsely.

"I heard," the boy replied. He glanced down at Jesse, his expression mirroring his mistrust. "I don't believe you, Reb."

"Take a look yonder. You know Burlock, you ought to recognize the dun in the stall."

Boy and girl shifted their focus to the dun gelding in the back stall.

"That his horse all right," Beckah said.

Tommy Lee raised up. He wore a coarse cotton shirt several sizes too big for him. The loose folds of the shirt he'd tucked in his overalls, which hung by a single strap across his shoulder. He studied the animal while Caitlin joined Jesse. Beckah seemed to brighten at seeing a woman.

"Come on down, honey. You must be nigh frozen," Caitlin said.

"Yes'm," Beckah said, and started to crawl toward the ladder. Tommy Lee had yet to be convinced.

"The horse don't mean nothin'. How come you know ol' Massa Burlock? How come you say he dead?"

Jesse shrugged. His expression hardened. "Because I killed him."

Morning broke clear and cold and as white as a virgin's wedding veil. A pristine carpet of powdery snow had settled over the meadow and the barn and drifted against the remains of a split rail fence. As the doors to the barn opened, the hinges on one side gave way, and with a silence-shattering crash, the door toppled to earth.

Jesse McQueen emerged from the shadowy interior. His breath clouded the still air. His boots sank into the snow. He guessed that about two inches of powder had fallen overnight. There were patches of ice under some of the snow and a rider would have to be careful.

Night had passed quickly enough. After serving up three helpings of biscuits and bacon for the young runaways and watching them polish off the entire jar of preserves, Jesse had bedded them down and then unrolled his own bedroll and fallen asleep. Sometime during the night, Caitlin had joined him for warmth. He awoke with her nestled beside him. It was a nice feeling but one he had not pursued with children present. In the morning, while Caitlin heated coffee and the last of the bacon, Jesse saddled the horses and readied them for the long ride to Memphis. There were few patrols during such weather, so Caitlin and the children would be safe enough. Caitlin had connections with abolitionists in Illinois and she assured both Tommy Lee and Beckah that she would find a home for each of them.

Jesse shielded his eyes as he looked out across the meadow. The snow seemed strewn with flakes of gold. The effect was dazzling. He heard footsteps

behind him and turned as Beckah, her dark pretty
features beaming with happiness, came up to hug
him. She halted, thinking her behavior improper.
Then she tossed propriety aside and hugged him
anyway. Afterward she shyly retreated a few steps.

"Thank you, sir, for helpin' us and givin' me
your blanket. It wears mighty warm," she said. And
looking around, she sighed. "It's all so beautiful.
Like angels been playin' here."

"You're welcome, Miss Beckah." Jesse grinned.
She trotted happily back to the horse that Tommy
Lee was leading out of the barn and leaped up
astride the animal. Then Tommy Lee mounted behind her. He walked the dun over to Jesse.

"You sure 'nuff is a funny kind of Reb. But if
you ever need me for somethin', you can look me up
in Cairo." He held out his hand and Jesse shook it.

"I'll remember that. Good luck, Tommy Lee."
Jesse noticed the boy gazing in apprehension at the
woods on the edge of the meadow. The eleven-year-
old had used up about all of his courage fleeing
from Burlock. "Nothing out there but trees, son,"
Jesse added. "And freedom."

Tommy Lee nodded and walked the animal out
of the barnyard and into the fallow fields. Caitlin
told them to wait for her as she emerged with her
own mount a few steps behind.

Jesse saw the worry in her expression and met
her halfway. She had a revolver and a shotgun, both
of which she knew how to use, and there was
hardtack and coffee to last the few days they'd be on
the road.

"You'll make it fine," he said reassuringly.

Anger flashed in her sea-green eyes. "I'm not
worried about me. You're the one who'll be standing
in the shadow of the gallows."

"I've been there before." Jesse kicked at the snow. He didn't much like the way she was saying good-bye.

"Come with me, Jesse."

"I still might be of use here."

"You're staying for that girl, for Miss Ophelia Tyrone. She'll get you killed, you softheaded idiot." Caitlin scowled and clenched her fists.

"I'm staying because it's what I have to do. And you know it." He patted her arm. "But I'm touched that you care."

"Oh, you impossible, arrogant, bonebrained ..." She stamped her foot, pulled him to her, and kissed him, then whirled around and climbed into the saddle.

"You're one of a kind, Caitlin," Jesse said, bewildered by her behavior. "And that's good because I doubt I could handle two of you." He brushed back his black hair and straightened his hat. Caitlin Brennan was an armful, for a fact.

"Watch yourself, Jesse McQueen."

Jesse nodded and mounted the roan. "With Baptiste dead, I haven't an enemy in the world," he said.

His bravura struck a false note. "Not an enemy save the whole Confederate Army," said Caitlin. "And everyone in Vicksburg and especially Captain Bon Tyrone and his sister." She leaned toward him and her eyes softened. "What do you think would happen if they learned the truth?"

"Tell Abbot that the ironclad the Rebs are building upriver is just a bluff. It's wooden-hulled and armed with Quaker cannons. Porter's gunboats have nothing to fear. It poses no threat. Do you understand?"

Caitlin sighed. She had tried her best. And in a

way, despite her concern, she was proud of him for staying. Back in New Orleans, a lifetime ago it seemed, she had thought a romp in bed had taught her everything about Jesse McQueen. But the events of the past night and his determination to remain behind proved her estimation of him shallow indeed. Maybe someday there would be time....

She turned her horse and rode toward the runaway slaves she would lead out of bondage. She was glad for the journey ahead. It took her mind off farewell.

Jesse watched them ride away and for one brief moment he had the urge to follow, to ride far and fast and put this terrible conflict behind him. He resisted the temptation.

"Hey!" Jesse shouted to the riders as they reached the trees. As his voice rang out he could see Caitlin turn and stop to face him across the frozen expanse. "Merry Christmas!" His voice reverberated in the still distance, returned to him, and joined, as if in chorus, with Caitlin's "Merry Christmas." The two voices lingered on the wintry air until they merged and became one "Merry Christmas" to warm a valiant rider on his solitary way.

Chapter Sixteen

Sergeant Doc Stark, with a soul like Lucifer's and a heart like molten lead, led his skirmishers up from the banks of the Mississippi River and over a ridge topped with red oaks and hickory trees then down through the woods on the other side. With Milo and Titus to left and right, Doc rode at a gallop and burst free of the timbered slope. Howling in triumph astride a bay gelding, he vaulted a thicket of wild grapes and charged into the farmyard at the base of the ridge.

It was a pleasant home site with a sturdy whitewashed two-story house whose porch needed a fresh coat of paint. There was a garden out back, a barn and hog pen set off to one side, and a creek flowing fifty feet from the porch steps with pastureland beyond. It was the kind of place most men only dream of owning, secluded and quiet and safe...on any day but this one, May 2, 1863.

Doc waved his hat to the woman in the doorway of the house. She wore a simple green dress, her hair tucked up inside a straw bonnet adorned with a yellow ribbon.

"Compliments of the Army of the West," Doc called out as the two dozen skirmishers fanned out across the farm. Several of the soldiers headed straight for the meadow, where three cows, several calves, and a mean-tempered old bull grazed in the shade of the sweet-gum trees.

"What do you want here?" the woman called out. She sounded worried and had a right to be. She was a plain, solid-looking woman, narrow in the chest, broad at the hips, and defiant in her bearing.

"Looking for Rebels," Doc said.

"Heard a Reb cavalry was hiding somewhere around here," Milo said, wiping a hairy hand across his beard. He grinned at the two children crowding the doorway to peek past their mother's skirt.

Titus reined in his skittish mare by the hog pens. "I found 'em, Doc. Looks like these Rebs are fixing to spring an ambush."

"You check the barn. I'll stop Johnny Reb," Doc replied, and trotted across the yard to the split rail fence that confined the hogs. As it was late spring, the sows were beginning to show some fat, but they wouldn't be prime until late summer. Only Doc didn't have until late summer. And if the hogs were a might on the lean side, at least there were plenty of them. He hauled out his Colt as Milo joined him.

"So that's what a Reb looks like. Darn near good enough to eat." He leveled his Colt revolving rifle. The two guns thundered in the yard and the pigs squealed in terror and tried to run from the terrible noise that dropped one after another, but the pen was their prison and their doom. When the last of the gunshots echoed down the hills, even the piglets were bloody and still.

"Stop it! Stop it!" the woman on the porch shouted. She had ducked inside and returned with a single-barrel shotgun. She stood on the edge of the porch and aimed the weapon right at Doc. "Leave us be, you blue hellions."

"Hold on now, missy. I admire a lady with fire," Doc said. He was stalling for time while trying to remember whether or not he had fired all six rounds at the goddamn hogs. "We're just poor hungry soldiers sent to gather food. Why, me and the lads are darn near faint from hunger."

The farm woman eyed Stark's gut that strained the buttons of his blue woolen shirt. "I doubt you've ever fainted from hunger a day in your life. Now you've done your harm and you'll ride off or be buried here. I doubt your Yankee bones will rest easy in Mississippi soil."

"Let me go!" A boy's voice rang out from the barn. Moments later Titus Connolly reappeared. He walked his horse out from the barn and continued over into the barnyard, followed every step of the way by an irate gander who squawked and spread its wings and extended its long neck as if preparing to nip at the horse.

Titus held a towheaded ten-year-old boy under his left arm. The lad struggled against the man's grip. He flailed away at the arm encircling his chest and kicked at the horse, but to no avail. Titus's slight stature was misleading. He was wiry and strong and no mere child was about to break his hold. He tightened his grip and the boy groaned as the pressure increased on his ribs. The rest of the troopers paused to watch. Titus halted alongside

Doc, keeping just enough distance to the side to be out of the spread of buckshot if the woman fired.

"You got your knife, cousin Titus?" Doc asked.

Titus grinned. "Right here." He raised his right hand. The sunlight glinted off the double-edged steel. He placed the blade against the boy's throat.

"Good. I'm gonna count to three. If Momma here don't put down that squirrel killer by the time I'm finished, you slit the boy's throat."

"Ear to ear just like skinning a rabbit," Titus said. He licked his lips and smiled. He nodded to Doc and then to Milo, who, despite his brutish nature, seemed appalled at the suggestion. It struck a sour note and he wanted no part of such a deed. He wouldn't stop it, but he wouldn't watch, either. Milo backed his horse away.

"One," Doc solemnly counted, his features impassive, his mouth a thin straight slash beneath his black bushy mustache. He never had to say "two." The boy's mother tossed the shotgun into the yard. It landed hard enough to trigger the weapon. Nothing happened. She had confronted them with an unloaded gun.

"Let him go. Please," she pleaded.

"You've got grit, I'll say that for you," Doc Stark gruffly conceded. He respected that quality in man or woman. So she had held him at bay with an empty shotgun. That was rich. At a wave of Stark's hand Titus loosed his hold on his prisoner. The boy hit the ground running and didn't stop until he'd reached his mother's side. Milo looked relieved.

"Appears cousin Milo's getting a might soft of heart."

"You shut up, Titus. Hell, you'd have *liked* to slit that boy's throat."

"Why wait and have to face him when he's old enough to carry a gun. Dead, he's a good Reb." Titus rubbed his forehead.

"I don't see any sense in talking on it." Milo refused to argue the point or be goaded into a quarrel.

"You've changed, Milo," Titus muttered. "Damn if you ain't taking all the fun out of this war."

"It quit being fun when we buried Emory," Milo retorted. The big man glowered at his cousin. "Then you never cared much for Emory, did you now?"

"Hell no," Titus said. "But that don't matter. I stand with family." His eyes narrowed. "I'd hate to think you're turning agin' me." Milo, for all his size and bearlike strength, wanted no part of his cousin. Titus was as dangerous as a coral snake, striking without warning, quick and silent and deadly.

"I ain't turning on you."

"You two quit your jawing," Doc called back to them. He broke down his Colt and replaced the spent cylinder with a loaded spare he kept in his coat pocket. "You find something we can use to haul those pigs back to camp?"

"Wagon in the barn," said Titus.

"Good." Things were going well, Doc thought. "Take three men and get those hogs loaded before they spoil. Put your knife to use and butcher one out. We can cook it up over the fire."

"What fire?" Titus glanced around, puzzled.

Doc reached behind his saddle and untied a hickory branch from the strips that held it in place. One end of the branch was wrapped in an oil-soaked cloth. He lit the torch and trotted past the farm woman, who filled the air with protests. Her other children, two girls, scampered out of the farmhouse and ran across the yard to clutch at their mother's apron. Doc tossed the torch through the first window he came to. In minutes, flames sprang up to devour the house from within. Doc rode back to his cousin.

"That fire."

Chapter Seventeen

Looking upon the Tyrone plantation from the emerald twilight beneath the towering red oaks, Jesse McQueen delved deep into his memory and spoke aloud for the benefit of the fluttering butterflies and red-winged blackbirds.

" 'Macbeth shall never vanquished be until Great Birnam Wood to high Dunsinane hill shall come against him.' " His father had insisted he read the classics. A worn collection of Shakespeare had become Jesse's favorite book. Every time he approached the Tyrone plantation, Dunsinane, the great tragedy of *Macbeth* never failed to come to mind. But it wasn't for literature alone that Jesse delayed his arrival at the plantation. The drive he had abandoned skirted a cotton field and led right up to the front porch, with its stately white columns and ivy-covered rock chimneys on either end of the two-story house. The path continued around the house and branched. The right fork led to the barn and stables. The left fork wound behind the house, past the summer kitchen, and down to the slaves' cabins, arranged in an orderly row on the far side of a three-acre garden.

But Jesse kept to the woods and followed a deer trail until he reached a clearing about a hundred yards from the plantation house. He walked his horse over to an oddly shaped hickory whose gnarled trunk set it apart from the other trees in the thicket. He glanced around to ensure his privacy, dismounted, and working quickly, dug a hole at the base of the twisted hickory. He removed a leather notebook from inside his coat, wrapped it in oilskin, and placed it in the freshly dug hole, then covered it over with dirt and decaying leaves. Whether entering Jackson or Vicksburg or paying a call on Ophelia here at Dunsinane, he always took care to hide the notebook. It was a necessary precaution. The drawings of fortifications around Vicksburg and Jackson and the calculated troop strengths for the entire delta could get him hung. A twig popped behind him. Jesse whirled and palmed his navy Colt. For a moment the tableau held. Jesse McQueen crouched, gun in hand, hammer pulled back, his finger curled around the trigger. A red fox, rooted in place, one white paw lifted above the brittle leaves that had concealed the twig. Keen eyes bore into the man it had surprised in the clearing. Jesse stood and returned the Colt to its holster. At the same instant, the fox became a fleeting red blur that vanished behind a patch of yellow wood sorrel that flourished where the sunlight lingered longest in the clearing.

Jesse gathered a handful of the delicate yellow blooms while the roan looked on.

"They're not for you," he told the animal matter-of-factly, and rode the stallion out of the woods. He had barely begun to cross the cotton fields when he realized what had been nagging at his thoughts since arriving at the plantation. No dark-skinned men labored in the fields beneath the hot Mississippi sun. No children played along the wheel-rutted road leading up to the house. No long-limbed ebony women, who might have been tribal queens had they not been brought in bondage to a strange new world or been born into that world and sucked on the breasts of mothers for whom slavery was their only memory. No such women tended the garden or lingered by their cabins or prepared food for the menfolk. The slave cabins were as devoid of life as the rest of Dunsinane.

Jesse began to feel uneasy and crossed the field at a brisk pace. The closer he came to the house, the greater the sense of dread that tightened his chest. For a moment he had a premonition of flames and crashing timber and the roar of guns. He gasped and brought the roan to such a savage halt that the stallion reared in protest.

"Jesse McQueen, what on earth? You looked about to ride that horse right up on the porch. I hope these flowers are for me."

His mind cleared, though the aftermath of those images left him unsettled. He could not explain what had happened. No doubt his half-breed grandmother would have an answer for him. Spirit talk, maybe from the fox spirit he had encountered in the woods. But fox was a cunning trickster, often leading men to ruin who were foolish enough to follow his dreams.

And yet he sensed that he had been given a warning. *No matter,* he told himself, *dwell on it later.* Miss Ophelia Tyrone was waiting for him, her back to a column. Jesse had to blink and rub his eyes. It had only been a week since his last visit, but in that time everything had changed. Ophelia was certainly not dressed like a belle of the South. Bon Tyrone's sister wore baggy canvas trousers, a butternut-colored shirt, and scuffed boots. Her hair was pulled back and tied with a leather string. Could this be the same Southern belle who in her silks and laces had danced the night away at Christmastime in Vicksburg? As if to make this strange transformation complete, Ophelia even had a smudge of dirt on her left cheek and the tip of her nose. Jesse wondered if this were another hallucination, the work of the trickster fox.

"Jesse, my heaven, you act as if you've never seen me before."

"Maybe I haven't," Jesse managed to say, climbing down from the stallion. No black stableman came forward to take the animal to a stall, comb it, and give it water and food.

"You best see to your horse. And wash up. I'm cooking dinner." Ophelia hurried down from the steps, patted Jesse on the arm, kissed him on the cheek, then headed for the summer kitchen—a hearth, two ovens, and a long oaken table and benches arranged beneath a pitched roof supported by four stout red oak posts. "I'll explain while we eat."

Jesse couldn't wait to hear.

Dunsinane was not as large or ostentatious as some of the fine manors in Vicksburg. There were three rooms downstairs. A spacious dining room was dominated by a rectangular black walnut table that seated ten and a glass-inlaid hutch and side-board that once displayed a variety of china and silver cutlery. Most of the silver had been sold to support the war. Across the main hall was the study and toward the rear of the house a sun parlor. In the center of the house, a plain, functional stairway led to the upstairs bedrooms. The master bedroom now belonged to Ophelia. A second bedroom across the hall contained several beds and was often used by Bon Tyrone and any officer guests that might have accompanied him to the plantation.

Indeed, thought Jesse McQueen as he stood on the back porch and surveyed his surroundings, Dunsinane was not so much a place as a way of life, a self-sufficient existence that for sixty years had stood apart from the outside world and the changing order of things. From the shade of the house he watched the shadows of the trees stretch like groping hands across the ground to ensnare first the weaver's cottage and next to it the tutor's cabin and beyond to the potter's workshop and reaching still farther across the garden to the slaves' quarters, where a few banners of smoke trailed from sagging chimneys.

There was the problem, the source of the strange stillness that hung over the plantation like a shroud. Word had come of the Emancipation Proclamation. "Father Abraham" in Washington had set the slaves free. With rumors rampant of Union troops approaching from north and south, every able-bodied man, woman, and child had abandoned the plantation three days past, leaving Ophelia to care not only for herself but for the elderly men and women who had been too frail to attempt the journey to freedom. Jesse found it ironic that Ophelia now cooked the meals and brought food to the old ones who had spent much of their lives toiling for the Tyrones.

Jesse watched Ophelia walk toward him through the garden. She had just taken food to a silver-haired black man sick with fever. She paused and knelt in the garden to check the snap beans whose green tendrils sprouted from the furrowed earth. By midsummer the vines would be chest-high and ready for picking. She stood and resumed walking. She passed rows of butter beans and tomatoes, summer squash and cucumbers, beds of parsley and mint and plantings of tiny green peppers hot enough to blister the tongue if some fool were to eat one raw. There'd be sweet potatoes later in the year, but the onions were ready to be pulled, purple and nearly as sweet as an apple.

Sweat beaded her forehead and streaked her features by the time Ophelia reached the back porch. Jesse was amazed at how unperturbed she seemed about having been deserted by the slaves whose presence was so essential to Dunsinane's survival.

"You appear almost happy," he said, after voicing this thought. "Yet you're alone. And such a plantation cannot be maintained with only a young woman to tend things."

"Well, I am not leaving. This is my home." She dabbed at her forehead with a white lace-trimmed kerchief incongruously tucked in the hip pocket of her dungarees, a touch of delicate femininity to off-set her plebian costume. She yawned and looked down at her blistered hands. For the past three days she had been working from sunup until well after dark. What she didn't know about farming she was learning the hard way, by trial and error. The weary young woman managed a brave smile. "In a way, I am almost relieved they're gone." She noticed his expression. "You don't believe me? It's true. Bon and I inherited what our parents built. But we neither bought nor sold slaves after Papa died. In truth, my brother and I were always uncomfortable with such commerce. Neither of us felt it was right to own someone, yet we were too . . . weak . . . to free those slaves we had. How could the plantation even exist without them?" Her eyes took on a dreamy quality as if she were trying to peer beyond the veils of time and see what the future held. "Now the matter has been resolved and I need no longer wrestle with my guilt."

"You begin to sound like an abolitionist," Jesse chided her. "Why do you and your brother fight to preserve an institution neither of you cares to maintain?"

"We fight because the Northerners are here in our homeland, trampling on our way of life and trying to tell us how to live and what to think and believe in." Ophelia shook her head. "Right or wrong, we must solve our own problems for a solution to last." She studied the man at her side. "But that's enough politics. We are alone here, Mr. Jesse Redbow McQueen. All alone and free to do anything we want." She lowered her face a moment and then looked up at him, a provocative glint in her gray-green eyes. "Anything."

Jesse gulped. His stomach started growling as he followed her into the house. He didn't know about supper, but dessert promised to be a handful and more. His mind already began to wrestle with his baser instincts. Ophelia was as courageous as she was lovely. And if she were willing to invite him to her bed, how could he refuse? But there had to be a way. *I must be mad*, he thought. For weeks he'd wanted nothing more than to take her in his arms. Now the opportunity was about to present itself and he was looking for a way out.

They entered the winter kitchen at the rear of the house and Ophelia continued through a side door into the sun parlor.

"I have to make an entry in Papa's ledger. That's the way he ended each day. I've picked up the habit. I'll only be a minute," she said over her shoulder. "Then we can get down to more important things." She disappeared into the study.

Jesse headed for the coffeepot, filled a clay cup with the bitter black liquid, and as quickly drained it. He slammed the cup down on the table in the center of the kitchen and clutched the edge of the table to steady himself. He sucked in a mouthful of air. Damnation, if she hadn't emptied near a quart of whiskey into the pot. Another cup of coffee like that and he wouldn't need an excuse. No doubt, it eased her aching muscles.

He rejected the easy way out and left the coffeepot on the woodstove. It was already late enough in the spring for the fire in the stove to make the kitchen uncomfortably warm. He blamed his discomfort on the smoldering log in the firebox and, thinking himself the grandest fool of all, went to find Ophelia.

The parlor was a familiar room, his favorite in the house, with its cane-backed furniture carved of sweet-gum wood and windows all around and a mahogany sideboard complete with bottles of sherry, brandy, and strawberry wine. But he resisted the temptation to linger in the room and entered the study.

Ophelia sat in a high-backed chair behind a desk that faced the front window. Her father had been a cautious man and, while working at his desk, preferred to keep an eye on the front drive. Again, she was her father's daughter. Jesse cleared his throat, found a shelfful of books to his liking, then cursing his cowardice, returned his attention to the task at hand.

"Ophelia ... I have grown quite fond of you these past months. No, fond is hardly strong enough. I deeply care for you. And would not hurt you for the world." He rubbed a hand across his stubbled cheeks. There was the rub—how to explain without revealing the truth, that he was a Union spy playing a deadly gambit in the Confederate heartland. "I am more than I appear to be."

Very good, Jesse. Now tell her how much you'd like to make love to her. And yet that would be the cruelest deception of all. She believes you to be someone you are not. Go ahead, lay the truth before her like a patient naked to the surgeon's knife and we'll see whether the patient lives or dies.

"Ophelia," he said, his resolve momentarily weakening. He crossed the room to stand alongside her. "Ophelia." She sat motionless, her head, drooped forward on her chest, rising and falling with each breath. Her father's ledger lay open upon her lap. A large undulating scrawl marked the spot where she had fallen asleep in mid-entry. Her hand still grasped the quill pen.

Jesse smiled, leaned down, and scooped her up. The long hours had taken their toll, and she was deadweight in his strong arms. Gently, he carried her from the room and out into the hall. The stairs creaked beneath his weight as he started up. He reached her bedroom without incident, carried her into the darkening interior, and fumbled his way to the big brass bed that dominated the spacious room. He lowered the sleeping woman to the feather mattress, and as he turned to go, caught a glimpse of his gray-clad reflection in the mirrored door of a chifforobe. In the dim light, the image startled him and he reached for his gun. Of course his mirror image made the identical move. His Colt had cleared leather in the time it took him to realize he was about to gun himself down. He slid the gun back into his holster and shook his head. The rug muffled his footsteps as he approached the mirror and studied his reflection in the faint light drifting in through the open doorway. He was older looking, his eyes deep set, betraying the strain he'd been under.

The role had begun to wear on him and he was uncertain how much longer he could play it. Eventually, he'd make a mistake. The information he had collected would be discovered and traced to him. Or perhaps Pike and Bascomb, the two soldiers who had survived his rescue of Caitlin Brennan, might somehow recognize him despite his efforts to conceal his identity. All it took was a hint of suspicion to land a man in serious trouble.

He fumbled with the buttons at his neck and opened his shirt to reveal the English coin hanging against his chest. He lifted the silver coin and rubbed his fingertips across its surface. Though it was too dark to see, he could feel the jagged initials George Washington had carved in the coin before presenting it to Jesse's great-grandfather as a unique medal of valor.

And Jesse began to understand that he wasn't alone in this damnable war. Three generations of McQueens were standing with him. His sacrifice was theirs. They had fought to preserve the United States. He could do no less. If that meant sacrificing himself and the feelings he harbored in his heart, so be it.

He turned from the chifforobe and crossed to Ophelia's bedside, where he knelt and leaned forward to kiss her forehead. Even in this innocent good-night, the medal dangled forward, coming between them, like a call to duty or a warning impossible to ignore.

"All right. All right," Jesse muttered. "I hear you." He tucked the medal back in his shirt and left the room and its slumbering occupant, the Lady of Dunsinane, undisturbed.

Chapter Eighteen

On the sixth of May, three horsemen made their way in the predawn hours along a deer trail that wound through the heart of a particularly dense stand of timber that the locals quite simply called "the thicket."

Captain Bon Tyrone had taken the lead, for he had been raised in this country and the dense stand of red oaks and sycamores, sweet gums and black walnuts held no mystery for him. The trees grew close to one another, vying for space. The sun would have to be well above the horizon before it could penetrate this thicket. Most men would have been hopelessly lost.

"Reminds me of the bayous below New Orleans," Spider Boudreaux remarked, eyeing the gloomy underbrush. An army of hobgoblins could be lying in wait among such shadows. "Only we aren't riding ankle-deep in muck."

"Thank the Lord for small favors," added Major

Peter Abbot in the humble disguise of a Congregationalist minister.

Bon Tyrone looked back at the fussy, bespectacled man dressed all in black with a stiff white collar around his neck, a flat-brimmed black hat on his head, and a worn leather-bound Bible tucked under his arm.

"Maybe you'll put a good word in for us with the man upstairs," he said with a grin.

"Count on it, my good sir. Why, encountering you and your men, Captain Tyrone, was nothing short of a miracle. Yes indeed, a miracle. I should have never made it past these woods but wandered in them till I died. Then my sister in Natchez would have to find someone besides me to marry her off."

"Glad to be of help, Reverend Pettibone," Tyrone said. The Gray Fox and his raiding cavalry, returning from a foray in search of Sherman's army, had crossed Abbot's path at sunset. Bon had dispatched his raiders east toward Jackson while he took a more circuitous route, one that would bring him to Dunsinane. He liked to check on Ophelia whenever possible. When Bon Tyrone suggested the major ought to accompany him to Dunsinane, Abbot was only too happy to accept. He needed to find McQueen, and Tyrone's plantation struck him as an ideal place to start.

"Is it often that you visit home, Captain Tyrone?" Abbot asked.

Spider chuckled. "It is nowadays."

"That's enough out of you, Sergeant," Tyrone said, dropping back to ride alongside Boudreaux.

"I don't mean any harm, Captain Bon," said the heavyset Cajun. "If I had a sister pretty as yours, and a good-looking fella I weren't quite sure of came around like McQueen, I'd worry, too."

"You talk too much." Bon glowered at him.

"Hell, yes. I reckon I was just born sociable and been jawing ever since."

"Spider!" Bon warned for the last time. He'd drawn the line and not even his friend had better cross it.

The Cajun shrugged, catching the officer's threat. He managed to change the subject without breaking stride. "Where'd you say you were from, Pettibone?" The man failed to answer. "Your name's Pettibone, ain't it?" Major Abbot blinked and looked up. The poor light hid his embarrassment.

"Quite so. Quite so, my good fellow. Yes ... uh ... my congregation—is in Oxford, back in the hills."

Boudreaux shrugged, attributing the minister's halting response to fatigue. "I rode through Oxford a few times."

"It is a splendid place. So peaceful ..."

The sergeant and the parson continued their pleasant conversation but Bon Tyrone paid them no attention. His thoughts were of Dunsinane and his sister. She was so headstrong and stubborn. Ophelia would never leave the plantation for the comparative safety of Vicksburg or, better still, their aunt's house in Richmond. She had been steadfast in her determination to remain. He wondered if a certain lieutenant had anything to do with her decision. What exactly were McQueen's intentions? Bon hadn't worried before. But ever since the mysterious rescue of Rosalie DuToit or whoever she was, he had been plagued with suspicions. There was no proof of her rescuer's identity. But Bon Tyrone had sensed McQueen's animosity toward Colonel Henri Baptiste. Their clash in Vicksburg had only been a manifestation of something deeper. Despite the fact that McQueen had stopped the train in Edwards and possibly saved the president's life, Bon could not rid himself of the notion that Jesse might also have been responsible for the death of the colonel in the attack on the mail car—which in turn linked him to the escape of a suspected Union spy. Yet it was all conjecture. Bon truly liked McQueen, and owed him a debt. He honestly hoped his fears were groundless. For the moment he would behave as if they were.

Golden sunlight filled the sky and chased away the last of the stars. It warmed Jesse's naked back as he hefted the ax in his strong hands and went to work. The woodpile was located just off to the side of the winter kitchen. Here was familiar work and a task all the more difficult for a willowy lady like Ophelia Tyrone. Jesse wondered if there was anything she wouldn't attempt. He doubted it. She was bound and determined to keep Dunsinane alive. He swung the ax in a mighty arc and split a two-foot chunk of cured oak then put another in its place, split it, and repeated the process. The bite of the blade and the splintering wood shattered the morning stillness. After an hour his bronze torso glistened with sweat. But the supply of firewood was nearly replenished. The work was simple and strenuous and cleared his head.

Jesse paused to watch the graceful antics of a flock of red-winged blackbirds darting and diving among the furrows in the garden. He considered shooing them away but decided they were probably after insects and changed his mind. Indulging in a moment's reverie, he allowed the pleasant warmth and the good smell of fertile earth to renew his spirit. The crank of the well handle behind him

ended his idyll. He glanced around and saw that
Ophelia had joined him. She raised a bucket of cool
water from the covered well that had been dug
between the winter kitchen and the rear of the
house.

Ophelia wore a pale yellow dress suitable for a
day in the country. The smudges on her nose and
cheek were gone. Her auburn hair was drawn back
in a bun. She took the dipper from the bucket and
brought him a cooling drink.

"Jesse . . . last night—"

"You're a brave lady, Ophelia, for whom I have
nothing but the highest respect."

"Please," she replied, "don't make it too high."
She lifted her eyes to the meadow and the distant
edge of forest. "Perhaps today—" Then her expression changed dramatically. "Oh!"

Jesse did an about-face. Tension rippled up his
spine at the sight of three horsemen riding toward
them. He set the ax aside and walked around the
woodpile to the table by the brick hearth in the
winter kitchen. He'd left his shirt, gray coat, and
gunbelt on the tabletop. The navy Colt was the first
thing he reached for. He caught Ophelia staring at
him, bewildered by his actions.

"Jesse, they're wearing gray. In fact, I do believe
it's my brother," she said, shading her eyes with her
right hand. "And a man in black—oh my, I think it's
a minister. There, you see, they're hardly enemies."

"A man can't be too careful these days," Jesse
said.

"Well, I doubt you have anything to fear from
my brother, silly."

Jesse pulled on his shirt and coat and buckled
his gunbelt around his waist, pausing as his fingers
traced the letters "CSA" stamped in the brass. If she

only knew. That was the problem; one day she would.

"A minister," Ophelia repeated, exasperated. "That means a real dinner. If you'll fetch me a ham from the smokehouse, I'll fix you the best meal you've ever eaten." She placed a hand on his arm. Standing close to him in the shade of the winter kitchen, the young woman felt his tension. "What is it, Jesse? What's wrong?"

He looked at her, searching—no, memorizing her pale oval face, her rose-colored lips and hazel eyes. A powerful current flowed between them, drawing them together—a current broken only by the medal . . . always the medal, the symbol of who he was and why he was here and what his first love must ever be.

"The time," he answered. And when she seemed puzzled, he added, "The time is wrong."

It should have been a bloodbath but instead they had dinner. Confederate raiders sat on one side of the dining-room table, their backs to the windows. The two Union agents sat across from them with Ophelia at the head of the table receiving the accolades for the dinner she had prepared. Jesse couldn't help but think how, if his and Abbot's loyalty were revealed, there'd be an exchange of gunfire instead of platters of corn bread, bowls of peas, and slabs of ham.

With the meal coming to an end, the "Reverend Pettibone" dabbed up the last of the sauce on his plate with a wedge of corn bread and plopped it into his mouth and sighed in satisfaction.

"Miss Tyrone, I shall forever be in your debt. I have never tasted a better ham."

"Why thank you, Reverend. I shall make you a supply of sandwiches when you leave tomorrow. That ought to see you through to Natchez." Ophelia looked around at the other men. "I'll make enough for all of you," she added, much to Spider Boudreaux's relief. Soldiers traveled as hungry as preachers, and the sergeant was loath to ride to Jackson on an empty belly.

"My heartfelt thanks, madam," Abbot replied. He smiled benevolently at all the other men at the table. "Good food and good company is the Lord's way of blessing the righteous." He looked at Jesse seated to his right. "Don't you agree, Lieutenant McQueen?"

Jesse met his gaze momentarily then shrugged. He shifted his attention to Bon across the table. Ophelia's brother still looked somewhat shocked over the departure of the slaves. True to his sister's word, he had also seemed relieved at first, as if a weight were lifted off his shoulders. Yet those feelings quickly changed to concern for Ophelia's well-being now that she was more isolated than ever. Spider had been all for chasing after the Negroes and returning them to Dunsinane. Bon would have none of it. But the nobility of his sentiments gave him precious little reassurance that all would be well.

"Oftentimes, righteousness is only in the eye of the beholder," Jesse told the phony parson.

"Are you saying there is no right or wrong?" Abbot asked, pressing the issue.

"I am saying this war is made up of Confederates who believe their cause is just and that God is on their side, and Federals who feel exactly the same way. We can't both be right. But we can sure as hell both be wrong."

"You sound disenchanted with your cause," Abbot said, studying the agent he had sent south. As he searched the younger man's expression lamplight reflected off the lenses of his wire-rim spectacles, which had slid down his nose. He pushed them back with his forefinger.

"I know what I believe," Jesse told him matter-of-factly. "I just don't have to use God as my crutch to see things through. I like to think there is a greater truth above the issues men contrive to kill each other over."

"Let the bloodshed fall on our heads, eh?" Bon grimly interjected. His expression became guarded. "Are you now the philosopher, Jesse? Just how many hats do you wear?"

"You'd be surprised," Jesse said.

"Maybe not," the Gray Fox retorted.

The two men stared at one another across the table for several seconds as if taking the measure of each other for the first time. Then Jesse slid his chair back and slowly stood.

"Your pardon, Ophelia, but if I am to leave tomorrow, I must tend to my horse. It has a loose shoe and I'd rather see to it here in your barn than on the Jackson road." He bowed to her, then nodded to the men at the table.

"You know your way around a blacksmith's forge, do you?" said Abbot, hoping to ease the tension.

"Yes, sir, Reverend Pettibone. It's a skill passed down through generations of my family," Jesse told the man, playing along with his game.

"Perhaps you might look at my mare. She started favoring a leg as we rode up." Abbot stood and excused himself. "I'll tag along with our philosophical friend here." He dusted the crumbs from his frock coat. "And when I return, we shall have that game of checkers, Sergeant Boudreaux."

"Why, I'd be glad to whup you, preacher." Spider grinned.

Bon watched the two men leave the room. His features grew pensive as McQueen and the preacher disappeared through the doorway. He listened to the rap of their boots on the hardwood floor and recognized the familiar creak of the hinges on the front door as it opened and shut.

"Bon . . . you say the queerest things sometimes," Ophelia told him.

"I don't know what you mean," he said.

"And your whole attitude, as if you begrudge Jesse's presence. He has been nothing but a perfect gentleman since he has been here." She scrutinized her brother and her defense of Jesse trailed off. "But that's not it. You aren't upset that we were alone here. Something else is bothering you. What is it?"

"No," Bon lied. And realized his mistake. Ophelia could see through him like a well-scrubbed window. "Colonel Henri Baptiste, before leaving Vicksburg, told me he was almost certain he had seen Jesse before, maybe in New Orleans. He thought there was some link between his prisoner, Miss DuToit, and Jesse."

Ophelia sat back in her chair, folded her hands in her lap, and stared at them. Finally she shook her head. "You think he is a spy? My God, Bon, talk like that could get him hung. Jesse is my friend and yours. How could you think such a thing?" Her protest was ardent enough, but failed to convince her brother. Jesse was a mystery to her in many ways. But somehow she believed that whatever secrets the man from the West held, she could trust him with her life.

"I don't know what to think," Bon replied at last.

"Then, dear brother, I suggest you keep your opinions to yourself," Ophelia snapped. She tossed her cloth napkin onto her plate, abruptly stood, and left the dining room.

Bon glanced at his sergeant, who had watched the entire exchange.

"She asked me, didn't she?"

Spider nodded and poured another glass of strawberry wine for himself. "Sure," he concurred. "And beggin' your pardon, Captain, you were fool enough to comply." He hefted the glass in salute and drained its contents. "Hope she ain't too mad to pack us them sandwiches."

Major Peter Abbot peered through a mud-grimed barn window at the plantation house with its lamplit windows so warm and inviting against the dark of night.

"They're nice people," he mentioned with a sigh. "It's a shame wars are fought by nice people, on both sides." He turned in time to see Jesse roll a barrel of nails away from the corner of a stall by the forge, then kneel and remove an oilskin-wrapped packet.

"I retrieved this from the woods while you and the others slept away the afternoon," Jesse told him. He hung an oil lantern on a peg jutting from a nearby post and turned up the flame as Abbot crossed to him.

"It was a stroke of luck running into Tyrone," Abbot said as he opened the packet. "Caitlin told me to look for you in Vicksburg or Jackson and here at the Tyrone plantation if I could find it. By the way, she reached Memphis without incident, though

I was mightily surprised to see her and those two youngsters...." His voice trailed off as he examined the drawings, maps, and estimations of troop strengths Jesse had compiled. "Sweet Jesus!" The color drained from Abbot's face. He quickly rewrapped the packet and tucked it away in his saddlebag that he had draped over the stall gate where he had left his mare. "This could get a man hanged," he muttered.

"Even a preacher," Jesse said.

"Especially a preacher," Abbot replied. He removed his spectacles and cleaned them with a kerchief from his coat pocket. He leaned against the closed gate. The mare behind him looked up then returned her attention to the mound of hay Jesse had left in her stall. A couple of moths began to circle the lantern, fluttering in ever-tightening spirals that brought them closer to death. "You have done well, Jesse. From what I can see you've got more than I ever expected. These notes will be invaluable to Grant." He knelt in the dirt and with a bent horseshoe nail traced a path in the hard-packed stable floor. "Here's the Mississippi and right here Vicksburg." He marked an "X" on the river line. Abbot looked up and found Jesse watching him in stony silence. "Grant's crossed downriver about forty miles or so. He aims to live off the land and sweep up to Jackson, dislodge the Confederates, and then approach Vicksburg from the east." He drew a diagonal line from the river to Jackson, indicating Grant's intended route and reeling off names like Port Gibson, Willow Springs, Rocky Springs, and Fourteen Mile Creek.

"What if Johnston combines his forces with Pemberton and waits for Grant in Vicksburg with both armies?" Jesse asked, hooking his thumbs in his belt.

"Then we'll have hell for breakfast," Abbot said. He stood and tossed the nail into the cold black forge. "If Johnston moves toward Vicksburg, Grant will have to change his course of action. There's the rub, my young friend. We have to know what General Johnston decides to do. And there's Bragg in Tennessee. He might push south to combine armies. What are his plans?"

"That's where I come in," Jesse wearily interjected. He was tired of the pretense and the subterfuge and longed to fight and die, if need be, in the uniform of his country.

"You are the only one who can help us." Abbot walked across the aisle and placed his hand on Jesse McQueen's shoulder. "I'm sorry, son. You've more than earned the right to quit this game. And if I am asking too much, then ride along with me and we'll find Grant together. And old Unconditional Surrender can take his chances and play the cards he's dealt." He stepped back and tried to look as earnest as possible. Jesse wasn't fooled for an instant.

"I'll stay. When Johnston makes up his mind, he'll need to inform Pemberton in Vicksburg, and I'm the best courier he has," Jesse said. "As soon as I learn something I'll come looking for you. Twenty thousand Yankees ought to be easy enough to find."

"It's forty thousand. Sherman's joined him. But just you be careful," Abbot replied. He was relieved to hear McQueen's decision. But he had to caution the young agent. "Things being as they are, you could get yourself shot by our own troops."

Jesse shrugged. "Hell, Major, if it was easy, everybody'd want to be a spy."

The door to the barn swung open, startling both men as Ophelia appeared from out of the night. She had a shawl wrapped around her shoulders and held a small hand lantern to light the way.

"The mare looks fine," Jesse said. "Just a bit of rock lodged under the shoe. Nothing to worry about now. It made the hoof a bit tender is all."

"Very well. I shan't worry," Abbot said. "Bless my soul, child. You should be resting after that sumptuous repast instead of wandering about at night." He continued on down the aisle and bowed to the young woman. Then he glanced back at Jesse. "Thank you again, Lieutenant McQueen, I can rest assured now."

"Best you be wary of Spider Boudreaux, Reverend Pettibone," Ophelia said.

"Oh, indeed." Abbot tried not to look alarmed. What did she mean?

"He is a notorious cheat at checkers," she told him.

Abbott relaxed and chuckled. "I am forewarned. A man can't know too much about his opponent." He hurried through the door. Ophelia stepped aside and watched him go. Jesse brushed his foot across Abbot's crude map, left behind in the dirt.

By the time he arrived at the barn door, Jesse had recovered his composure. "And what brings you out here, Miss Ophelia?" he asked. All the good smells of baking clung to her clothes and mingled with the scent of lilac water on her neck and behind her ears.

"I thought we might walk together," she said. She put her arm in his.

"Sounds like a splendid idea," he said. They left the stable arm in arm and strolled out into the warm spring night. The chickens in the henhouse fluttered and seemed to sense someone was afoot. Hogs watched them from behind the slats of their pen, blunt faces frozen in anticipation. They were hoping for kitchen slops, certainly an infrequent feast these days with Ophelia cooking only for herself and the elderly slaves that had been left behind.

As Ophelia and Jesse rounded the garden a loping shadow detached itself from the edge of the forest and started toward them. Jesse spotted it and momentarily stiffened before realizing it was only a hound on its way up from the cabins of the field hands. The hound lifted its head, caught and identified Ophelia's scent, and came on through a blizzard of fireflies to snuffle at her outstretched hand and receive a scratch behind the ears. The hound's unerring nose caught the scent of a rabbit in the garden and he took off like a rocket, baying as he bounded over the butter beans and young stalks of corn.

"Get him, Mose," Jesse muttered as he listened to the sounds of the chase resounding in the darkness. "Give that old blood a critter to chase and he's happy."

"Dogs are simple. They're lucky. It doesn't take much," Ophelia agreed. Standing in the night, well away from the glare of the lantern-lit windows, she began to relax. The plantation house had become for her the eyes and ears of her older brother, watching her every move, eavesdropping on her intimate conversations. The night and distance ensured her privacy. "Bon thinks you might have helped that woman spy escape," she matter-of-factly said.

"What do you think?" Jesse coolly replied.

"I don't want to know." She suddenly turned in Jesse's arms and kissed him. He was glad to reciprocate, but an awkward discomfort tempered his passion. He enjoyed the moment, but not the accompanying guilt.

"What was that for?" he gently asked as she rested her head against his shoulder.

"My way of saying good-bye," she answered in a hushed tone more suitable for church. Then again, she was standing beneath the littering vault of heaven itself, so why not speak with reverence? The world was changing all around her. Nothing would ever be the same again, including this night.

Jesse's heart was filled with all the words his devotion to duty would not allow him to speak. As she had told him once, the word came back to haunt him. *Someday, yes, maybe someday.*

He pressed his face against her auburn hair and held her close and whispered, "Good-bye."

Jesse and Ophelia remained in one another's arms. Transfixed by the magical display of earth and sky, they might have been lovers, poised between fireflies and the stars.

Chapter Nineteen

It was morning, the ninth of May, and Jesse McQueen had been dreaming he was once more standing in the fields of Dunsinane with Ophelia in his arms, when a Confederate sergeant stopped outside his tent near the corrals on the outskirts of Jackson. The sergeant roused him from his sleep and informed him he was wanted in the command headquarters of General Joe Johnston within the half hour.

Jesse pulled on his boots and stumbled out of his tent. He blinked and rubbed the sleep out of his eyes and studied for a moment the men around him as they crawled from tents, lit their cook fires, dressed, and grumbled about the various officers whose sole purpose was to make the lives of their subordinates miserable. Jesse buckled his gunbelt around his narrow waist and settled his sweat-stained gray hat on his head. Johnston's couriers were quartered together in a cluster of tents near a corral and a gutted barn that had been commandeered from its former owner for the duration of the Confederates' stay in the vicinity of Jackson. Johnston kept a half-dozen men attached to his headquarters, ready to ride at the drop of a hat, night or day, in fair weather or foul.

Two of their number had been dispatched to Richmond with reports for President Davis. Another was up in Tennessee looking for General Bragg, and a fourth was down with a twisted knee. Jesse glanced toward the only other courier besides himself who was ready and able to ride if required, but the officer, a fellow lieutenant, was snoring in his tent.

Jesse headed for the corral, whistled softly, and the roan broke from the rest of the herd and dutifully trotted over to be rewarded with a pat on the neck and gentle words of praise.

"This might be the day, old friend. I sense it in the air." Jesse climbed into the corral, took a bridle he'd left on the fence, and slipped it over the stallion's head. He saddled and led the horse out of the corral and around the remains of the barn. To the east the sun appeared on the horizon like a dipper of molten gold that spilled its contents across the sprawling city of Jackson, with its factories and warehouses, the capitol building and houses of state government, foundries and machine shops, arsenals and public stores. Church spires jutted skyward against a backdrop of vermilion and amber. Ruby clouds gradually paled, became pink then cotton white in the dawn of a new day.

General Johnston had bivouacked his army in defensive positions east and south of the capital. With only six thousand men, there was little he could do to defend the city until General Bragg dispatched reinforcements from the Army of the Tennessee.

Jesse had expected those reinforcements to arrive any day now. Once "Old Joe" Johnston had a substantial force at his command, he might well be able to join with Pemberton and stop General U. S. Grant in his tracks. Jesse's mind wrestled with the possibility of such a disaster as he followed the wheel-rutted road to Johnston's headquarters in the home of a family friend, Eliza Farley. Farley, a widow, had built her house outside Jackson a stone's throw off the Vicksburg road. Jesse had only met her once but found her to be a sweet-tempered woman with a hearty appetite for life. Her husband had been a friend of Johnston's before the war. After his death, the widow had sold off all her land holdings and retired from any of her social obligations. She had moved out of Jackson to this small but comfortable cottage, though she spent most of her time now traveling to see her sons, one of whom was in Petersburg and the other in Charleston, and her daughter, who was managing alone with three children on a plantation outside of Meridian. Two weeks ago Farley had turned her house over to Johnston and his staff and left to join her daughter.

The cottage was set back a dozen yards off the Vicksburg road. Confederate infantry was bivouacked throughout the area. Three hundred cavalrymen were also stationed in the vicinity. Jesse had counted troops from Alabama and Georgia and several from Mississippi, including the hard-riding, hard-fighting hellions of the First Mississippi Volunteers. He was surprised to see them back so soon. Tyrone had been dispatched to reconnoiter Grant's army and keep Johnston informed of the federals' progress.

The Gray Fox and his men had been anxious to harass the seemingly unstoppable tide of Union troops marching up through the heartland of Dixie. But Johnston was holding them all in check, unwilling to chance any losses without a battle plan. Resigned merely to play watchdog to the advancing federal army, Tyrone had evidently abandoned his mission to make a report.

Jesse turned off the road as the scent of woodsmoke, frying salt pork, and boiling chicory coffee filled the air. He started up the drive toward the widow's house nestled in a grove of pecan trees. Several officers were congregated on the covered porch, two of whom Jesse immediately recognized. General Joe Johnston was seated in a cane-back rocking chair, a cup of coffee in his hands. He appeared to be absorbed in the opinions of his junior officers, one of whom wore a cocked-brim gray hat sporting a black plume. Captain Bon Tyrone sat with his back to the drive, one leg crooked over the railing. A major and two other captains had also arrived to meet with the general who had roused them from their sleep for breakfast and this early-morning council of war.

Besides Tyrone and the general, Jesse McQueen noticed that another courier, Lieutenant Abram Mitchell, had arrived from Tennessee. Had Bragg answered Johnston's call for reinforcements? Mitchell appeared to have been excused from the council, for he descended the porch, gathered up the reins of his lathered mount, and proceeded down the drive toward Jesse. A few moments later, the two couriers drew abreast of each other. Mitchell touched the brim of his battered gray cap.

"Glad you made it safe, Abram."

"Careful, Jesse. Old Joe's in a powerful bad

mood," Mitchell replied, dabbing the sweat from his sunburned features with a swath of cloth torn from an old shirt. His uniform was caked with dust from his ride. "Bragg ain't sendin' doodly-squat! The general's fit to be tied."

The two men continued on past each other, their interchange ended.

Bon Tyrone stood and leaned his husky frame against the wall of the house as Jesse approached the porch and saluted the general. Johnston nodded and then continued speaking to the other officers on the porch.

"There's real coffee on the stove inside. It will probably be the last we taste for a while, unless I can impose on Captain Tyrone to raid the Yankee supply lines up north." The officers chuckled and filed inside the house, where a black servant showed them to the kitchen. Bon lingered outside on the porch. He and Jesse exchanged civilities. It disturbed Jesse how Ophelia's brother seemed so cool toward him of late. If indeed Bon suspected his loyalty, he was unwilling to charge him in public without proof.

General Johnston glanced at an orderly who had remained at the opposite end of the porch, bent over a lap desk, his pen scratching across the paper, dipping into a brass inkwell shaped like a teardrop with a flat base.

"Have you finished that dispatch, Lieutenant?"

The orderly rose from his chair and brought the hastily transcribed dispatch over to the general. He placed the lap desk in Johnston's hands. The officer quickly scanned the dispatch and nodded. "Very good," he said, and signed the bottom of the page, folded it, wrapped it in oilskin, and tucked it in a leather pouch. He stood and tossed the pouch to Jesse McQueen.

"I have repeatedly warned Pemberton that Vicksburg is a trap. Yet he refuses to abandon the city. So be it." Johnston raised his red-rimmed eyes and stared past his courier to the Vicksburg road winding off to the west. "Well, when he reads this, General Pemberton will know how alone he really is. Perhaps it will inspire him to rethink his situation before Grant bottles him up." The general lowered his gaze and focused on Jesse. "You carry a dispatch of vital importance, Lieutenant. I pray you are up to the challenge."

Jesse met the general's stare. "I promise to personally deliver it into the appropriate hands," he said. And he meant every word. The appropriate hands belonged to General Ulysses S. Grant. This was the dispatch Jesse had been waiting for. It was time to ride into battle beneath the flag of his country. It was time for *Captain* Jesse Redbow McQueen to return home to Old Glory, the Stars and Stripes.

"Then you are dismissed, sir," Johnston said.

"General—perhaps I ought to keep the lieutenant company," Bon said. "What with a Union Army to our south, Grant is bound to have sent out patrols."

"I am sure Lieutenant McQueen is more than capable of completing his mission."

Jesse waited, steeling himself for the accusation he was certain to come. Escape was impossible. If the matter came to a head, he knew he wouldn't get ten feet down the drive before the troops on either side filled him with lead. He looked up at Bon Tyrone standing on the porch and without batting an eye said, "I appreciate the offer, Bon. Tag along if you've a mind, if you're all that worried for my safety."

"Nonsense," Johnston said. "Captain Tyrone here needs his rest. Come tomorrow, I intend for him to lead a column and strike at Grant's supply lines." He stood and walked toward the front door. "Be on your way, Lieutenant. And godspeed."

"Yes, sir." Jesse saluted. He spun on his heels and leaped astride the roan, figuring to put a good five miles between himself and the Confederate encampment before striking out in search of the Union Army. He ignored Bon's continuing stare and tugged on the reins to bring the stallion about, heading for the Vicksburg road. He did not want to appear too anxious to leave and kept the stallion to a brisk trot. But with Bon's eyes boring into his back like a slug from a .44 Colt, Jesse felt like a human target all the way down the drive. It was the longest ride of his life. He held his breath and didn't suck air until he was clear of the cottage and the guns of the man who had been his friend.

"What the devil are you up to?" the heavyset Cajun asked as he elbowed his way through the underbrush to the tether line where the First Mississippi Volunteers kept their horses. Spider had left the troop back by the road, forty tired, bearded men with nothing but sleep on their minds. But if Bon had given them the order to ride, the men would have crawled from their bedrolls, saddled their weary mounts, and followed him.

The Gray Fox finished cinching his saddle. He'd chosen a fresh mount, a high-stepping brown gelding from the Fifth Alabama Mounted Infantry, and spirited the horse right out from under the none too watchful eyes of those troopers encamped near his men.

"That's horse stealing, Captain Bon," Spider reminded the officer. Then, his eyes twinkling with mischief, he added, "I'll go and fetch me one from the same place you catched the brown." He started to leave. Bon caught him by the arm.

"Not this time old friend. I go alone. You stay with the troop. There's no sense in both of us getting into trouble with the general."

Spider cocked his head to one side and assessed the merits of Tyrone's argument. A big, solid, simple man, the Cajun was smarter than most folks took him to be.

"I saw Jesse McQueen ride by." Spider Boudreaux scratched at his jowls and rubbed his dirt-streaked neck. "You aim to follow him."

"All the way to Vicksburg, if need be, or wherever he leads." Bon leaned on the saddle. "I have to know, Spider. He's my friend, and my sister is falling in love with him. I must have the truth."

"Why don't you just turn him over to the authorities?"

"Because I owe him for Ophelia's life." Bon reached over and clapped the sergeant on the shoulder. "Get some rest. I'll be back before you know it."

"Just be back before Gen'l Johnston hears of it." Spider shook his head. "Jesse's got him a pretty slim lead ... been ten minutes or so that he came past."

"I'll catch him. And track him. And after today there will be no more doubts."

Spider ruefully wagged his head from side to side. He spat a stream of tobacco juice on an anthill at his feet. "I don't like it, nary a bit," the Cajun said. But Bon had the upper hand. And the rank.

The sergeant was powerless to stop the officer even for his own good. "As I see it, you got two questions need answering, Captain."

"Oh?" Bon climbed into the saddle.

"Yes, sir. The first being, whether or not your friend is a spy."

"And the second?" Bon asked, looking down.

"If he is a spy, can you kill him?"

Bon freed the reins from the sergeant's grasp and made no reply as he walked the gelding beneath the shade of the pecan trees and out toward the Vicksburg road.

The Gray Fox was weary of questions. He needed answers. And he knew where to find them.

Chapter Twenty

Jesse McQueen shifted his weight in the crook of the red oak and grimaced as a knob of bark jabbed his posterior. He repositioned himself yet again and, finding a comfortable perch, at last raised his spyglass and adjusted the focus until the blurred images became an armed host, General U. S. Grant's Army of the West. Forty thousand men had converged on a plantation in the heartland of Dixie. Soldiers and livestock, freight wagons and caissons had swarmed across a cotton field and turned it into an arena of dust. No doubt the main house had been commandeered by Grant and his staff for the night. Jesse doubted the army would tarry longer.

Regiments of soldiers had unrolled their bedrolls and begun to make their camp upon the plowed earth. Skirmishers were beginning to fan out from the encampment, taking up the perimeters to guard against a night attack. Jesse shifted his gaze to a column of infantry marching at double time along a wheel-worn drive leading up to the red-brick plantation house. They fanned out near the front porch and began to stack their rifles and gather in groups of three and four to start cook fires, light pipes, and relax on woolen blankets.

Artillery men set up a half-dozen Napoleans, the twelve-pounder cannons that were the workhorses of Grant's armaments. The remaining eighteen field pieces were hitched to the caissons and left in the center of the encampment. Horses had been ground-tethered for the most part, although some of the officers had brought their mounts into the barn.

A creek ran alongside the western edge of the cotton field. It flowed out of the thicket of red oaks and sweet gums concealing Jesse a couple of hundred yards away. A stone's throw from Jesse's vantage point among the branches, the headwaters of the spring-fed creek bubbled out of the earth and spread a shadowy pool of icy water across lichen-covered stones, shallow tree roots, and black mud.

It was early afternoon. Jesse tucked the spyglass in his coat pocket and resolved to ride into the Union camp under a flag of truce. Suddenly a flurry of crows and blue jays exploded from a treetop north of him. Jesse stiffened and cursed softly. Earlier in the day he had glimpsed a plume of dust along his back trail and once he had waited in the lee of a deserted cabin for his unseen companion to reveal him- or herself. He had waited in vain. Nevertheless, he had a pretty good idea as to the identity of his pursuer, although he had expected the proud, brave fool to abandon the hunt once the combined federal force under Grant and Sherman came into sight.

"Blast him anyway," Jesse muttered as he descended from his perch and returned to his horse on the edge of the glade. Sunlight glimmered on the surface of the shallow pond like strewn diamonds. Water lilies drifted on the surface, and dragonflies darted to right and left, then hovered above the surface. Here was a place of tranquillity and peace. Jesse wished he could lie down on a bed of rushes and dream away the war. What had begun as a great adventure had become acutely painful now that he had lived among his enemies and called them friends. He led the roan back among the trees and tethered the stallion to a burr-oak sapling that struggled to find the sun in this world of emerald twilight.

He had just returned to the edge of the spring and stepped out from behind the red oak when Bon Tyrone, astride his brown gelding, emerged from the shadows on the other side of the clearing about fifty feet away. The two men confronted one another in a brittle silence that Jesse was first to break.

"Bon...I'm sorry it's you. Turn and ride out. These woods are full of Union patrols," he said.

"Not without that pouch from Johnston," Bon retorted, and drew his pistol. The LeMat blossomed flame as the Confederate drove his heels into the gelding. The animal charged forward and hit the pool of water at a gallop as Bon continued to fill the air with hot lead. Jesse dived for cover behind the red oak. Slugs flattened against the bark and ricocheted off among the trees.

Water erupted in a fine spray to either side of the gelding as the sturdy animal splashed across the pool. The animal faltered as its hooves sank into the muddy bottom of the pond. Bon yanked the gelding's head up and the sturdy mount cleared the icy-cold water and reached dry ground. Bon rode past the red oak and fired at what should have been Jesse McQueen. But his intended victim had vanished.

He thought he glimpsed movement to his right. The LeMat spoke twice. Again, nothing.

"Spider's right. I *am* a piss-poor shot," Bon grumbled. He held the pistol ready and mentally tabulated the rounds left in the cylinder. The gun held nine and he had fired six...or was it seven? "Show yourself, Jesse! Damn you! I knew it, but I didn't want to believe it. You were working for the Union all along. And like a fool, I trusted you." He heard a twig pop, whirled, fired, and missed a brown squirrel by inches. The terrified creature scampered up a tree and vaulted from branch to branch as it fled to safety.

A clump of bark landed in the bushes to his right. Bon faced this new threat. Even as he turned, the Rebel sensed he'd been tricked. He twisted to the left and tried to bring his pistol to bear as Jesse leaped from behind a curtain of vines and slammed into him, knocking him from the saddle. Bon groaned as McQueen landed on his chest, wrenched the LeMat from his grasp, and tossed it out of reach. Bon shoved Jesse aside and struggled to stand. Jesse wrestled free, lifted the larger man off his feet, lost his balance, and toppled into the spring. Both men shoved clear of each other and stood, sputtering and streaming water.

Bon swung with a solid right but Jesse ducked beneath the blow and came in low to drive a solid left jab to the Rebel's groin. Bon gasped, and as he doubled over in agony, Jesse straightened. Like a battering ram, the top of his head caught Bon flush on the chin. The Confederate officer staggered and sank down in the mud. His eyes went blank. Somehow he managed to splash his face with water and kept from losing consciousness.

"Goddammit, Jesse. You don't even fight fair," Bon grumbled.

McQueen looked at the big man he had felled. Bon was larger by a couple of inches, had a longer reach, and weighed more. "I fight to win," Jesse replied, catching his wind. "Remember, I'm part Indian. That was a fair fight for a Choctaw." He sloshed from the pond and sat down with his back to a red oak. "Take your horse and ride out. You made enough noise to alert Grant's whole army. The woods will be crawling with Yankee cavalry and any minute now they'll—"

"I'm not leaving without that dispatch and you," Bon growled. He dipped his face into the cold water and rose up dripping. "What kind of man are you?" He gingerly prodded his jaw with his fingertips. It wasn't broken but he'd have a hell of a bruise. "You have no honor."

"This isn't a game, Bon. I fight my war, the same as you fight yours." Jesse wasn't in the mood for a lecture. Warfare was a nasty business, and trying to cloak it in terms of civility and proper conduct was a waste of time. "Captain Tyrone, you're a good man, but what you stand for is wrong. I'll stop you any way I can."

"We'll see about that," Bon said. Drenched to the bone, he managed to stand and lumber from the pond. His intent was perfectly clear. Jesse glanced at the man's clenched fists and sighed. Didn't the blasted Rebel ever quit? He drew his navy Colt and pointed it at the big man's chest. Bon never even batted an eye.

"You won't shoot me."

"Why not?" Jesse replied.

"Because then you'd have to explain to Ophelia how you killed her brother."

"Damn," Jesse whispered beneath his breath. The man was right. He scrambled to his feet as Bon charged.

Gunfire filled the air and geysers of mud erupted between the two men. Powder smoke drifted among the trees. Jesse and Bon slowly turned to face a dozen blue-clad Missouri volunteers, their weapons drawn and aimed at the two men. Jesse became acutely aware of the color of his uniform. The patrol's leader, a burly, mustachioed sergeant, walked his mount forward a few steps. Jesse's eyes widened with recognition.

"Oh, no," he muttered.

"By heaven, what have we here?" Doc Stark said aloud. Milo and Titus broke ranks to join him. Milo grinned and brought his Colt revolving rifle to bear.

"Looks like we caught us a pair of Rebs trying to sneak into camp." He licked his lips.

"Hold it, Doc," Jesse said. "You're about to make a big mistake."

"I'll live with it." Doc smiled.

"But you won't," Titus added, training his own gun on Jesse McQueen.

"Friends of yours?" Bon asked, paling.

"From home," Jesse replied.

This has nothing to do with the war, Bon sensed. The Gray Fox had the distinct impression he was standing smack dab in the middle of a blood feud. And in the middle was the worst place to be.

"I might even get a medal for shooting a turncoat like you," Doc said.

"A firing squad more than likely," another voice said from across the clearing. Major Peter Abbot rode into view. Doc looked up in surprise, baffled by the officer's remarks. Abbot ordered the Missouri volunteers to holster their weapons, then walked his horse across the pond, further clouding the water with sediment from the muddy bottom. A hint of a grin touched Abbot's face as he glanced at Jesse. Bon recognized the Reverend Pettibone and inwardly groaned. Were there any honest Confederates left in Mississippi?

Abbot placed himself between the Stark brothers and Jesse Redbow McQueen.

"I was just gonna shoot me a Johnny Reb, Major Abbot, sir," Doc explained, taken aback by the Union officer's warning.

Peter Abbot, with ever a flair for the dramatic, removed his wire-rim spectacles and cleaned them on a cotton scarf then donned them again. He glanced over his shoulder at Jesse and fixed Doc Stark in a hard-edged stare.

"Ah...but you see, this 'Johnny Reb' works for me."

He turned and rode back to the two mud-drenched combatants by the spring as Doc Stark led his foragers out of the clearing, grudgingly relinquishing the field.

"My compliments, Captain Tyrone," Abbot said, saluting the Confederate officer. Bon scowled and lowered his head.

"Well, how about it, turncoat," Abbot said, looking down at the eldest son of Ben McQueen. "Are you ready to rejoin your command?"

"You'll never know how ready," Jesse replied. He started back toward his horse and stopped in his tracks. "What about Bon?"

Bon glanced up sharply. "Don't you worry about me, you bastard," he snapped.

Abbot shrugged. "That is a problem. We can't

let him go and have him warn Pemberton or Johnston about us."

"Then he can come along with us," Jesse said. The alternative was executing the officer on the spot. He wasn't about to allow that to happen.

Abbot looked skeptical.

"As my prisoner," Jesse added.

"I'd rather be dead," Bon growled, incensed at the notion. His pride had suffered a near-mortal wound at having been taken in by both McQueen and the major.

"Perhaps so," Jesse said. "But you'll learn to live with it." He motioned for the Rebel officer to follow along. At the first opportunity Bon Tyrone would probably try to kill him—as would Doc and Milo Stark and Titus Connolly.

Jesse McQueen sighed. It was good to be home.

Chapter Twenty-One

Jesse found the two Union generals a study in contrasts. General William Tecumseh Sherman, tall and angular, his deep-set eyes constantly in motion, scrutinized first McQueen, then Major Abbot, then the commander of the Union Army. General Ulysses S. Grant, at forty, was a rumpled little man whose stooped-shoulder stance and scruffy, bearded face hardly inspired confidence. He kept a cigar clamped between his teeth and a bottle of scotch on the camp table. He took his time and weighed each man's merits before shifting attention from one individual to the next. At the moment Captain Jesse McQueen was the object of the general's scrutiny.

"So you are the young man Abbot has been bragging to us about," Grant said. "I was expecting a real fire-eater, ten feet tall. Why, Mr. McQueen, you appear quite human." The general glanced at Abbot and chuckled. "Though I suppose size isn't everything." Grant was the smallest man in the tent. His military coat was unbuttoned to reveal his undershirt, suspenders, and blue woolen trousers. A moth had found its way into the tent along with a particularly pesty cloud of tiny black gnats that continually harassed the officers.

Sherman handed Grant the dispatches from the Confederate commander in Jackson. "We have already seen your previous list of Pemberton's troop strength and your sketches of the fortifications around Vicksburg."

"Quite so," Grant interjected as he read the letter from Johnston to Pemberton. "Invaluable..."

Contrary to Jesse's expectations, Grant had refrained from staying in the plantation house where enemy ears might overhear his plans. The commander of the Northern army was more comfortable seated on his cot among his fellow officers. The troop of Illinois regulars surrounding his headquarters ensured his privacy as well as his safety.

"I have arranged for you to be assigned to the general's staff," Abbot said, placing a hand on Jesse's shoulder. "At least for the time being."

"Until we can safely send you both back to Washington," Sherman added. "Where, Major Abbot, you will no doubt conjure up some new schemes to befuddle the Rebs and win glory for your young friend here." Sherman took a sip of coffee and glanced at Grant as the Union general slapped his hand on the tabletop.

"That's it! By God, Captain McQueen, but you have brought me excellent news." Grant stood and leaned forward on his knuckles as he stared at Sherman. "Bill, it seems that Johnston is abandoning the capital to us, Pemberton is keeping himself bottled up, and Bragg is hog-tied in Tennessee. He refuses to send Johnston reinforcements." Grant walked around the table and stood in the doorway of the camp tent. A soft breeze fanned his cheeks and cooled his perspiring forehead. He stuck his head out and ordered an adjutant stationed outside to fetch the rest of his staff. Then he returned to his place behind the camp table.

"I'd better bring John MacClennand and Jim McPherson in on this." He held up the stolen Confederate dispatches and smiled. "Gentlemen, we have a ways to go, but the outcome is inevitable. Vicksburg is ours."

Jesse could see now how first impressions were deceiving. Grant might look like a store clerk but there was another quality to the man, a subtle tenaciousness that had won him victories on the battlefield and would do so again.

By the time the tent was crowded with officers, Jesse managed to win permission to leave. He slipped through the entrance as Sherman argued the merits of striking at Jackson and razing the capital's factories and warehouses, a plan everyone agreed on. Jesse was grateful that Dunsinane lay farther to the north and that Ophelia was out of harm's way. It was a comfort to know.

At sunset, Cicero knelt on the muddy creek bank and peered down at his black features mirrored in the water. He liked what he saw, the face of a free man. And the Starks were going to help him stay free, and make him rich in the process. Splitting the Tyrone fortune even four ways was better than crossing to the North with only the shirt on his back. It was Doc who convinced the Union officers that Cicero could prove himself an invaluable scout and an aid to the foragers. Thus Cicero found his place among the Starks. Doc had even given him a long-barreled Patterson Colt that had to be held with a two-handed grip when fired since it kicked like a Missouri mule. But it was his gun, no matter that the hammer was loose or that the cylinder was cracked. The gun was his.

The runaway slave stood and continued to study his reflection.

"Say, buck, look at you. Doc done got you a new blue shirt and army-issue britches and found you a pair of boots." Cicero nodded to his reflection. "Yes, sir, I looks proper." He hooked a thumb in his suspenders. "Ain't no field hand. Ain't ever gonna be again." The black man patted the gun butt jutting from his waistband. He straightened and looked proud, then started up the embankment.

The Army of the West spread out before him. The dogs of war had been unleashed upon these fertile fields, and when they left, nothing would ever be the same again. A pall of dust blanketed the meadow and draped the distant trees in a brown shroud. Grit stung his eyes and worked its way between his jaws and made a grinding sound whenever he closed his mouth. Cicero had never seen so many men gathered in one place. The presence of so many Yankees made him feel secure and he wondered when the time came if he would be able to leave with the Starks. He chided himself for being such a coward. Of course, he'd be able to leave. He wanted his share of Old Marse Tyrone's treasure. He had earned his share by the sweat of his brow and the bondage he and his people had endured. Nothing would keep him from what was rightfully his.

Cicero kept to the edge of the field, on his way

to rejoin Doc Stark, whose foragers had pitched camp in the shade of a pecan grove, when he spied the lone prisoner who had been brought in from the woods. Captain Boniface Tyrone had been shackled to the wheel of a canvas-sided ambulance and left with the medical personnel.

Bon Tyrone waited out the dusk in the shade of the medical wagon, his back against the spokes of a rear wheel, his knees drawn up and head nodding forward, the very picture of dejection. Cicero continued to watch the Gray Fox through a haze of dust, and slowly, Tyrone rose up as if sensing the black man's presence from about fifty feet away. Bon's gaze settled on the black man, who straightened his spine and walked proud. He wanted to approach the Confederate captain and confront him, but old habits died hard. Though he was miles from Dunsinane, it was difficult to overcome the servility that had been bred in him from birth. Mustering the last of his courage, Cicero approached the Gray Fox.

"Well Marse Bon, you ain't so high and mighty now," he said, staring down at the man in chains, squatting by the ambulance.

Bon ignored the black man.

"You look at me when I talk. You the one wearin' chains now. Not me." Cicero grinned and placed his hands on his hips.

"You never wore chains at Dunsinane," Bon remarked.

"Might as well have. I wasn't free. A man ain't free then it be the same as chained." Cicero batted at a swarm of gnats that had begun to plague him.

Bon frowned. "Maybe you're right."

"Don't you worry none, though." Cicero grinned.

"You and Miss Ophelia gonna get to set things aright."

"What the devil are you talking about?" Bon warily inquired.

"My pa tole me about the well and what it hold." Cicero could not help himself. "Gonna use that gold to buy my freedom. Ain't nobody ever gonna tell this colored what to do, ever again."

"There is no gold," Bon tried to explain, but the black man cut him off.

"I can read your lies, Marse Bon." Cicero nodded. "Me and my friends, we aims to have it. Ain't no army gonna stop us. Not Johnny Reb, not Billy Yank."

"You're mad. You and your friends," Bon replied. He struggled to rise. Cicero backed away beyond his reach. "Come back here, Cicero. Wait. You don't understand!"

"Hold it down there." Major Harlin, the chief surgeon poked his head out of his tent flap. "Or I'll have you muzzled, Reb. And you, Cicero, leave that prisoner be. Go on. Go on, now."

"I'm jes' as good as you, Marse Bon," Cicero muttered as he turned to go. "Better even, 'cause I got the gun now." He patted the Patterson Colt tucked in his wide leather belt. The Missouri volunteers had claimed a corner of a turnip patch near the plantation house and had stripped the garden bare. There'd be pork jowl and greens for supper.

Cicero's belly began to growl as he continued on to the Starks' campsite, reaching it in time to find Doc Stark, his brother, and Titus waiting for him with their horses saddled.

"What took you so damn long?" Milo grumbled. Doc warned him to lower his voice.

"It's time we go," Doc said, handing the reins

to Cicero. His voice was almost a whisper. "The army will be in Jackson tomorrow. A man could get himself killed." He turned and nodded to Milo and Titus, then all three men climbed into their saddles.

"I'm pow'ful hungry, Doc," Cicero said. Greens and salt pork smelled mighty good.

"Tomorrow night you can eat your fill," Doc replied. "In Dunsinane."

The dying sun painted the Mississippi sky in pastel pinks and purples and etched the clouds in crimson. Field sparrows soared and dipped and glided among the campfires in constant search of food scraps left by the soldiers as they finished their hastily prepared suppers. It was a warm night and mosquitoes continued to swarm. Soon the Union troops were slapping and brushing the pesky insects from their faces and necks. It was as if the countryside itself was attempting to repel the invaders and send them back across the Mason-Dixon, back to the cooler climes far away from the sacred soil of the South.

Jesse McQueen ambled restlessly through the Union camp. Most of the soldiers paid him no mind, considering him just another officer. But now and then he passed a group of men who had witnessed his "court-martial" and seen him stripped of his ranking. Now here he stood in the trappings of a captain. Accounts of his exploits behind the Confederate lines had begun to spread, passed along from one campfire to the next. By morning the entire force would have heard the stories, and after they had been embellished by half the army, Jesse doubted he'd recognize himself in them.

He slowly circled the plantation house, pausing

from time to time to gaze at a darkened window, sensing that he was being watched by some member of the family whose name he had been told but didn't care to remember. It was easier to plunder the property of strangers. And he already knew the enemy too well. It had made his decisions all the more painful.

With that in mind, Jesse noted the physicians' tent and ambulances about thirty yards from the house and resolved to check on Bon Tyrone. Jesse had no doubt as to the reception he'd receive from the Gray Fox. In the distance, the voices of freed slaves rose in songs of joy and thanksgiving that drifted above the settling camp. How fleeting this freedom, for tomorrow the army would march off and life would continue, for the most part unchanged. Grant had refused them permission to follow an army that might charge into battle on any given day. Most of the ex-slaves understood, but it didn't change the fact that tonight they felt free, tonight they sang.

Bon Tyrone glanced up as Jesse entered the radiance of the campfire. He held a plate of roast chicken and beans, a tin cup on the ground by his right thigh. At another campfire, a trio of orderlies dined on the remainder of the chicken and beans. The oldest of them looked to be about eighteen. Young and inexperienced, they had been sternly warned against fraternizing with the prisoner and had taken those orders to heart despite the fact that Tyrone was the first live Rebel soldier they had ever seen. The novelty was bound to wear off before long, Jesse thought.

Bon set the food aside and with stomach growling returned to his place by the wagon.

How like Pacer Wolf McQueen was Bon Tyrone.

Jesse's thoughts drifted to his big, rawboned younger brother with his shoulder-length red hair and flashing eyes. Like Pacer Wolf, Jesse thought, in size and temperament, as proud and headstrong. Perhaps it was this similarity that had formed a bond between the two men in the first place.

"You come to gloat, Captain McQueen?"

"You know me better than that." Jesse scowled.

"Hell, I don't know you at all," Bon said. He tugged at the eight-foot-long chain tethering him to the wheel. "Maybe you're here for absolution. Well, I'm fresh out."

"I did not come here looking for forgiveness. I just came to ask if there was anything you needed."

Bon snorted in disgust and held up his shackled wrists. The dull iron links rattled each time he moved. "It isn't right a man be kept like this."

"First, I need your word that you won't try to escape."

Bon looked away. A simple lie would buy him his freedom. But the price was too high. His word was his bond and he intended to do everything in his power to escape . . . except dishonor himself. He stood and stretched to his full height. Jesse McQueen was not overawed. He'd been cutting big men down to size most of his life.

"I promise to try to escape every chance I get," Bon said. "And if I can break your skull in the process, so much the better."

Jesse hooked his thumbs in his gunbelt and nodded. "Then keep your chains, Bon Tyrone." He offered a salute. "Good night."

The words were hardly out of his mouth when a ripple of gunfire sounded from the woods north of the plantation. The encampment immediately came to life. Men scrambled out of their blankets and grabbed for their muskets. Officers bolted from the uncomfortable confines of their tents and hurried off in the direction of their commands.

Close at hand, Major Harlin, the chief surgeon, and two of his subordinates stumbled from the hospital tent where the officers had been enjoying a clandestine bottle of brandy.

"My God, are we attacked?" Harlin shouted. He was a corpulent man with ruddy cheeks, a bushy gray beard, and thick eyebrows, arched in indignation. He spied Jesse and hurried over to him. "Is it General Johnston and the Confederate Army?"

"I doubt it. The firing has already stopped." Jesse remained near the ambulances. They were close to the drive that led to headquarters. Something had alerted the pickets. Jesse wondered what had caused them to open fire. An answer wasn't long in coming. Three Union soldiers came riding at a gallop through the camp. As one of their number continued on toward the plantation house, the other two men angled off the drive and rode right up to the hospital tent. A lean young private leaped down from his mount and hurried around to catch his companion as the soldier slumped to the side and slid out of the saddle. One of the surgeons and an orderly hurried to help him. They took the wounded man inside the hospital. Major Harlin called the other young soldier.

"What's your name, son?" he asked.

"Private Washburn, sir, L. James Washburn." He appeared quite rattled and had all the look of a youth who had never been in combat.

"What happened?"

"Joe's been wounded; the big man, the forager that's been riding with the Missourians, the one everybody said was part Cherokee—"

"Stark!" Jesse blurted out.

"Yes, sir, that's it, Sergeant Stark. Him and that colored and two others tried to ride around us." Washburn wiped a forearm across his brow and then he realized he had blood on his shirt, though the stain had been left there by his friend. "Joe and me and Corporal Cutter, he went on ahead to make his report, we hollered for them to hold up. Weren't nobody supposed to leave camp and we told 'em." Washburn stopped and gulped air before continuing. "Joe Baker, he's my friend. We grew up together in Illinois. Anyway, he tried to stop them. Walked right up to Sergeant Stark and blocked his horse. And asked to see the sergeant's orders." Again Washburn paused to catch his breath as he rattled off his tale. "Stark shot him. And then, that big one with the Colt rifle, he commenced to shooting and me and Corporal Cutter dove behind an ol' hickory tree. We shot back but I don't think we hit nothing. And they rode off like, just like that. Sure was in a powerful hurry." Washburn excused himself and hurried back to the hospital tent as the rasp of a bone saw and the animalistic howl of a wounded man filled the night and put dread in the hearts of every soldier within earshot.

Major Harlin shoved his hands in his unbuttoned coat. His breath was thick with brandy. However, to his credit, he seemed clear-eyed and steady.

"What an unusual occurrence. Three soldiers and that colored man Cicero shooting their way out of camp. Bad . . . very bad. I wonder where they've gone."

"I know," Bon said behind them. He was standing near the campfire, the chain shackling him to the wagon wheel pulled taut. Anger and defiance had left him. He was helpless and desperately worried—

and had every right to be. "They've gone to Dunsinane."

"Why?" Jesse asked, walking back to his prisoner.

"Cicero was born at Dunsinane. He knew of the gold my father came by long ago, a chest of Spanish gold. Cicero all but came right out and told me he was going after it and said he had help."

"Spanish gold would catch Doc Stark's attention right enough," Jesse conceded. Now he, too, was beginning to worry.

"I used every last coin to outfit my troop. There isn't a glimmer of it left," Bon continued. "When your deserters realize it, there'll be hell to pay."

"And Ophelia's all alone." Jesse's blood ran cold. Stark was as unpredictable as a tornado and just as savage.

Major Harlin was obviously confused by their interchange. "I can't fathom what you're so concerned about, Captain McQueen. But I do know one thing: Grant has ordered that no one leave the camp. And he isn't the kind to change his mind." The surgeon shrugged. "I'd report this bit of news to headquarters, nonetheless."

"Yes, sir, I'll get right on it," Jesse told the officer. Another scream of agony erupted from the hospital tent.

"Damn butchers," Harlin muttered, and trotted across the clearing, past the ambulances, and disappeared into the tent.

The orderlies had returned to their campfire, oblivious of everything but the chickens they were roasting over the flames. Jesse turned and caught Bon by the arm and led him around the ambulance. The length of chain permitted him to reach the shadows. He raised his prisoner's wrists and fumbled with the shackles, fitting an iron key in the lock. A quick turn and the black metal bracelets clattered to the ground.

"What are you up to?" Bon said.

"You think we can find some horses and sneak out of here without getting shot?" Jesse said.

"Hell, Jesse. I've been riding through Yankee lines for nigh on two years." The Gray Fox grinned. "Nothing to it."

Chapter Twenty-Two

For the second time that night General Grant had been awakened by gunshots and he was furious. His nerves were on edge. It didn't matter that his reports indicated there were no significant Confederate forces in the immediate vicinity. Every time the pickets opened fire the general came stumbling out of bed with his pistol in his hand and panic in his heart, fearing that somehow he'd made a miscalculation, that his plans were flawed and he was on the verge of losing his entire force to the Confederates.

"Relax, Ulysses," Sherman told him. Sherman had been awakened by the same gunfire, but he was more perturbed than worried. He peered from the entrance to the tent. "Here comes Major Abbot now. He'll verify what's happened."

Grant wore a sweat-stained undershirt and his army-issue trousers. His suspenders hung loose and flapped against his thighs as he began to pace before his camp table. He filled a shot glass with whiskey and tossed it down. The liquid burned a path to his gut. The spreading warmth calmed him. Sherman frowned.

"Don't be a mother hen, Cump," Grant said. "One drink won't harm me, and besides, the reporters are nowhere around to write of my dissolution in their damn newspapers."

Sherman chuckled and said, "You have a point, my friend." He yawned and rubbed the back of his neck. The tent flap was swept aside and Major Peter Abbot reluctantly entered. He'd rather have been whipped naked through the streets of Richmond than face General Grant's stern, unyielding gaze.

"You sent for me, General?" he lamely inquired.

"Yes, Major. I've heard some disturbing news. Perhaps you can shed some light on the matter. It will help me...sleep." Grant emphasized the last word in a solemn tone of voice. "I've had precious little of it so far."

"Yes, sir," Abbot replied in a conciliatory tone. He tried to smile and looked at William Sherman, whose features seemed set in stone. *No help there,* Abbot decided, and focused on Grant again.

"Correct me if I am in error, Major," Grant said. "An hour ago, three deserters and a former slave slipped out of camp. Now Captain McQueen has also deserted. And he has taken Bon Tyrone with him. We held the Gray Fox prisoner for all of six hours!" He slammed a fist against the tabletop and chomped his cigar clean through. The cigar fell from his mouth. He scowled and spat out the remnant of tobacco still between his teeth. "Is that about right?"

Peter Abbot gulped. "Jesse didn't desert, General. From what Major Harlin told me and what I already knew of Tyrone's situation...well...sir... there are extenuating circumstances."

"I've ordered out a troop of cavalry to bring them back. Perhaps I'll hear McQueen's explanation from his own lips," Grant said. He searched in his coat pocket and found another cigar of cured Virginia tobacco, the last of a supply smuggled into Cairo. "Then again, why don't you enlighten me, Major Abbot. And take your time; no doubt we have all night."

Abbot lifted his spectacles and rubbed the bridge of his nose, scratched his head, and tried to come up with the most plausible explanation, one good enough to keep himself from being demoted to private and Jesse McQueen from a court-martial— for real this time.

"Well, you see, General Grant, our agents' missions by their very nature must be...uh...secret...."

"Nothing to it?" Jesse glowered. He had a bullet hole in his sleeve, another in his saddle, his hat had been shot away, and blood oozed from a flesh wound on the neck of the dun gelding he'd stolen.

Bon Tyrone gingerly probed the spot where a ricocheting slug had clipped his ear. His long gray coat had been riddled with bullets as it trailed, unbuttoned, behind him as he galloped through the Union picket lines. The two men had ridden unchallenged out of the Union camp. The soldiers guarding the north road were still rattled by the desertion of Doc Stark and his companions. One moment they called out to the two approaching horsemen, and seconds later, before Jesse had a chance to reply, the federals had opened fire. Jesse McQueen and Bon Tyrone had hugged the shadows and raced through a gauntlet of flying lead. Orange tongues of flame lapping at them from the darkness were a vivid memory. Only by the grace of divine providence had they emerged alive and for the most part unscathed.

"Well, I usually have more men," Bon retorted. "And if you had let me create a diversion—"

"Blowing up a powder wagon, not hardly," Jesse replied. "Setting you free is liable to land me in prison. I don't want to be shot in the process."

Bon shrugged. "It was worth a try." He continued to study the night-shrouded landscape for any sign of pursuit. A troop of Yankee cavalry had made a valiant effort to catch them, but Bon's knowledge of the countryside had prevailed. Now, a couple of miles from the plantation that played unwilling host to the federals, there was no trace of the pursuers.

"Lost 'em," Bon added with a self-satisfied smile.

The two horsemen sat astride their mounts by a cottonwood tree. Jesse took his bearing from the stars. The countryside might not be as familiar to him as it was to Bon, but he knew that a man need only head due north to cut across the Vicksburg road to Jackson road, follow it west and later north and across country to Dunsinane. He was loath to waste even a minute, but there was something he had to find out.

Jesse reached in his saddlebag and produced Bon Tyrone's LeMat revolver and offered it to the Confederate.

"I don't intend to ride to Dunsinane looking over my shoulder at you, so if there's to be trouble between us, let it be here." Jesse's hand dropped to his navy Colt as he waited for Tyrone to make his move. The Gray Fox buckled his gunbelt around his waist. His right hand closed around the walnut grip. At this range, the twelve-gauge underbarrel would cut Jesse in half. But there were other considerations. From what Jesse had told him, Doc and Milo and Titus were a rough bunch. Bon would need all the help he could get if he was to rescue Ophelia from these deserters. Of course, there was always the chance that when they discovered the gold was gone, they might panic and leave Ophelia and Dunsinane unharmed.

Sure, and pigs can fly, he thought. Bon's hand dropped clear of the LeMat. "Whatever's between us can wait." He swung his horse about and pointed the animal north. A twig dropped from a branch overhead and struck Jesse's hand. He glanced up, and in the shadowy foliage he spied a raven, eyeing him from a juncture of branch and tree trunk. The moon poked its silvery head out from behind a cloud bank and bathed the raven in a lustrous light as it preened its wings and tail feathers. The raven appeared to be studying him as it hopped to a lower branch.

"Grandmother," Jesse softly called, his voice full of warmth. "Be with me."

Bon waited at a discreet distance. He was uncertain what was delaying the Union spy. Jesse Redbow McQueen was as much a mystery now as he ever had been.

"You coming with me?" Bon asked his enemy.

McQueen looked one last time to the branches above and found them empty. The raven was gone.

"All the way," Jesse replied, his resolve as dangerous as a loaded gun.

Chapter Twenty-Three

Roughly a mile from Dunsinane, Jesse knelt in the road and, with a twig, prodded the clump of horse dung he'd found. Here in the middle of the wheel-rutted path that years of travel had trampled and packed into a road, the noonday sun sent a shaft of sunlight through a gap in the branches of the red oaks. For the last couple of miles and continuing on to Dunsinane the towering red oaks spread their limbs above the road like a canopy. Jesse and Bon had ridden their tired mounts through a patchwork of amber light and sea-green shadows. The road was peppered with the tracks of iron-shod horses, but Jesse was only interested in the most recent ones.

"These droppings are fresh," he told his companion. "The Starks are just ahead." He tossed the twig aside, stood, and returned to his horse. He'd ridden this road numerous times as a courier in gray. It felt odd to be here in the uniform of a Union officer—sort of like wearing a target. "I think we ought to cut through the woods and ride in from the east."

Bon nodded in agreement. "We'll be able to watch the front and rear of the house." His eyes were red-rimmed from lack of sleep. "Before we go on, there's something you better know," he said, watching Jesse remount. The rebel hesitated. Why warn McQueen? The man was a Yankee spy. He'd betrayed them all. Let him get what he deserved. McQueen had taken a fool chance in leaving the Union camp; let the chips fall where they may. Somehow the arguments didn't hold water. Jesse had freed the Gray Fox at the risk of his own career and placed himself in harm's way for Ophelia's sake. Bon couldn't let him ride into a trap.

"What is it, Bon?" Jesse asked. He wiped a forearm across his face, drying the sweat. Red squirrels chittered at them from the safety of the oak trees. Raucous jays announced the presence of the two men to the rest of the forest.

"Spider Boudreaux said he'd check on Ophelia while I was gone. He might be at Dunsinane right now, with a patrol." The Confederate looked up the road as if he were envisioning such an occurrence.

"Yeah . . . ?"

"I'd be duty bound to make you my prisoner," Bon concluded with a shrug, his cheeks reddened. "I figured I ought to tell you, in case you wanted to turn back."

Jesse pursed his lips a moment and scratched the back of his neck as he considered the possibilities. In another hour he might be dead or a prisoner of the Confederacy. Neither prospect held much appeal. But Doc Stark was bad blood. It was time to put an end to it.

"Me turn back?" His eyes narrowed and his gaze hardened. "Sorry, Bon, that dog won't hunt." He flicked his reins and the horse left the road and started into the woods.

It was a quarter past noon and the kind of warm spring day when the earth seemed alive underfoot. This dark, rich soil could grow anything in the world. Every time Ophelia worked the garden, she marveled at the forces of nature awakened beneath the freshly turned sod. She was happy to be a part of such a renewal. It gave her a sense of purpose.

Milo Stark found her kneeling in the garden, crumbling the dirt beneath her fingertips and indulging in a moment's reverie that his gruff voice shattered.

"Clean that mud off you and you'd be as pretty as you was in Memphis," Milo hungrily observed.

Ophelia spun around in alarm and recognized the big man looming over her as the same lout who had assaulted her in the alley in Memphis. Behind him stood Doc and Titus, strangers to her, but from their looks they meant trouble. She was surprised to see Cicero again. He seemed unable to meet her gaze. Milo had left the others by the well and had come down into the garden to bring the woman in. It was a task he enjoyed.

"Even in that man's shirt and rolled-up trousers, you look fittin'," Milo added. He waved a hand and motioned for her to join him. Ophelia glanced toward the cabins across on the other side of the cotton field.

"I see something in your eyes I don't like," Milo said. "You're thinking maybe you can outrun me. Well, maybe you can. But this here Colt rifle of mine has you beat hands down." He leveled the long-barreled gun at her midsection. "The man with the game leg is my brother Doc. The other one is my cousin Titus. Keep clear of him 'cause he ain't got any idea how to treat a woman." Milo took a few steps toward her and grinned. "I do." He cocked the rifle. "Now get your pretty little self up to the house."

Ophelia shrugged, dropped the hoe, and walked out of the garden. Milo immediately fell into step behind her. His boots kicked up clouds of dust as he tramped over the dry earth. He followed her into the shade of the summer kitchen. The Starks and Titus had discarded their uniforms on the way north and now wore civilian garb, linsey-woolsey shirts and woolen trousers. Doc and Milo kept their army-issue hats. Titus, on the other hand, had stolen a battered broad-brimmed hat off a scarecrow. Even Cicero had reverted to the clothes he had worn as a slave, though he kept the Patterson Colt tucked in his belt.

"Good afternoon, Miss Tyrone," Doc Stark said, twisting the ends of his bushy black mustache. Perspiration glinted on his scalp beneath the thinning strands of his black hair. "We mean you no harm, my dear."

Ophelia noticed the men had left their mounts in front of the house. That was why she hadn't heard them as they rounded the house on their way to the well by the winter kitchen.

"What do you want here?" she asked them. She looked at Cicero. "I never thought you'd be back, Cicero. It appears you have fallen in with bad company."

"You don't need to never mind about that, Miss Ophelia. You always treated me good. You can't help what old Marse Tyrone did. No more'n I can change the color of my skin." The former slave at last met her gaze. "I reckon I gots as much claim to that gold as anyone. I come for it."

"What gold?" Ophelia stared at the men in amazement.

"Spanish gold," Doc Stark said. "A family treasure your father had his father"—he indicated Cicero—"hide in the well. We came to emancipate it."

"But that's gone. My brother spent it outfitting his volunteer cavalry troop, and what was left we used to buy medical supplies that we smuggled down from Cairo."

Titus's lean, hungry features took on a worried frown. "You mean we come all this way for nothin'?"

"She's lying like her brother. They never took it." Cicero looked at his companions. "That chest is still there, hid about fifteen feet down, right in the wall, a black iron chest I seen myself before I left from here."

"Did you open it up?" Doc asked, his thick brow furrowed and his brooding gaze hardened.

"Well, no," Cicero stammered. "I—uh—there wasn't no room. I would have had to carry it up to the top and someone might have seen me...."

Doc nodded. "Maybe you better go and bring it up then. Milo can lower you down." Doc patted his gut and sighed. "Why don't you fix us some food. My cousin will walk you to the smokehouse over yonder. Pick us out a nice ham for dinner. I aim to leave this place on a full belly."

"C'mon," Titus told the woman, and his lips parted in a feral smile. Ophelia could see she had no choice and did as she was told. Milo left her in the open-air kitchen and sauntered over to the well. Cicero gingerly climbed over the waist-high stone well and caught hold of the bucket rope. He appeared anxious. Milo flexed his muscles, then gripped the crank with both hands. "Don't worry. I'll take it nice and slow," he said.

"I'm ready," Cicero told him.

Milo released a catch and began cranking down the bucket. Cicero wrapped his legs around the thick hemp rope, slipped over the side, and planted his feet against the slippery walls. Keeping a firm hold on the rope, he began the laborious task of walking down the inside wall. Doc Stark scratched the back of his bull neck and strolled over to the well. Milo grunted with each turn of the handle as the gears clanked and groaned at the added weight.

"The darkie weighs enough," Milo grumbled. He continued to turn the crank. Sweat beaded his beard and dripped from his forehead. His broad back rose and fell with each turn of the handle. Sounds of boot heels scraping the wall and of harsh breathing drifted up from the darkness.

"Hold it now. I gots to go slow. Feel right along...here. Yes sir! I got it! Bring me up!"

Doc nodded to Milo who began to crank in the opposite direction. Again the gears protested. Again the man complained that he was having to do all the work. Doc ignored his brother. His attention was fixed on the dark hole in the earth, and the former slave dangling on the end of a rope who slowly came into view, and the iron strongbox he held under his right arm.

Titus slipped a knife from his belt and cut a length of sausage hanging from the low ceiling. He began to eat while watching Ophelia. The inside of the shed was filled with the mouth-watering aroma of pork and beef and smoked hens with dark reddish-brown skin.

"Milo's right. Dress you up in silks and gew-gaws, you'd be a woman to make a man proud." Titus carved another mouthful from the summer sausage. "What do you think about that, huh?"

"I think that sausage is tainted and you're fixing to be sick to death," Ophelia replied.

Titus spat out what he was about to swallow and wiped his mouth on his sleeve. He spat again, trying to clear out even the faintest residue of what he had been eating. Then he saw Ophelia laughing at him. He'd been tricked.

"You bitch," he muttered. He tossed the sausage aside and advanced on her. He brandished the knife as Ophelia retreated toward the rear of the smokehouse.

A gunshot rang out. Titus cursed beneath his breath and stumbled out into the daylight. Ophelia, carrying a ham in a straw basket, brushed past him and hurried across the yard to the summer kitchen. She felt relatively safe from Titus as long as Milo was close by. Not that the big man was any sort of savior, Ophelia thought. She was in trouble and had yet to think of a way out.

A few yards ahead, Doc Stark stared down at the strongbox he had blasted open with his Colt. The gunshot still reverberated over the quiet land. In the warm sunlight, blackbirds circled the garden with keen and watchful eyes. Down by the cabins an old hound lifted its head at the sound of the gun, but the sun's warmth lay heavy on the land and the morning had brought rabbits and squirrels to chase and the hound was too sleepy to investigate the sound.

Before the last echoes faded, Jesse McQueen

caught Bon Tyrone by the shoulder and pulled him down behind a dewberry bush as the Rebel started back to his lathered mount. Bon tried to twist free but Jesse held him fast. They had left their horses well back in the trees east of Dunsinane and crept forward through the thinning shadows until they had a clear view of the plantation house, the rear grounds with the summer kitchen, the tutor's cottage, smokehouse, and abandoned outbuildings.

"Goddammit Jesse," Bon hoarsely whispered. "Get out of my way."

"Wait," Jesse cautioned.

"That's my sister over there!"

"And you'll get her killed, yourself too, charging in. They'll have a good sixty yards of open ground to shoot your lights out." Bon slowly relented, seeing the wisdom in McQueen's words. It didn't make waiting any easier. Both men were on edge and bone weary. The long ride from the Union camp had been uneventful but grueling. Their horses were about winded, though Jesse felt the animals had one more burst of speed in them, one more run. The Starks' horses looked in similar condition at the front of the house. No one was leaving Dunsinane, not for a while, and some of them weren't leaving it at all. Ever.

Doc knelt by the strongbox as Ophelia returned from the smokehouse. He was oblivious of her presence, staring into the box at an assortment of oilskin wrapped documents, deeds to Dunsinane and storefront properties in Richmond and Petersburg.

"I told you," Ophelia said, setting down her basket. "Smuggled guns and black powder and medicines bring a high price." She sighed with some regret. "It took everything we had."

Milo left his place by the well and joined his older brother. When he saw the contents of the strongbox, his bearded features paled. "We joined a damn army and dodged Rebel bullets and got the Yankees after our necks for deserting and all for a worthless bunch of papers." He trembled as he spoke. Milo's dreams of wealth had come crashing down and he wanted to lash out at anyone or anything.

"You're welcome to the ham," Ophelia told the two men, the equivalent of rubbing salt in their wounds.

"Shut the hell up, you Rebel bitch," Milo growled. His hairy callused hand caught Ophelia with a vicious slap that spun her around and sent her staggering into the shade of the summer kitchen, where she sagged against the oak table.

"Cousin Milo, you do have a way with women." Titus Connolly chuckled. His narrow, angular features were flushed with a mixture of excitement and anger.

"No! Stop it. Miss Ophelia ain't done nothin'!" Cicero blurted out. The sight of the empty strongbox was almost more than he could bear. Bon hadn't been lying. The gold had been spent. Cicero would begin his life of freedom as dirt poor as when he had labored at Dunsinane. He would end it the same way. The gunshot came without warning.

Doc Stark palmed his Colt and, still kneeling, fired over the top of the strongbox. The slug caught Cicero in the chest, glanced off his sternum, and ripped through his vitals. He fell stiff-legged against the well and sat in the dirt, arms limp against his side. His head dropped forward, his chin touched his chest.

Ophelia was stunned by Doc's vicious act. Milo

had leaned his Colt rifle against one of the oak supports close at hand. She lunged for the weapon, but Titus, behind her, read her intentions and caught her by the hair and hauled her back against the table.

"Take up your rifle, you damn fool," Titus shouted at the big man. Milo retrieved the weapon and laughed as Ophelia managed to turn and rake Titus's cheek with her fingernails. He yelped and released her. She bolted toward the rear door of the plantation house. This time Doc Stark limped over to block her path. He caught her by the arm and jabbed his gun in her side and she quieted down.

Back among the trees, Jesse scrambled to his feet. "The hell with a plan," he growled, and slapped the Confederate on the shoulder.

Bon Tyrone had already reached the same decision. He had the longer stride and the two men reached their mounts and swung into the saddle as one. Neither man spoke, there simply wasn't time. The horses leaped forward and charged from the forest. Jesse and Bon opened fire as they galloped into sunlight. Bon loosed a wild Rebel yell. Jesse rode low in the saddle and let the navy Colt in his hand speak for him.

"What the hell is going on?" Milo bellowed. Doc glanced up as the riders cleared the trees. "Jesse McQueen!" he roared. "Damn him!" Doc tried to level his pistol at his attackers, but Ophelia continued to struggle in his grasp and threw off his aim. Doc's arm encircled her. He used her as a shield and dragged her toward the back steps of the house.

Milo overturned the oaken table in the kitchen

and used it for a barricade. He propped his elbows on the edge and the rifle in his hands spat flames. It thundered twice and belched acrid black smoke that soon obscured the big man as he continued to fire through the haze.

Titus liked the idea of taking cover within the house. He took off after Doc, who had already climbed the back steps and ducked inside. About twenty-five feet from the plantation house, Titus howled in agony as a chance shot from Jesse's navy Colt shattered his knee and dropped him in the dust. He groaned and rose up on his good leg and took aim. Jesse slipped from horseback. Titus held his fire. The riderless animal blocked his view. Jesse rolled to the left and, belly down in the dirt, shot twice. The first shot doubled Titus over. He straightened and tried to bring his revolver to bear and took Jesse's second slug alongside the first. He clutched at his belly and emptied his revolver as he fell forward, blasting a furrow in the black earth as he died.

Bon Tyrone's horse staggered, shot through the heart, and went down. The Rebel tried to kick free, but his boot caught in the stirrup as the animal collapsed and rolled on its side, pinning the Confederate officer to the ground. Bon groaned and tried to pull himself out from under. He spat dirt and gulped in a lungful of air and renewed his attempt to work his leg free. He didn't think it was broken, though his ankle hurt like the devil. A lead slug thudded into the belly of the horse. Bon sank back, gripped the LeMat with both hands, and looked up as Milo stood with the Colt revolving rifle in his hand.

Bon flicked the hammer on his gun, squeezed

the trigger, and blasted a load of shot that knocked Milo backward over the table. The rifle went flying from his fingertips and clattered off the brick hearth behind him.

Bon propped himself up on an elbow and waved Jesse away as the man started toward him.

"I'm all right. Help my sister!"

Jesse waved at Bon, turned, and loped toward the house. The back door looked too inviting. Jesse resisted the temptation, altered his course, and headed for the front drive and the horses the deserters had left tethered to a hitching post. He rounded the corner of the house as Doc Stark limped onto the porch between the whitewashed pillars.

"Jesse!" Ophelia shouted, and aimed her shoulder into Stark just as he fired. Again, she spoiled his aim, the bullet shattered the study window.

Jesse flinched and brought up his gun, but all he saw was Ophelia in his sights as Stark ducked back inside and dragged the woman with him.

Ophelia struggled and twisted until Doc lost his hold on her. She wrenched free in the foyer and grabbed a cane from a stand by the door and cracked Doc across the side of his neck. The cane shattered. Stark howled and lashed out with his gun hand. The barrel of his Colt clipped her temple. Ophelia sagged in the double doorway to the dining room. The world spun and she tried to hold on as blackness engulfed her. Doc Stark caught her as she fell and carried her into the dining room and deposited her on top of the long table.

He grabbed a crystal oil lamp from a sideboard, lit the wick, turned up a nice flame, then hurled the vessel against the wall. Flames sprang up along the floor and engulfed the curtains and lapped at the ceiling. Doc studied his handiwork and the girl sprawled helplessly on the table.

"This ought to distract you, Jesse," he muttered.

He heard the front door crash open as Jesse kicked it in. Doc grinned and took up his position.

Bon began to claw at the dirt beneath his leg. His hands dug deep in the Mississippi soil. He strained and worked his foot back and forth as best he could. Finally he felt the leg slide an inch, then another. Yes, he thought. And bit his lip to keep from crying out. He dug and pulled and continued to work his leg and gained another few inches. He sensed motion out of the corner of his eye and stared in dismay as Milo Stark crawled across the overturned table and stumbled toward him. Blood streamed from half a dozen flesh wounds, and his skull was bloody where he struck a table leg as he fell.

Milo pulled a broad-bladed carving knife that he had found near one of the ovens. There was nothing subtle about his approach. He gripped the carving knife in one meaty paw as he advanced on his helpless prey. Bon grabbed for the LeMat and Milo hesitated until he heard the hammer strike an empty cylinder.

"Just you wait, Johnny Reb," he muttered. "I got something for you." Fifteen feet, then ten, his heavy frame plodded onward, the knife before him, raised now and ready to slash the pinned man.

"Should have stayed a prisoner, Tyrone," Milo said with a rueful wag of his head. Bon grabbed the pistol by the barrel and swiped at his assailant, but the Gray Fox was at a distinct disadvantage. Milo had no trouble avoiding the blow. In fact, the attempt amused him.

"Gonna carve you like a Sunday chicken." The man with the knife chuckled. He jabbed and slashed Bon's shoulder.

A single gunshot thundered. Milo stiffened, squared his shoulders, and puffed out his chest. His mouth formed an "O" as the knife slipped from his grasp. He rose up on his toes then fell forward, sprawling across Bon and the dead horse. Bon shoved him aside and looked across the yard at Cicero, who sat with his back to the well, legs straight out before him, blood-drenched, the life ebbing from him. But the black man held the Patterson Colt with both hands, smoke curling from the barrel.

The two men faced one another, former owner, former slave. Bon nodded his thanks. Cicero weakly smiled. He lowered the gun. It was too heavy for him to hold any longer. He choked and coughed blood, then whispered in an anguished voice, "Now I be free." And he died.

Jesse entered the main house of Dunsinane crouched low, his reloaded navy Colt cocked and ready to blast Doc Stark out of existence once and for all. He squinted through a haze of smoke, swung his gun to cover the study to his left, then the stairway straight ahead, and then the dining room. Heat fanned his face as he eased to the doorway and peered into the room. About a third of the room was engulfed in flames. The blaze was spreading fast. In minutes the entire room would be an inferno, with Ophelia stretched out upon the table like a dead queen upon her funeral pyre.

Jesse, reacting on instinct, lunged through the

doorway and hurried to the unconscious woman's side. He shoved the chairs out of the way and reached out to scoop her in his arms. Smoke seared his lungs. Flames singed the back of his coat.

He sensed a danger other than the flames and whirled about to face the kitchen as Doc Stark's burly frame filled the doorway. His gun bucked in his hand. The slug knocked Jesse to the floor. His navy Colt skidded across the floor and beneath the armoire in the corner whose china display was framed in fire. The stained cabinet went up like kindling.

"Too bad, Jesse," Doc said, holding a damp cloth over his nose and mouth as he entered the room. He leveled the gun at the man lying helpless on the floor. The pain in his left shoulder kept Jesse conscious. He concentrated on the pain and the darkness receded from the fringes of his vision. Doc kicked McQueen's left foot. Jesse groaned and looked up.

"Wake up. I want you to see this coming." Doc steadied the revolver. He chuckled, looming over the wounded man sprawled at his feet. "You and your high-and-mighty family. Well now, who's lookin' down at who, eh?" His finger tightened on the trigger.

Beneath the armoire, a tendril of fire ignited the loaded chambers of the Colt .36. Three chambers exploded in rapid succession. Doc Stark glanced up, distracted by the gunshots, thinking himself under attack.

Jesse reached to his right boot and palmed the Smith & Wesson. When Doc turned to finish him, Jesse fired up into the deserter's face. Doc screamed and clutched at the blood spewing from the socket where his right eye had been. He staggered back and

Jesse emptied the .22-caliber pistol into him. Doc shuddered under the impact of each bullet, then with a hand to his face and the other flailing wildly, he toppled back through the window and fell through a shower of glass and a rush of fire and smoke into a flower bed.

Jesse rolled on his stomach and brought his knees up under him. He heard coughing, then two slender, soot-smeared arms encircled his waist and helped him to stand.

"A Yankee. Somehow I knew it," Ophelia said in a hoarse voice. She was bruised and bloody and more than a little dazed. But she saw Stark die and saw who killed him.

"I wanted to tell you," Jesse yelled, striving to be heard above the roar of the fire. He glanced around and added, "Maybe we ought to talk outside."

Bon watched in horror as the flames exploded the upstairs windows. A fireball swept up over the cedar-shingled roof. He gave one final herculean effort and pulled clear of the dead horse. He attempted to stand, but his twisted ankle refused to accept his weight. No matter. He'd crawl, by heaven, and started to do it when he spied Jesse and Ophelia stumble around the side of the house. They were both battered and singed but alive. And beyond them, riding at a gallop down the drive to Dunsinane, came Spider Boudreaux and a dozen men of the First Mississippi Volunteers.

Jesse managed to reach Bon a minute ahead of the Confederate column. He stood swaying a moment. "Looks like you win," he said. He left Ophelia at her brother's side and staggered over to the summer kitchen. He turned the table upright and slumped down onto a bench seat. Ophelia hurried over to him and began to bandage his wound. The slug had ripped his shoulder across the top, but it had missed the bone. It was painful though not fatal.

"Why did you come back here?" she asked.

"You ought to know."

Ophelia shook her head. The complexities of war were one thing, the intricacies of the human heart quite another. Yes, she did know. And that was the reason why she could not bring herself to hate him.

Jesse watched as Spider and the others circled Bon. Some of the men noticed McQueen and the color of his uniform and covered him with their carbines and dragoon pistols.

"What the hell happened here?" Spider said. "We seen the smoke and come at a gallop. Looks like we missed the whole blasted ball."

"We had a bit of trouble." The roof crumbled inward in a shower of sparks.

"Trouble hell, it looks like Armageddon," the Cajun replied, the glare of the flames reflected against his grizzled features. "Johnston's pulled out of the capital. Vicksburg's on its own. We been ordered to the east. Looks like we'll fight the Yankees another day, I reckon." Spider frowned and looked at Jesse. "What about him?"

"I'll handle it," Bon said, and limped past his men, who at a glance from the Gray Fox retreated from the summer kitchen. Jesse stood as the Confederate officer approached.

Ophelia glared defiantly at both her brother and Jesse. "The first one who starts something will have to answer to me!" she warned.

Her outburst broke the tension. Bon shook his

head, and despite all that had happened he had to smile. "By God, she means it."

"I believe her," Jesse added. Then he looked at Bon. And waited.

"I'll take Ophelia to Richmond. She can stay with her aunt," Bon told him.

"I'm not going anywhere. I can live in the tutor's cottage until we can rebuild." Ophelia sounded determined. "This is my home. And the old ones need me. I'm staying."

"I'll hang around to bury the dead and...to help out," Jesse said to Bon. "Unless you figure to try and take me with you."

Bon looked from his sister to McQueen and threw up his arms in exasperation. His options were clear; he'd have to kidnap his sister and kill Jesse.

"Ahhh..." he growled, and limped over to one of the horses the deserters had stolen from the Union camp. He climbed into the saddle, not without effort and taking care not to further injure his ankle.

"What about General Grant? You've got a lot of explaining to do," Bon said, settling astride the horse. Another of his men retrieved his pistol.

"These deserters will help smooth things over," Jesse replied. "I'll leave the rest for Major Abbot to handle."

The Gray Fox glowered. It still galled him to think he had been tricked not once but twice.

"So be it," he said, and turning to Ophelia, reached down to take her hand in his. "I'll be back from time to time. Just keep watch for me, sister." He kissed her hand.

"I will. Take care."

Bon looked at Jesse. "I aim to plague you Yankees yet."

"No doubt you will," Jesse told him. "Though for today let it be said of us that we met as enemies but parted as friends." Captain Jesse Redbow McQueen offered his hand. Captain Bon Tyrone clasped it in a firm and honest grip.

And as the Gray Fox rode away at the head of his column Ophelia stood at Jesse's side and wondered aloud, "What will happen now?"

Jesse put his arm around her. "Who can tell?" he answered.

A kind of peace had returned to Dunsinane, marred only by the crackling flames as something old gave way to something new.

Author's Note

General Grant took Jackson on the fourteenth of May. Four days later he had brought his army to the fortifications around Vicksburg. After a siege of forty-seven days the city surrendered on the Fourth of July in the year 1863. It was a blow from which the Confederacy never recovered.

Although the McQueens are a fictitious family, some of the exploits depicted in this story are grounded in fact. A Union agent whose name has been lost to history allowed himself to be publicly court-martialed and drummed out of the army. He became an officer in the Confederacy and acted as a courier for General Joe Johnston. Throughout the invasion of Mississippi, this daring agent kept General Grant supplied with plans of attack and defense personally drafted by the Confederate military hierarchy. But he was only one of many brave and gallant souls who fought and sacrificed and endured that dark and bloody time we call the Civil War.

Turn the page for an exciting preview of the fourth volume in best-selling author Kerry Newcomb's saga of an American military dynasty.

WARRIORS
OF
THE NIGHT

This Bantam original will be on sale December 1991. Look for it wherever Bantam books are sold.

The scent of blood drew the big cat to the sunbaked ridge overlooking the Rio Grande. The mountain lion moved with swift sure grace, a fleeting tawny shadow among the stark upthrust layers of volcanic rock. With a body as long as a man was tall and armed with fang and claw and powerful muscles capable of ripping an enemy to shreds, the panther of the Big Bend country had never known fear—until now. . . .

The lion leaped from boulder to boulder and alighted atop a ledge of compressed ash, where with calm, patient resolve the predator waited. His keen eyes surveyed the dry wash wherein the past, flash floods had scrubbed the smooth worn limestone walls of the arroyo and littered the floor with palm-sized pebbles in a variety of earthen colors, dark shades of red and gray, white, brown, and black. There had not been a spring shower in the past week, so the arroyo should have been bone dry. But today, in the mid-morning heat, a rivulet of blood traced a crimson path along the watercourse. The "headwaters" of this grisly stream were the mutilated remains of a mestizo goatherd and his son. Man and boy lay stretched across a flat outcropping of table rock, their chest cavities slit open and hearts ripped out.

The stench in the watercourse was no stranger to the lion, nor were the buzzing flies and the shadows that swept across the corpses and the blood-spattered rocks as the vultures located the kill and began to circle in ever-tightening spirals against the hard blue dome of sky.

Another time or place the lion might have hurried to the feast. But something old and dark and terrible had passed this way and left a trail of death that even a prince of predators was loath to follow. As if warned by some deep-rooted instinct against an evil as ancient as these weathered hills and wind-sculpted peaks, the big cat did not enter the arroyo but turned its back upon this place and crept away.

A gust of wind sighed among the desert mountains like some final, faint agonizing cry, stirred the dust, then like the panther, departed in silence.

Three hundred miles away, Doña Anabel Cordero de Tosta had problems of her own. She was a slim, dark-eyed young woman with raven hair pinned back; she wore a flat-brimmed sombrero. Anabel was dusty and tired and certainly not looking for trouble. But trouble she'd found. Or rather, it had found her in the menacing form of a Quahadi Comanche war party. Though the Comanches were an ever-present danger in the Chisos Mountains of the Big Bend, it was highly unusual for the braves to be raiding so close to San Antonio now that a company of Texas Rangers had set up quarters in town. But here they were, eight fierce-looking warriors and Anabel in the thick of them.

Carmelita had warned her against going alone to visit the grave of her father. "At least if you will not wait for your vaqueros, take your brother," she had said. Ah, but Anabel was impatient, and as for her brother Esteban, of what use was a priest in her present situation. Beneath her lap blanket, her hand read around the trigger of a sawed-off shotgun that had belonged to Don Luis, her father, a stubborn, hard-bitten bandit who had fought the Anglos until his death a few weeks past. He had been laid to rest near the ruins of a mission ten miles north of San Antonio on land that had once belonged to the Corderos and was now considered part of the Texas republic. Don Luis Cordero de Tosta had never recognized

Texas's independence but considered the republic to be part of Mexico. From his lair in the Chisos Mountains, El Tigre—the tiger of Coahuila—had fought to the bitter end to drive these Anglo invaders from his country's sacred soil. He had hoped to restore his family's wealth and influence in the process. His dreams were worm food now, and he had left his unfinished business as a legacy for his daughter.

On this second day of May in 1845, Anabel was more concerned with living through the next five minutes than with the weight of her inherited responsibilities. She had gone to her father's grave site searching for answers. Her quest might well prove fatal. However, there still might be a way out. Anabel knew the lead brave, Spotted Calf. During a visit last year to her father's retreat in the desert mountains, she had watched Don Luis conduct trade with the Comanches. If the chief remembered her, Anabel might be able to reason with him.

One of the Comanches struck her horse with his war lance in an attempt to startle the brown gelding hitched to her carriage. Several of the braves followed his example. They ringed the carriage, whooping and waving their weapons as Anabel fought to keep the gelding under control. Gripping the reins in her left hand, she refused to give in to panic. The shotgun beneath the blanket was some assurance, but she'd need more than buckshot to survive the day. Don Luis Cordero, her father, had established a formidable reputation among the Quahadi Comanches in the mountain country. They had respected his strength. Don Luis had many vaqueros riding for him, men skilled with the gun and knife, each man an experienced Indian fighter. Unfortunately these vaqueros were probably miles away.

Outnumbered by a contingent of Texas Rangers, Don Luis and his men had scattered after the running fight that had claimed the life of El Tigre himself. Anabel knew they'd find some way to return to San Antonio and contact her. For a fleeting second she even entertained the hope they might come riding down out of the hills, guns blazing as they charged, past thickets of mesquite and mountain cedar. The howling savages surrounding her put an end to that fantasy. They knew she was alone.

The Comanches, eight lean and wiry-looking warriors, were painted for war. Their coppery features were hidden behind masks of red and yellow war paint. The rumps of their sturdy mountain-bred ponies bore the mark of the snake, the sign of the Comanche.

Spotted Calf led them, but there was little in the way of attire to indicate his leadership save for three turkey feathers fastened to a topknot of shiny black hair.

He wore a brown brocade vest (no doubt the prize of some raid) that hung open to reveal his naked chest. A blue breechclout and long-fringed buckskin leggings covered his lower limbs. His calf-high moccasins were decorated with tiny glass beads and elk's teeth.

Some of the warriors were armed with muskets, some with war lances. All of them carried the short, highly lethal orangewood bow prized by every Comanche. The war party continued to circle the carriage. Men rode up and counted coup on the frightened gelding with their bows. And still, Anabel kept the horse under control.

Impressed, Spotted Calf broke from the ranks of the taunting braves and walked his mount up to the carriage to confront what he understood to be a helpless young woman.

"The daughter of my enemy is foolish to come alone among these hills," said Spotted Calf. He was close enough now for Anabel to see the bear-claw necklace the brave wore around his neck and to smell the dried bear grease on his buckskin leggings.

"Enemy?" The woman made a show of her surprise. "The Quahadi have always traded in peace with Don Luis Cordero." If the Comanche didn't know of her father's death, the señorita wasn't about to tell him.

"In the time of the new calf moon, your father came with many men and stole my horses," Spotted Calf told her. "And killed Whistler, the dream walker."

Anabel refused to be cowed by the warrior. She remembered the incident well. "El Tigre de Coahuila only took back the horses your braves stole from him."

The brave ignored her reply. He would not hear the truth in her words.

"It was a bad thing, to kill the dream walker. Only Whistler could see beyond seeing. His magic was strong. But now his voice is silent. His songs no longer hold back the dark spirits of the old ones." Spotted Calf turned to the braves surrounding the carriage and raised his rifle gripped in his strong right hand. At his signal his followers quieted and ceased their failed efforts to spook the señorita's horse. Then the war chief leaned forward and peered into the carriage.

"I will take you with us."

"My father is close by. He will bring his vaqueros and hunt you down and kill you," Anabel warned.

"I do not think so." Spotted Calf seemed wholly unconcerned. "Because then I will kill his daughter. No. I think you will be worth many horses and guns." Spotted Calf reached for the reins she held. The time for talking was finished. Anabel steadied herself and, with a quick flick of her wrist, tossed her lap blanket over Spotted Calf's head then struck him square in the face with the twin-barreled shotgun.

The Comanche howled in pain and lashed out at the blanket covering his head. His horse reared and the war chief lost his purchase and landed on his backside in a thicket of prickly pear. Anabel slapped the rump of her horse with the reins as the braves in front of her tried to block her path and bring their muskets to bear. Other warriors notched arrows to their bowstrings. All of them were unprepared for what happened next. The shotgun roared and buckshot toppled from horseback the three braves blocking her path. The shotgun's recoil knocked Anabel back against the leather walls of the carriage. The gelding bolted forward, carrying the woman through the powder smoke and racing away from the startled Comanches. A couple of shots rang out. An arrow glanced off one wheel as the carriage rolled up and over a rise and dipped out of sight. In its wake, one brave lay dead on the side of the road. Two others sporting flesh wounds struggled to bring their skittish ponies under control and remount. Spotted Calf, his broken nose a gory fountain of crimson, exhorted his warriors to pursue the carriage as it disappeared from view, leaving a trail of white dust to settle on the wheel-rutted road. The braves responded slowly. The momentary loss of their chief and the death of one of their number had left them numb. Spotted Calf treated his companions to every insult he could think of, calling them helpless women and the offspring of camp dogs. He caught up the reins of his horse from Little Coyote, who had kept the animal from running off. Spotted Calf leaped astride the animal. Then he winced and, reaching beneath himself, plucked nettles from his buttocks.

"Dancing Horse is dead," said Sees the Turtle, the stern-featured older brother of Little Coyote. Spotted Calf listened as he probed his nose. Pain seemed about to split his head in two. He sucked air through his mouth and struggled to will the pain into submission. The death of his companion Dancing Horse only added to his anger. Spotted Calf wrapped a strip of buckskin around his face and covered his nose in an attempt to stanch the flow of blood. Once accomplished, he grabbed a war lance from Sees the Turtle. The weapon, fashioned of bois d'arc, was seven feet in length tipped with an iron lance head bound to the shaft with sinew of rawhide thongs. A half-dozen turkey feathers were attached near the butt of the lance.

"I will have her scalp," said Spotted Calf.

"We are too close to the village of the white eyes," Sees the Turtle cautioned. "The Rangers are camped there."

"My vision has led us," Spotted Calf replied. "Our band has been driven from the mountains by the dark ones. Now we tremble before these 'Rangers'? Have we become old women afraid to leave our lodges?" The war chief glanced past Sees the Turtle and addressed himself to the other dispirited braves.

"Are there no men to follow me?"

"I will follow," Little Coyote spoke up. He was bold and brash and eager to fight. He met his brother's disapproving gaze and refused to be swayed. Full of a young man's pride, Little Coyote wanted to prove himself the equal of those he rode with. The remainder of the war party raised their weapons and shouted war cries. Spotted Calf grinned and looked at Sees the Turtle, who shrugged and nodded his willingness to continue the pursuit.

"Our horses are swift. She will not escape us," Spotted Calf reassured his rival. The blood had ceased to flow from his flattened nose, but he left the makeshift compress in place just to be on the safe side. "She will not escape . . . me," he repeated, making it personal. He struck his horse with the butt of the lance, the animal lunged forward, and in a matter of seconds was galloping full out. Roused to action once more and despite the bad omen of their initial losses, Sees the Turtle, Little Coyote, and the rest of the war party joined in the hunt. Like coppery-skinned wolves, they would not close the chase until the "pack" had made its kill.

Minutes later and a mile and a half down the road, Anabel Cordero met Lieutenant Ben McQueen. It happened without warning as is the way of that coyote trickster—fate—who turns a man or woman's life inside out on a whim.

Every gulley she crossed, every hill she passed brought Anabel closer to San Antonio. The carriage lurched from side to side like a storm-tossed ship. Her pursuers on horseback were slowly gaining on her. Once she cleared the hills, though, the Comanches might abandon the chase rather than risk a run-in with the well-armed Rangers. For once, Anabel was almost thankful for their presence in the town.

She clung to the carriage as the wheels jumped from rut to rock and somehow kept herself from being thrown from the seat. The gelding was galloping full out now and Anabel began to figure she had the edge when she skidded around a chalky-white stone outcropping, rode a precipitous incline across a dry creekbed, and had just begun a climb between two scantily wooded knolls when a long-limbed, red-haired horseman in a dusty blue uniform dashed from a cedar break and in a matter of seconds had brought his sleek brown mare up alongside the gelding.

The officer in blue leaned from the saddle and with the practiced ease of a natural-born horseman caught the gelding's harness and forced the animal to a swift stop. The gelding stood with sides heaving, nostrils flared in the rising heat as the sun continued to climb toward noon.

Ben McQueen turned and flashed a broad smile at the woman he thought he had rescued. "There you go, ma'am. I believe that's got him under control. Snake spook your horse? I heard a gunshot and—"

Her buggy whip cut him short. He reacted with hawklike quickness, surprising in a large man, and managed to shield his square-jawed features from the stinging kiss of the whip.

"*Imbécil! Idiota!*" Anabel was furious. He had cost her precious moments.

"You've one hell of a way of thanking a man who has just saved you from a broken neck. A runaway horse on a road like this—"

"Not runaway. Running away!" She pointed back along the road toward the rise she had just crossed. "From them!" In an example of perfect timing the war party swept over the rise and, without breaking stride, loosed a volley at the couple on the incline ahead.

Ben McQueen had envisioned himself the gallant rescuer. Indeed he'd been enjoying the role of hero, especially after the señorita proved to be as pretty as a summer sunrise. Alas, with the arrival of the Comanches, his fall from grace was brutal and complete. Hero one moment, *idiota* the next. Ben's sun-bronzed features paled and his green eyes grew round and wide.

A bullet nicked the leather frame of the carriage, feathered arrows sprouted from the rubble underfoot. Ben slapped his cap across the gelding's rump and the horse bolted forward. "I'll lead them away," he shouted. "They won't catch me!" His words were no sooner spoken than the brown mare staggered and swung halfway around as a lead slug, by a stroke of sheer misfortune, plowed into the animal's side and punctured a lung. Ben kicked free and slid from the saddle as the mare went down. The soldier looked over his shoulder and saw that the señorita had once more halted the carriage. Ben turned toward the howling Comanches. Well, he could stay and die or run like hell. A whirling arrow missed him by inches. Another buried itself in the road at his feet. Ben was armed with an army-issue carbine, a saber, and a pair of .36-caliber single-shot percussion pistols. He ought to be able to make a heroic stand lasting all of thirty seconds. The hell with it! Ben turned and dodged another volley of flint-tipped arrows all the way to the carriage.

Anabel used her whip on the gelding as Ben crowded onto the seat. The gelding responded, sprang into action, and climbed the rise ahead while back along the road Spotted Calf led his braves across the dry wash and started up after his quarry. Once again the carriage momentarily disappeared from view. Spotted Calf raised his war lance over his head and called to his braves to double their efforts. His surefooted stallion climbed the last few yards. The carriage was just ahead. He had closed the gap.

He didn't know who the white man was or where he had come from, but it had been plain to see the man was alone. And that made him fair game for a Comanche lance.

The carriage churned a thick cloud of dust in its wake. Spotted Calf and his warriors ignored the grit that stung their eyes and burned their lungs. It was time for the kill before the carriage cleared the foothills and reached the grazing lands along the San Antonio River. This was the moment and now was the time. Thirty yards became twenty then ten as the Quahadi war party closed in for the kill. Muskets were loaded by braves who rode at a gallop without breaking stride. Arrows were notched and loosed with such velocity they pierced the carriage's folding cover. Muskets blasted holes in the back and sides. Spotted Calf rode up alongside the carriage and jabbed his spear in a killing thrust that sawed helplessly at the empty air above the riderless seat. The rest of the war party swarmed over the carriage and brought the gelding to a halt.

Little Coyote had his arrow all ready to make a kill. He eased the sinew string and stared at the carriage. Sees the Turtle spat a rifle ball down the barrel of his musket and tamped it in place by striking the gun butt against his thigh. Spotted Calf raged and shoved his war lance into the leather walls, hacking through the sides and back in a series of savage attacks until the folding cover lay broken and shredded in the road.

"What trickery is this?" said Little Coyote. "What spirit has carried them off?"

"This is a bad thing," one of the wounded braves added. Spotted Calf studied the winding road as a sudden gust of wind swept the settling dust once and, like an unfolding curtain, parted to reveal the hill behind them fringed with post oaks and cedar. The war chief ignored the superstitious complaints of the braves around him. His attention remained riveted on the wooded slope. The war party fell silent. Even Sees the Turtle ceased his complaining. He waited like the others and watched the hills.

"I think we've lost them," Ben said, peering over the jumble of limestone rocks and cacti that formed a natural barricade among the deep green scattering of cedars halfway up the slope.

"You don't know Comanches," the young woman beside him coldly remarked.

"No, I don't," he admitted. "Lieutenant Ben McQueen, at your service." He touched the leather brim of his cap and smiled, hoping to thaw her chill reserve.

"I don't want you at my service."

"So I noticed. You just about took my ear off with that buggy whip."

Anabel sighed, unable to cling to anger. She did not trust these Anglos. Yet this man had placed himself in harm's way for her sake. And his idea of abandoning the carriage once they were out of sight of the Comanches had bought them a little extra time. She softened and, with guarded emotions, introduced herself.

"I am Anabel . . . Obregon." No one in San Antonio, save her brother and Carmelita, knew her real identity, that Anabel was none other than the daughter of Don Luis Cordero de Tosta, the tiger of Coahuila, whose death cried vengeance from the grave.

"Pleased to meet you," Ben said. He removed his cap and wiped the perspiration from his forehead. His thick red mane was plastered to his skull. His blue flannel uniform was unbearably hot and the spiny thickets that dotted every hillside and choked the gulleys had played havoc with his trouser legs.

Ben McQueen scrunched his big-boned, six-foot-four-inch frame down behind the rocks and tried to take stock of the situation. He knew Choctaw, Cherokee, and Creek, the legacy of a youth spent in the Indian territory. But of the Comanches he had only heard rumor and tall tales since disembarking in Galveston. The squat leathery-looking warriors gathered in the road below were providing his first encounter. If the soldiers he had left to escort retired General Matthew Abbot into San Antonio were only here . . . no, of what use blame? Flights of fantasy weren't going to see him through this dilemma. It would take powder and shot and cold steel, not to mention nerve and a wagon load of luck. He felt a hollow pit form in his stomach and struggled to ignore the sensation. He concentrated on seeing that his weapons were loaded and primed. He couldn't help but notice the practiced ease with which Anabel bit open the paper cartridges and loaded the twin barrels of her shotgun. She sensed his interest and shifted her dark-eyed gaze.

"What is it?"

Ben's square-jawed features split with a grin. He wiped a hand across his stubbled jaw and then with a wry look told her.

"There's some ladies in Philadelphia that would be most impressed by your talents." Anabel looked with disdain.

"A woman must be able to do more than braid her hair and wear silk dresses to live here," she remarked. Anabel worked a metal ramrod down each barrel, tamping the loads in place. Her riding skirt was torn at the hem and her black boots were scuffed. The hill rose gradually for another twenty-five feet before playing out beneath a sheer wall of limestone too steep to climb. To reach the crest they'd have to follow the contour of the hill around to where the cliff had eroded and broken off into rubble. The hill was slowly being reclaimed by mesquite trees whose twisted roots and branches seemed able to thrive in even the most arid of soils. Unfortunately, any attempt to climb the remaining slope would require crossing open ground.

Ben removed his blue cap and slowly eased himself onto his knees. He set aside his saber and carbine and edged around the barricade nature had provided for them and, once in place, studied the war party. The warriors in the distance were framed by the spiny pads of a prickly-pear cactus. The Comanches had started to backtrack but had yet to pick up any sign of their prey. The ground was so hard-packed and broken, Ben doubted he had left any tracks for the war party to follow. His hopes began to rise. He crawled back behind the rocks and crouched alongside Anabel.

I think we're safe here," he whispered with confidence. Then he saw the rattler.

It was a big diamondback, six feet of cold-blooded nightmare thick as Ben's forearm, and devil-nasty. The rattlesnake had been sunning itself on a ledge above them. Something had disturbed the reptile and caused it to retreat downhill. Ben didn't care about the reasons, only the immediate danger of the creature. The rattlesnake noticed the two intruders blocking its path and coiled itself within striking distance. Charcoal gray and black, with black-and-white bands at its buzzing tail, the rattler continued to warn the humans in an attempt to drive them away. The rattler's mouth opened once to reveal a pair of poison-drenched fangs as Ben tossed a handful of pebbles in the snake's direction, hoping to force it to retreat.

"Don't move," Anabel whispered. "Maybe it will go away."

"Good Christ, señorita," Ben hoarsely replied. The rattler looked like it had no intention of "going away." Ben eased his hand toward the hilt of his saber. A gunshot would alert the war party below. But Ben figured if he could just free his sword, silent steel might save the day. He gripped the scabbard in his left hand and, with his right hand curled around the hilt, began to slowly slide the blade out where it would do some good. Sweat beaded Ben's forehead and rolled down into his eyes, stinging them. The buzzing of the rattles seemed deafening in the confines between the jumble of rocks and underbrush and the base of the limestone cliff. Anabel started to caution the lieutenant, then reconsidered. She did not want to run the risk of distracting him. The rattler's head wavered between the man and woman as if uncertain which to kill first. Then it struck.

Even expecting the attack, the savage swiftness with which it came so startled Ben he leaped to his feet. He parried those gaping fangs with the length of his scabbard and struck with the saber, slashing again and again at the writhing creature. The tip of the sword shattered against stone. Ben didn't care. He continued to hack at the rattler until it lay dead upon the blood-smeared rocks. Then with the adrenaline still pumping through his veins, he slowly turned, sword in hand, as the hairs rose on the back of his neck. My God, he was standing completely in the open. He looked downslope and found himself staring into the upturned faces of the Comanches, who had seen the glimmer and flash of his saber as sunlight glinted off the blade.

The author of **In the Season of the Sun** and **Scalpdancers**
begins a multigenerational saga that will span the history of
America, as seen through the lives of one family.

THE MEDAL
by Kerry Newcomb

*From a nation born of strife and christened with patriots'
blood, there arose a dynasty of soldiers. They were the
McQueens of America -- a clan hungry for adventure; a
family whose fiery spirit would kindle the flame of a
country's freedom. Keeping that flame from blazing into
tyranny through the generations would take more than
merely courage and determination. It would take a
sacred secret: the proud legacy they called*
THE MEDAL.

Look for the first two books in this series,

THE MEDAL BOOK ONE: GUNS OF LIBERTY
THE MEDAL BOOK TWO: SWORD OF VENGEANCE

on sale wherever Bantam Domain Books are sold.

AN239 -- 9/91